Ann Granger has lived in cities all over the world, since for many years she worked for the Foreign Office and received postings to British embassies as far apart as Munich and Lusaka. She is now permanently based in Oxfordshire.

Ann Granger is the author of three other hugely popular crime series: the Mitchell and Markby novels; the Fran Varady series and the Victorian mysteries featuring Scotland Yard's Inspector Ben Ross and his wife Lizzie. For more information about her crime novels visit www.anngranger.net.

Praise for Ann Granger:

'Characterisation, as ever with Granger, is sharp and astringent' *The Times*

'For once a murder novel which displays a gentle touch and a dash of wit' *Northern Echo*

'While Ann Granger's novels might be set in the familiar mode of traditional country crime stories, there is nothing old-fashioned about the characters, who are drawn with a telling eye for their human foibles and frailties. Granger is bang up to date' *Oxford Times*

'Her usual impeccable plotting is fully in place' *Good Book Guide*

'The plot is neat and ingenious, the characters rounded and touchingly credible' *Ham and High*

'Entertaining and lifelike characters . . . a satisfying and unexpected twist' *Mystery People*

'Lovely characterisation and a neat plot' *Yorkshire Post*

ANN GRANGER
ROOTED IN EVIL

HEADLINE

Copyright © 2017 Ann Granger

The right of Ann Granger to be identified as the Author of
the Work has been asserted by her in accordance with the
Copyright, Designs and Patents Act 1988.

First published in Great Britain in 2017 by
HEADLINE PUBLISHING GROUP

First published in paperback in 2017 by
HEADLINE PUBLISHING GROUP

1

Cataloguing in Publication Data is available from the British Library

ISBN 978 1 4722 0462 2

Typeset in Adobe Garamond by Palimpsest Book Production Ltd, Falkirk, Stirlingshire

Printed and bound by CPI Group (UK) Ltd, Croydon CR0 4YY

Headline's policy is to use papers that are natural, renewable and recyclable products and
made from wood grown in sustainable forests. The logging and manufacturing processes are
expected to conform to the environmental regulations of the country of origin.

HEADLINE PUBLISHING GROUP
An Hachette UK Company
Carmelite House
50 Victoria Embankment
London EC4Y 0DZ

www.headline.co.uk
www.hachette.co.uk

This book is dedicated to Eileen Roberts, Kate Charles (Carol Chase) and all who have made the first twenty-three years of the St Hilda's College Crime Fiction Conference in Oxford so memorable. Also to all the friends from across the world I have met there over the years, all of them crime-fiction lovers to their fingertips!

It is also in fond memory of my agent for twenty-six years, Carole Blake. She was always so full of enthusiasm and encouragement; and so suddenly taken from us all. God bless, Carole.

'For the love of money is the root of all evil.'

– Epistle of St Paul to Timothy,
King James Bible

Chapter 1

It was raining in Oxford, as it was in most of the rest of the country. Would-be passengers scurried along the row of bus stops in Magdalen Street, scanning the listed numbers on the metal flags beside each one. A hopeful violinist was serenading the pedestrians, but they didn't care about him. His own decision to seek shelter in a covered gap between shops didn't help, because he was hidden in the shadow. The plaintive notes drifted out of his retreat, but no one stopped to drop a coin in his violin case open on the ground.

Carl Finch saw him. But Carl didn't pause to give him any money, either. Carl was particularly short of cash himself. He appreciated the busker's attempt to earn a crust, even though the scrape of a fiddle had never appealed to him. But, he thought grimly to himself, unless he got his hands on the money to which he was entitled – and Carl did not doubt he was rightly so under any natural law – he'd be reduced to desperate measures himself.

He was in his early forties, solid in build, with long, tawny-blond hair and fair skin. Scowling as he was now, he suggested a Norse warrior who had just leaped from a longship and was splashing through the water towards the undefended shore, sword in hand. People got out of his way.

But Carl was a worried man. He was not the attacker. He had more in common with the terrified monks of some storm-battered abbey who had received news of invaders. No monk could have prayed more fervently than Carl did for a deliverer.

A bus drew into the stop he was passing and he saw that it was going up the Banbury road, so he jumped on. No seats were available. He stood, pressed in unwished familiarity against the other rain-soaked passengers: old women with plastic carrier bags, young mums with infants, bewildered tourists and one elderly man with the air of having had something to do with the University at some time and who now seemed as angered by the world as Carl felt.

He jumped down at Summertown, set off briskly past the shops before turning off into one of the side roads and, some five minutes later, arrived at his destination, a trim Victorian terraced cottage. It was set back from the pavement by a low brick wall and a tiled forecourt. The curtains were already drawn because, although it was still technically afternoon, the light was failing. A lamp had been turned on within, its mellow glow escaping through a chink. Edgar Alcott valued his privacy. But he also liked to peep out and see who was at his front door demanding admission.

He had recognised Carl, opened the door and was ushering him inside. 'My dear fellow, what a dreadful day. So good of you to come.'

Carl divested himself of his wet Barbour, hung it on a hook in the narrow hallway, and followed his host into what Edgar liked to call his 'drawing room', even though it was postage-stamp sized. But Edgar was a meticulous sort of person and liked things 'right'.

2

Rooted in Evil

He was a living example of this dictum. At any time of day he was always smartly turned out: clean shirt, carefully knotted tie (selected to go with the shirt of the day), trousers with knife-edge creases, highly polished shoes. There was something highly polished about Edgar himself, too. It was impossible to tell his age. He had the fresh, unlined skin of a much younger man and his hair, though silver, was thick and bouncy.

Carl did not believe that the other man had always had the name Edgar Alcott, not even half of it. No doubt there were plenty of people with the surname, but Carl didn't know any. He seemed to recall that his stepsister, when young, owned a book called *Little Women* by a woman called Alcott, but that was it. He also suspected that 'Edgar' was an adopted moniker. He had no reason for thinking this other than it didn't suit the man, somehow. At any rate, Edgar Alcott never gave any information about himself and, somehow, one couldn't ask. He was beaming at Carl and politely enquiring whether the visitor would like a cup of tea – or perhaps something stronger? Strangers passing him in the street probably judged him a harmless old fellow. But Edgar wasn't harmless. The pale blue eyes beneath the arched silver eyebrows glinted like steel.

Carl asked for a whisky, because he needed it. Edgar poured it for him, but not a tumbler for himself.

'Too early for me, old chap. Soda? Or water, perhaps? A terrible fellow once asked if I had any ginger ale. Naturally, I never did business with *him* again!'

Carl replied, thank you, but he would drink his whisky neat. Edgar shook his head slightly but did not otherwise object. Watching him, Carl thought resentfully that his host was a past master at controlling people and situations. Carl always had to make the journey to Oxford to discuss business with him, however urgent, because Edgar, who did not drive, claimed he abhorred train journeys as 'unhealthy'. Besides trains, Edgar also abhorred cats. This had given rise to the one and only occasion on which Carl had seen him lose control. A friendly moggy had perched on Edgar's low wall. Carl was stroking it when Edgar had burst out of the house in a rage, face flushed red, eyes popping, screaming at the animal to 'get away!' The cat had wisely fled. The incident had lasted a few seconds and then Edgar was his old-maidish self again.

'Such unhygienic creatures,' he'd said to Carl, leading the way back indoors.

Now Edgar, having politely handed the glass to Carl, sat down on a Victorian hooped-back chair, crossed his ankles, folded his very white hands, and asked, 'And have you brought me glad tidings? Better still, something tangible? I do hope you have. It's been such a dreary day, and I do need something to cheer me up.'

'I haven't brought any money, Edgar, sorry. It's just been impossible to raise that amount of cash. I've tried everything.'

Edgar sighed. 'I had such confidence in you. Yet you have let me down quite unforgivably. My dear chap, whatever went wrong?'

If Carl had replied honestly, he'd have said, 'Just about everything!' But he knew it was important to remain outwardly confident. 'You'll get your money, Edgar. But it will mean waiting rather longer than we first thought. The company had not anticipated local opposition. But it is being sorted out and if you'll just have patience . . .'

'Have I not been patient?' Edgar asked, in that mild way that always sent a shiver down Carl's spine.

Carl flushed and drew a deep breath. He had to sound calm and self-assured. His whisky glass was empty and he desperately needed another tot. But Edgar showed no sign of refilling it. 'I have lost money, too,' Carl went on. 'Please understand that I simply haven't—'

But Edgar interrupted. 'Enough is enough, Carl. I really must have my money, you know. I am a businessman, not a charitable institution. However, I am not unreasonable. You can pay me in two instalments, but the first must be paid before the end of the month.'

In desperation, Carl blurted, 'Look, I'm setting up a meeting with my sister—'

'You have mentioned your *step*sister before. She'll advance you the money?' Edgar's eyes glittered like icicles in a ray of winter sun; and the emphasis was a reminder that the speaker liked accuracy.

Carl flushed. 'No, not straight away. The fact of the matter is, there is the property, the Old Nunnery. I may have mentioned it to you before. It's becoming a burden to Harriet and I do believe she'll listen to what is a very sensible plan. Sell the whole damn lot, house and land. It's the obvious thing! She'd share the proceeds with me! I'm sure of it. After all, there would be enough to see us both right. I know I'm asking a lot of you, Edgar. But let me talk Harriet round. Eventually, you'll get the lot back, believe me.'

'My dear Carl, perhaps you are being optimistic?' Edgar was shaking his head. 'Grasping at straws, as they say? Yes, you have mentioned this property before and I have made enquiries. But you don't own it! You wouldn't be the vendor, dear boy, if it came on the market. Even if it made *very* good money, none of it would be yours.'

'But it should be!' Carl insisted passionately. 'My stepfather never intended to cut me out of his will and leave me with a measly few thousand! He raised me as his own kid! And he left a fortune, Edgar, a fortune!'

'But you weren't his child, were you?' Edgar still spoke in that unrelenting mild voice. 'Not his flesh and blood? As I understand it, he merely married your mother when you were already a little boy.'

'He regarded me as a son! He always treated me as such. He paid the school fees. He bought me my first car. We did everything together as a family, he and my mother, Harriet and me. When my mother died, he was there for me in every way. But he was a very sick man in his last years and he was influenced. Somehow, he was persuaded to cut me off with the proverbial shilling. Not by Hattie, my sister – she wouldn't have done that to me. It was her husband, Guy. I see his hand in it!'

'Nevertheless, your stepfather did not leave you a share in the property and you cannot be sure of persuading your stepsister, especially if, as you say, her husband would be strongly against any idea of sharing any profits with you.'

'I can talk Hattie round,' Carl insisted. 'We were always close. She won't let me go to the wall. She doesn't want to end up bankrupt, either, and the way Guy is behaving, they will be. Yet the money is sitting there in the shape of a valuable asset. She'll agree, Edgar. It would be the best thing for both of us.'

Edgar rose to his feet and went to peer through the chink in his front window curtains. 'I really don't like violence, Carl. Truly I don't. But I dislike being taken for a ride even less.'

His back was turned to Carl, who, for a split second, was tempted to leap up and brain the old devil. It wouldn't help. Someone would have seen him arrive here, or would see him leave, perhaps a neighbour also peering through the curtains. His fingerprints were probably all over the place. He didn't have that kind of luck, the sort that let you get away with murder. Nor did he have that kind of nerve. Anyway, the paper trail would lead the police to him.

'As I was saying, I've been in touch with Hattie.' He tried to keep his voice under control. 'She's agreed to meet and discuss it. We're brother and sister – all right, not by blood, but we *were* brought up together and we *are* very close, especially since my mother died. Anyway, she's not as besotted with Guy, her husband, as she was. She'll listen to me this time. I can get her to sell, I know I can, and once the house and the property are sold, believe me, Edgar, she won't say no to divvying up the money.'

'I do hope so, dear fellow. How dark it has got; and it's raining again.'

Carl left the house feeling a desperation he would not have imagined possible. He had to win Hattie over, and it had to be soon. Not only because he didn't want his legs broken but also because that cuckoo-in-the-nest, Guy Kingsley, would talk Harriet into another of his hare-brained schemes. The Kingsleys would eventually go bust; Harriet knew that. She wasn't a fool. All that money the old man had left would go down the drain, and the house and property would be sold to meet *their* debts. Carl could kiss goodbye to seeing even a penny. It just wasn't fair. Harriet and Guy's marriage was on the rocks. Everyone knew that. Carl was family; he had sound business sense, unlike Guy's loopy ideas, even if, lately, luck had run against him. Dad would never have cut him out of his will like that if Guy hadn't been there to influence him all those months he lay sick; and to influence Harriet, too.

'I need,' muttered Carl, 'to get rid of blasted Guy Kingsley.'

Chapter 2

The mud-splashed Range Rover turned through the weather-worn pillars flanking the entrance, sending up spectacular twin sprays as it jolted through a deep puddle in the gravel. Small stones rattled against the bodywork. Harriet Kingsley, gripping the wheel, progressed noisily to the top of the drive and stopped before the house.

She put up her hands to push back her thick, dark blond hair and her fingers brushed the moisture pearled on her forehead. She had to get control of herself before she went indoors, before Guy saw her. He wasn't the most sensitive of men, goodness only knew, but even he would see that his wife was badly upset about something.

Harriet continued to stare at the Old Nunnery for some minutes, trying to calm down. The day was cold and damp. The interior heating of the car provided temporary respite, but she still felt an inner chill that was nothing to do with the temperature and all to do with shock and panic. She was shivering and sweating, crazy though that seemed, and her heart was pounding in her chest. She was lucky she'd been able to drive home without there having been a worse incident than almost forcing an oncoming SUV into a wall, just below Crooked Man Woods.

That other driver, the one in the SUV, would remember her,

worst luck! Where had he been heading? Perhaps even to the woods? No, no, not on this damp, chilly day. He must have been on his way somewhere else. But supposing, just supposing, he had been intending a stroll through the ancient woodland? Suppose, just suppose, he'd turned off into the car park and had chosen to walk down that path, of all the possible routes through the trees, and he'd stumbled upon . . .

'Stop it, Hattie!' she ordered herself aloud sharply. Why on earth should he have been going to the woods? No one went there much except at weekends and during milder times of the year. In springtime, when the wild flowers, above all the bluebells, spread a colourful carpet between the trees, whole families descended on the spot, and in mid-summer, when the woods offered a cool retreat. At this time of year, late January, the wildlife pretty well had the woods to itself.

Immediately, she thought that this wasn't quite true. Not only walkers visited the woods. Forestry workers, doing routine maintenance, had been there recently and might have come back. Some were volunteers and some employed by the trust which owned the woods. The volunteers were likely to turn up at any time. But there was absolutely no reason why any of them should be there today. No reason at all. She hadn't seen anyone.

No one except him, and he was still there.

She made a last effort to pull herself together. She had to appear normal. She peered through the windscreen at the house, in all its ramshackle familiarity, with its haphazard mix of architecture built of mellow stone.

It had once been a real nunnery, standing foursquare against the elements on this open hillside, surrounded by high walls.

When Henry VIII had ordered the dissolution of the monasteries, most had been pulled down. The wealthy wool merchant who had got his hands on this desirable property had demolished only the chapel, the site marked by mossy remnants of foundation stones sunk in the turf.

The house had eventually passed into other hands and continued to undergo extensive modifications over four centuries. A new wing, built in what a Victorian owner had believed the Gothic style, represented his ambition to have a ballroom. No one had danced in it since the First World War, when the son of the family perished in the Flanders mud. The house and contents had passed to a niece. Since then, three direct generations of Harriet's family had lived here, descended from that niece. If you included that wavy line in the descent, they'd been there since Georgian times.

'And I,' said Harriet aloud, 'will be the last.' Whatever happened, she could be sure of that.

She felt she could face Guy now. Her heart had stopped pounding. She still felt slightly nauseous but, overall, she was in control. No more putting it off.

Harriet drove sedately around the house to the old stable yard to the rear and slightly to the left of the main block. She parked up well away from the stacks of building materials. From within the complex that had once been divided into tack room, loose boxes and a hayloft came the sounds of hammering. Further back from the stables stood the stone cottage that had been the accommodation for the outdoor staff in a vanished era. It showed signs of recent drastic renovation; its exterior had been scrubbed yellow. The tiny window frames of the upper floor, replaced and painted glossy black, peeped out from beneath the gutter of the tiled roof.

She paused, after getting out of the car, to cast a critical eye over the alterations. If you had a walking stick, you could stand outside the cottage, reach up and tap on the upper windows the whole place was so tiny. How short in stature our ancestors were, she thought; Lilliputians to whom the present vitamin-stuffed generation would appear a race of Gullivers.

The stable block, too, was being converted into guest rooms for the bed-and-breakfast business Guy was certain would be a roaring success. It was odd how alike Guy and Carl were, both so full of schemes, confident of elusive riches just around the corner. Perhaps that was why they'd never got on. More likely it was because their individual schemes always seemed to depend on her putting money into them. You can only cut a cloth so many ways. She'd told Carl that, more than once.

So far, the cost of the conversions had begun to alarm even Guy. The plan was for four en suite units in the cottage and six in the stable block, each comprising sleeping and sitting space, with a 'breakfast nook'. The sofa in the sitting area would open out into an additional bed and allowed each unit to be described as a 'family accommodation'.

If guests didn't want self-catering, the breakfast part of a B-and-B deal would be offered in the main house, where the small sitting room would be turned into the visitors' area. It had looked all right on the plans, but Harriet felt a frisson of doubt.

Every business plan Guy had ever come up with always looked all right on paper. He was always so enthusiastic, that was the trouble. He would never listen to any doubts expressed by her, or anyone else. Small, practical details troubled him not a jot. He just swept them aside. 'It will be all right on the night', the theatrical phrase, might have been coined for Guy. Everything always would be all right and, when it wasn't, and the record so far showed a distinct lack of success, Guy simply discarded that brilliant plan and steamed on to the next one. Just like Carl.

'How?' Harriet sometimes wondered when depression settled. 'How did I end up financing a pair of losers?'

Her father had warned her, whispering painfully from his sickbed, 'I shall be leaving you pretty well off, Harriet. I am telling you this now so that you will be on your guard. If you are known to have any money, there will always be someone eager to help you spend it.'

Had he meant Carl but shied away from naming him aloud out of respect for Nancy's memory? Her father had continued, 'If you did not have Guy to protect you, I would have considered a trust fund. But as long as you have Guy, I know you will be well advised. Guy loves you. He won't let you come to any harm.'

All his life so shrewd in business matters, her father's judgement had failed him at the end. He'd liked Guy, admired him for his army career, and had been swayed. Guy did love her. Her father had been right about that. What he had not anticipated was that without Queen's Regulations to guide him, Guy was adrift in the civilian world.

The riding stables had been the first brainwave to grab Guy's imagination. 'Obvious, darling! Look, the stables are already there!'

That had folded under the cost of finding suitable horses and feeding the hungry brutes, together with the sheer hard work of looking after them, and all that even before the accident. A horse had bolted with an inexperienced rider in the saddle. Pretty quickly out of the saddle, actually. Dislocated shoulder, broken pelvis and loss of income on the part of the injured rider. He had turned out to be a high-flying young lawyer in the business sector and they'd ended up being sued heavily by him. They'd had insurance, of course. But even so, they'd had to pay out considerable damages. Then, as after any such serious accident, the cost of insurance had gone up. End of that venture.

Then came the restaurant, set up in the old ballroom; that hadn't lasted long, either. The kitchen had not been of the standard for a commercial enterprise. Tiling the walls and installing new worktops and equipment had cost much more than they'd expected. Experienced chefs proved temperamental and expensive. Guy's cheerful suggestion that Harriet might like to 'take over the cooking' was met with such an outburst on his wife's part that even Guy had realised that hadn't been a wise suggestion. He still assumed, however, that she'd cook all those breakfasts for the guests who would fill the newly adapted stable block and cottage.

The antiques centre had been the next thing to grab Guy's imagination. 'We've got a house full of old stuff. We can start by selling some of that.'

My old stuff! Harriet had thought but not said aloud.

The fatal flaw in that plan had been that neither of them was an expert in antiques. Nor did they find the boxes of china and bric-a-brac, all wrapped in faded newspaper, as Harriet remembered from childhood exploration of the attics. It had probably been dispersed to jumble sales and charity shops, perhaps by her stepmother. Lingering in the attic, draped in cobwebs, was furniture, mostly the sort of thing that languished in salerooms all over the country because it was out of fashion. There were boxes of books by writers no longer read and, in one suitcase, her mother's wedding dress, the lace discoloured, the waist unbelievably tiny. So much for Guy's dream of the attic contents fetching a small fortune. They'd had to go antique hunting and, despite all those programmes on the television, it was not as easy as it looked. They'd nearly ended up in court again, due to Guy being unable to tell the real thing from something made in China last year. The unsold 'old stuff' cluttered the former ballroom, briefly restaurant, and gathered dust. Some pieces still had yellowing price tags on them.

The hammering stopped and male voices were raised in argument. Harriet recognised her husband's and that of Derek Davies, the carpenter.

'He's not a practical man, is he, your husband?' Derek had once remarked to her over a mug of tea. 'Got lots of ideas, mind! I'll give him that.'

She couldn't face whatever dispute had arisen between Derek and Guy. Not just now. Harriet turned away from the sound of argument and made for the house. She marched briskly through the kitchen, dragging off her jacket as she went and hurling the garment on to a hall chair, from which it promptly slithered to the floor. She ignored it. She had to speak to someone else. She couldn't keep the morning's awful events to herself. After a moment's hesitation, she thought of Tessa. Tessa would understand.

Harriet grabbed the phone, but the sound of the dialling tone in her ear made her panic again. What was she doing? What would she say? She slammed the receiver down.

As she walked back towards the kitchen the phone rang shrilly in the hall behind her, making her jump out of her skin. Reluctantly, she returned to pick it up.

'Did you just try and ring me?' asked her friend's breathless voice in her ear. 'I was outside in the yard. You rang off before I could get to the phone.'

'Something awful has happened and I don't know what to do,' Harriet said bluntly.

'What sort of thing?' Tessa's voice had sharpened.

'Carl's dead.'

There was a shocked silence. Then Tessa said, 'I don't know what to say. When? How? Was it an accident?'

'No. He's – he's shot himself, in Crooked Man Woods.'

A gasp. 'But that's—' Tessa, true to form, went on the offensive. 'Why would he do such a daft thing? Not that Carl wasn't always one for the dramatic gesture. Sorry, won't speak ill of the dead and all that . . . if he really is dead. When did this happen? I hadn't heard anything. Are you sure?'

'Oh, yes,' said Harriet, surprising herself by how calm she now sounded. 'I've just found his body.'

'Where? In the woods, you said? But you're at home now, aren't you? You rang me from your landline number. Look, sweetie, are you sure about all this? This isn't some ghastly mistake? Do you mean some poor devil has shot himself in the head? Or in the chest?'

'No mistake. Quite sure it's Carl. Shot in the head, lower part of the face all gone, just a horrid bloody mess. But the eyes, forehead, the hair . . . yes, it's Carl.'

A pause, then Tessa, ever practical, asking, 'Have you made a statement to the police?'

Oh, damn, thought Harriet. The police . . . She hadn't even

16

thought about them. 'No, no, I haven't. I've literally just found him, Tessa. I panicked and drove home.'

'Is Guy there? You've told him?'

'No, of course I haven't told him! He'd ask why I was in the woods, and if he found out it was to meet Carl and discuss money, well, he would hit the roof. He's outside now, having words with Derek Davies over some carpentry problem. But when he comes out into the yard he'll see the car and know I'm home. I told him at breakfast I would be popping into Weston to the supermarket there.'

'Stay there and have a hot drink, tea or something. I'll be right over,' Tessa's voice said briskly. 'Don't, for pity's sake, hit the bottle!'

The admonition brought her out of the fog of panic. 'I'm not going to, am I?'

'Good!' said Tessa and slammed down the phone at her end.

Of course, now that Tessa had ordered her not to have a drink, she wanted one desperately. But tea, that was the thing for shock, wasn't it? But if she went back to the kitchen there was a possibility Guy might walk in. She had to head Tessa off before she reached the house. They had to talk first, without the danger of Guy blundering through the door mid-explanation.

Harriet let herself out of the front door and ran down the drive to the gate. She waited on the road, huddled under the wall that formed a boundary to the property. Atop the gateposts twin lions stared smugly towards the outside world. Perhaps they'd originally looked fierce. Time and weather had worn their features to those of amiable pugs. There had been a time when the house had been a place of safety, happiness and protection. When had all this changed? When her father died? Or had it been before that, the reassurance it offered slowly slipping away unnoticed until it was gone?

Harriet shivered. She'd left her jacket on the hall floor and her sweater offered no protection against the sharp bite of the wind. I'm still in shock, she thought, wrapping her arms around her body. I should have had that drink. Her next thought was that when Guy came into the yard he'd see the car. He'd assume she was in the house, probably go indoors and call out to her. He'd wonder where she'd got to.

'Oh, Carl' she muttered, remembering the ghastly sight. 'You idiot. Why has it all ended in this dreadful mess? There must have been some other way. Things couldn't have been that bad, could they?'

Yes, they obviously had been. He'd asked her so often over the past months to help him, his emails, messages and calls to her mobile phone ever more desperate. She couldn't even blame Guy for urging her to ignore Carl's pleas, because the contact with Carl had been secret. Guy couldn't get into her computer. He didn't know her password. Carl, in financial trouble, had always turned to her. This time, she'd been determined to refuse. The responsibility for what lay in the woods lay with her entirely.

'Come on, Tessa!' she cried.

Her friend lived only four miles down the road, after all. It wouldn't take her that long to get here. As if in answer to her words, a mud-splashed jeep bounced around the corner and drew up in front of her, spraying her with grit so that she had to jump aside. Muffled barking from within was followed first by the driver climbing out and then the eruption of a thick-coated sable and white rough collie. The collie greeted Harriet with enthusiasm, wriggling, whining and pushing its long muzzle into her hand before it bounded away through the gateposts and ran up the drive towards the house.

'Fred!' shouted its owner in vain. 'Sorry, Hattie, he thinks we're going indoors. Are we?' As she spoke she was subjecting Harriet to a sharp scrutiny and followed her words with a hearty embrace. 'Hold up. Don't go to pieces, whatever you do.'

'We can't go into the house, not yet, anyway. I've got to tell you what happened first. Can we sit in the car?'

'OK,' said Tessa when they were safely in the vehicle. 'Let's have it. Are you certain about all this? If his head was the mess you described, you could be mistaken and it's some other poor sod.'

'It was Carl. There was enough . . . enough to tell. Anyway, he was wearing Carl's scruffy old Barbour. He was slumped on the ground, propped against a felled tree trunk. It was so – grotesque, unreal. I wanted to tell him to stop messing around and stand up! That was stupid, because he was so obviously dead.' Harriet briefly pressed her hands to her face, as if that would keep out the image of the dead man.

'But you've been avoiding Carl, haven't you? What possessed you to meet him, and in Crooked Man Woods, of all places?'

Harriet hunched her shoulders unhappily. 'Lately, Carl's been in financial trouble and pestering me about bailing him out. I couldn't help him, Tess, even if I wanted to! Guy and I are sinking so much capital into converting the stables. I decided the only thing was to meet Carl face to face and, even if it meant a real ding-dong argument, I would get it into his head that I would not, under any circumstances lend him any money, much less sell the Old Nunnery.'

19

'Sell the house?' squawked Tessa. 'Is – was – Carl bonkers? Hasn't your family lived there for ages? Your father left it to you so you could carry on there, not sell it to bail out Carl.'

Harriet leaned forward and said desperately, 'It sounds so simple when you say it. But it wasn't like that; you know it wasn't! Carl thought it should have been left to us jointly. He claims – claimed – that it was always Dad's intention.'

'Why should it have been?' was the growled reply. 'Carl wasn't any kind of blood relative, just Nancy's kid from her previous partnership!'

Harriet gestured through the car window towards the house. 'Things have been made worse by the failure of all our business ventures, Guy's and mine. Carl said I was throwing away all Dad had built up. I know Guy's plans don't work out, or haven't worked out in the past. But this holiday accommodation idea might. Other people do it.'

She hunched her shoulders. 'I suggested to Carl we meet in the woods so that Guy wouldn't know. Guy would insist on being there and they'd both fly into a rage. Carl would insult Guy and then . . . oh, you know how they are. They were, I mean,' Harriet amended her words miserably.

'Insulting Guy isn't difficult,' replied Tessa mildly. 'I insult him all the time, even though he is your husband.'

'He doesn't mind *you* insulting him. He quite likes it. Carl is – was – a different thing altogether. Look, let me finish before he comes wandering down here looking for me. I thought Crooked Man Woods would be perfect, because at this time of the year there's seldom anyone there during the week. We could have a good shouting match and no one would be any the wiser. I'd had enough of him sniping away about Dad's will. But now it isn't about the will or the house, it's about Carl doing such a dreadful thing. He must have been so desperate, Tess, and I feel so guilty.'

The reality of it almost overwhelmed her. Harriet muttered, 'It was horrible. He's seated on the ground with his back against a felled tree trunk. Shotgun lying across his body, just this awful empty, scarlet hole where his nose, mouth and chin should have been.' She put her hands over her face again and stifled the sob that threatened to break out.

She was enveloped in her friend's long arms and pressed against Tessa's sweater, which always smelled of horses and dog. 'Don't crack up, sweetie. Listen to me. You have to tell the police. You can't just find a body – a dead body – and drive off without saying anything. Was there anyone else in the woods?'

'I didn't see anyone, hear anyone. But there was a car . . . an SUV, silver. As I drove away from the woods it passed me on the road. I was driving like a mad creature and I forced the other car right over and nearly into a wall. He'll remember me.'

'All the more reason to report this. It's got to be done. Eventually, the body will be found.' Tessa scowled, her nose wrinkling and her lips pursed. 'But it doesn't have to be reported by you!' she said suddenly. 'Look, go on back to the house and say nothing. Where in the woods is this felled tree trunk and – and Carl?'

'Just down the blue footpath.'

'Fine. I'll drive down there with Fred. No one will think it odd if I walk him in the woods. I do it often. I'll find Carl, or whoever it is, and I'll phone the police and report it. You could still be wrong about it being Carl. At any rate, you don't have to be involved. This other driver, he didn't see you at the woods, only on the road, right?'

'He might have been going to the woods.'

'Much more likely he was taking the back road into town. Right!' Tessa, mind made up, was not going to hear any more quibbles. 'Let's fetch my crazy dog and I'll be off. You go indoors and act normally.'

'I don't feel normal. I'm shaking inside.'

'Tell Guy you think you're coming down with something. There are all sorts of bugs going around at the moment. Wait until I've had a chance to get there and take a look.' She drew a deep breath. 'You're very shocked, sweetie, but you've got to listen to me and remember what I say.'

Harriet nodded, her eyes fixed on Tessa's face.

'When I find him, whoever he is, I'll phone the police like a good citizen. I'll have to wait there until they come. Then I'll make my statement and leave. I'll come back here and, if I don't think it's Carl, I'll tell you.

'If I agree that it *is* Carl, I'll seek out Guy and tell him first, and suggest we tell you together. He'll probably want to be the one to break the bad news, but I'll insist on tagging along. All you need to do is act shocked when we give you the news. The state you're in, that shouldn't be difficult. The main thing is, don't give any hint that the news *isn't* a complete surprise. Guy won't suspect you were ever there, not unless you tell him! *No one* need know you were there. You'll have heard the bad news from me – and Guy.'

Harriet said in a very small voice, 'I'm very grateful, Tessa, but I can't let you do it. Can't we just wait until someone else finds him?'

'And if no one goes down there for the rest of the day? We can't just leave Carl sitting there stiffening. The police have to be informed. Let me handle this, OK?'

Tessa pushed her out of the car. 'Go on, in the house with you! *Fred!*'

Chapter 3

'You're either prone to catching colds, or you're not,' the family doctor had informed Tom Palmer's mother. Or so his mother had always insisted. His mother had had great faith in the medical profession. That her son had later chosen to study medicine had been, for her, the pinnacle of achievement – hers.

Tom didn't remember the doctor saying the words. He had been ten years old at the time, red-nosed, red-eyed and sniffling, with no interest in anything other than getting out of the surgery as fast as possible. The doctor had clearly wanted him out of the place, too.

He could, through the haze of memory, picture the doctor: a tall, spare man with thinning hair. Young Tom had supposed him very old. Possibly he had not even been middle-aged.

'Probably,' croaked Tom, staring at the mirror, 'the same age as I am now.'

An older version of that wretched ten-year-old was reflected back to him, red-nosed and resentful beneath the untidy mop of black hair. Tom was running true to the medical's man's prediction.

He had a cold and it was a stinker.

Mindful of his duty, he had gone to work the previous day. His colleagues had received his arrival much as the family doctor had done all those years ago. They'd all spent the rest of the day trying to persuade him to go home.

Inspector Jess Campbell called by at the morgue in the afternoon with a query and joined in the chorus.

'Look,' she said to him briskly. 'You're just spreading your germs around. The clients you've got here can't catch it, but everyone else can. You're not helping yourself! For goodness' sake, at least take some time off. Stay in bed. Drink lots of fluid. Take vitamin C.' She'd added: 'You're a doctor, you ought to know better.'

So Tom had gone home early, interpreted 'plenty of fluids' as a couple of large whiskies and gone to bed. To be fair, he'd slept like a log. But he'd awoken that morning with a thumping headache – and still with the cold. His fingers scrabbled for his smartphone on the bedside cabinet. He peered at it. It was nearly eleven o'clock. Automatically, he checked his messages. There was one from Jess, hoping he had taken her advice and was at home. She would call by that evening. The other one made him wonder for a second or two whether the cold had affected his brain and he was imagining it.

It was from Madison in Australia. Well, that was turn-up for the books and no mistake! He hadn't heard from his former girl-friend in six months. He had not been expecting to hear from her again, ever. But there it was, brief and to the point.

Hi, Tom! Hope you're OK. I'm coming home at the end of the month. Looking forward to seeing you and catching up.

'Oh, are you, indeed?' growled Tom at the screen. 'What's up? Had enough of the sunshine? Year's research up and temporary work permit expired? Whatever love life you found hit the buffers? Coming back to dear old England and steady old Tom, are you?'

A hot shower made him feel slightly more human but didn't

dispel the feeling of baffled rage Madison's text had left simmering in him. He pulled on some clothes and stomped morosely into the cramped nook described by the estate agent as a 'fully equipped kitchenette'. There were two eggs in the fridge, enough milk for a couple of cups of tea, and some dried-up ham. He tried a cupboard. Tea, soggy cornflakes, two tins of beans and a tin of tomato soup. He took down the soup and poured it into a pan. The bread bin yielded up a dry end of loaf. It was too late for breakfast and too early for lunch, so from these poor offerings he managed to conjure up a sort of brunch. He retired with the tray, laden with soup and brittle toast, to his living room, where he switched on the television.

An American lady judge was lecturing the defendant in some case. The defendant was putting up a spirited rebuttal to all charges, but the wretch hadn't a chance. The whole thing put Madison back in mind and set him reflecting on their relationship.

Tom did occasionally wonder if his early experience of doctors' waiting rooms had contributed to his adult decision, once suitably qualified, to concern himself with investigating those already dead. His mother had certainly never understood it. 'I suppose,' she had said to him eventually, 'they give less trouble than patients who are alive.'

This was not necessarily so, but he had left her happy with her explanation. Certainly, the dead didn't complain, and they were always interesting. Tom liked the exactness of the discipline of investigating causes of death, the hunting-down of elusive clues and unexpected discoveries. Bodies couldn't speak, but it was amazing what they could tell you, even so. True, when he told people what he did for a living, they tended to look alarmed and, thereafter, conversation veered between the stilted and the unhealthily curious. Several young women had freaked out.

The two exceptions in recent memory were Jess – because she was in CID and thus able to consult with him on professional matters but, in private life, still maintain a separate friendship. The other exception had been Madison.

Jess was a friend, though none the less valued for being only that. Madison had been much more. She carried out research into exotic diseases and so hadn't worried about dating someone in his line of work. They had other shared interests. They liked the same kind of music. They had belonged to the same walkers' club. It really had seemed that things were working out very nicely. They'd even discussed, tentatively, moving in together. Not in his place (too small), or in hers (even smaller), but perhaps somewhere larger, conveniently situated . . .

But the offer of a year's research scholarship in Australia had proved a stronger lure than shared domesticity. Hikes across hill and down dale, or a concert or two, certainly didn't compete. Madison had departed for the other side of the world, and the subsequent infrequent contact had given him the impression she wasn't interested in coming back again.

But something, apparently, had changed all that and now Madison was buying her ticket for a flight home.

'If she thinks,' said Tom hoarsely to the lady judge, 'that she can waltz in here and we'll pick up from where she dumped me . . . she's got another think coming!'

The toast scratched his sore throat so that he had to soak it in the soup to get it down, and that made it squashy and disgusting.

He didn't feel well. He wasn't well. But being cooped up in his flat, brooding on the Madison problem, was only adding to his woes. He went to find his walking boots and weatherproof jacket. When faced with any kind of personal problem, walk.

Just being out in the countryside helped his mood enormously. He drove carefully through back roads and winding lanes. Cresting a hill, he saw the valley spread out below him like a hand-worked rug, patches of dull, wintry green, brown trees and grey farmland awaiting the urge for spring growth. Beyond, the terrain rose gently and trees crowned the high point. They marked, he knew, the limit of Crooked Man Woods. They covered the whole far side of the hill, and when he crested the summit the mass of them appeared to his right, swooping down to the valley.

He'd met no other traffic so far. But as he began the descent, he met an oncoming car. The road was narrow here and Tom's SUV took up room. But the other vehicle was larger, a Range Rover. If both drivers took care and slowed down, they should be able to pass without too much trouble. But the driver of the Range Rover careered straight towards him and swerved only at the very last moment. Tom was forced almost into a low stone wall.

'Oy!' he croaked, twisting in his seat. 'Bloody idiot! What do you think you're doing?'

The Range Rover roared away, and the driver, Tom was pretty sure, was not 'he' but 'she'. He had caught a glimpse of long, fairish hair surrounding a grimly set face. Despite having nearly caused an accident, she did nothing to acknowledge the other driver. It was as if she hadn't even seen him. In his mirror, he watched her career over the hill and disappear from sight.

'And thank you, too, madam!' growled Tom.

He drove on, rattled by the encounter and by unabashed reckless driving on the part of another motorist.

To get to the woods you had to turn off down a gravel track leading to a visitors' parking area. There were no other cars there; only, Tom saw, a bicycle. Its owner had chained it to a fence post, but there was no sign of the rider. Tom parked, got out, and checked the side of his car to make sure it hadn't suffered any scratches. All was very quiet, and his footsteps, crunching on the gravel surface of the car park, sounded unnaturally loud.

The paintwork was unblemished. He heaved a sigh of relief and made for the kissing gate into the woods. A display panel alongside it provided useful information for visitors.

'This is ancient woodland and protected,' he read. 'There are varying explanations for the name. Foundations of a Saxon settlement were discovered nearby, when fields were ploughed in the late 1890s. There are indications of a later medieval boundary bank on the southern perimeter of the woods. Arrows (red, blue or yellow) indicate routes through the trees. Don't light fires, leave litter or remove wild plants or flowers. Respect your countryside.'

Tom manoeuvred himself through the gate and set off down the red route. In less than a minute he was out of sight of the car park and the trees closed around him. He felt they were watching him. It was as if he had walked, unannounced, into a roomful of people and they had all turned their heads without leaving their positions. Traditionally, woods and forests had always been the haunt of magical creatures (mostly sinister) and real creatures (also unfriendly) in the form of outlaws and robbers. He stopped to listen. The air was full of faint but myriad sounds he couldn't identify: a crackle here and a snap over there. Birds rustled above in the bare branches and dead leaves fluttered down around his head. He peered into the ranks of the trees to either side, as into the nave of a dark Gothic church, its aisles marked by receding pillars. In warmer months the undergrowth would be too dense even to see that much. He had a momentary, illogical impulse to flee, a sense of being a trespasser.

He told himself not to be daft and set out again. It had rained recently and underfoot the terrain was sodden and squelchy, his boots making deep imprints that immediately filled with water. Some creature scuttled away into the shrivelled, frost-blackened tangle of blackberry spines to his left, its flight marked by an almost imperceptible movement of the mass. It might have been a rabbit. There was a large burrow on the far side of the woods, in the meadow there. At this time of year they were more often active at dusk or in the early morning, and they were not, strictly speaking, woodland animals; but perhaps this one had been driven by hunger from its snug burrow and the frosty grass. More likely, it had been a rat.

Tom was more at ease now. The woods had accepted him. His cold symptoms had abated. He breathed more easily. His eyes didn't itch. His throat was still sore but it didn't seem to matter so much. He really did feel better. Even Madison's impending return had slipped out of his mind. The near-miss with the other car still niggled, but he thrust it resolutely from his thoughts. He'd come out here to feel better: and better he was determined to feel!

Tom was not the only person wandering about the woods that morning. An hour earlier, Sally Grove had cycled here from her rented cottage just outside Weston St Ambrose with the intention of taking some photos of a possible subject for a watercolour painting she was planning. Sally belonged to an informal group calling itself 'Countryside Artists'. They were none of them professionals, of course. Gordon Ferris might dispute that, because Gordon had spent his working life teaching art and crafts in various educational institutions; even, briefly, to prison inmates. Some of the cons had been surprisingly talented, but Gordon had not felt at ease in their company and he'd relinquished that project. But he missed having a group to whom he could demonstrate his knowledge of the subject and his artistic skills and so had formed Countryside Artists.

As students, Gordon had at first found them unruly and apt to question his advice. But once they'd all settled down, shed their inhibitions and found their preferred medium and subjects, things had worked out well.

None of them felt at ease working *en plein air*. Gordon occasionally set up his easel in promising spots but disliked passers-by stopping to scrutinise his *oeuvre* and offer unsought comment. So he took his sketchpad and scoured the countryside for subjects then took the results back to his studio, a converted shed. After all, he argued, it's what Constable had done. Not that Constable had worked in a former garden shed with odds and ends left over from its former use scattered about.

Sally did not aspire to do as Constable had done. She liked trees. Each tree, she saw as an individual. They were survivors, every twisted branch and knot in the bark telling a tale. She took her mobile phone out with her and snapped possible subjects to work up later in paint in the comfort of her kitchen.

Having a free morning, she'd cycled out to Crooked Man Woods. It wasn't the first time she'd come here and she'd always been perfectly happy wandering about. But today was different. From the very beginning, as soon as she had set foot among the trees, she had felt a presence. She was not superstitious. She put her unease down to lingering indigestion working on her imagination. She shouldn't have reheated that week-old lasagne last night. It had been in the fridge, but the fridge wasn't working as well as it should and she would have to replace it when she had scraped together the money. Also, the sound of a gunshot had unsettled her. It had come from the far side of the woods and she had heard it while chaining up her bike in the car park on arrival. It was not permitted to use guns in the woods but sportsmen or farmers occasionally took potshots at pigeons out in the fields behind the woodland. Then there was the clay-pigeon range; you heard a racket from there from time to time. But that was behind her, way over to the left, and you didn't hear single shots. Sally put it out of her mind and doggedly snapped away with her phone camera at anything offering a likely subject.

Her concentration was broken by a sharp snapping sound away to her right. Her heart gave a painful leap. She peered into the thicket. Nothing. Probably something falling from a tree. Then, to her surprise, she heard a car engine. Although you couldn't access the woods from the car park by motor vehicle, there was another way in on the far side, down a track used by maintenance traffic. Visitors' cars were not allowed to use it, so this must be a Trust worker. The engine was cut. Sally decided to move to a different area. There was too much going on here, and she couldn't focus her mind. She found her way out of the trees on to one of the marked paths, crossed it, and plunged into the trees on the further side. For a while all went well; until she heard a noise unlike any other. It sounded as though someone or some creature was panting and groaning in considerable distress. The noises stopped. Then they began again, as if whoever or whatever was doing it had just paused to catch breath.

Sally's instinct was to turn and run. But that would be to admit that the origin of the sounds was something bad and dangerous, and she would never be able to come to the woods again, for fear of another encounter with 'it'. She had to find out what it was because, obviously, she reasoned, there was a simple explanation. Once she knew it, her fears would be dismissed, all would be well and she'd be able to wander the woods with her phone camera as before.

She made her way cautiously towards the sounds, camera held up at the ready. But the noises stopped again. Sally snapped off a couple of shots anyway. She was nearly back at the walkers' path. The trees were thinner. *Click*, *click* with the mobile. If anyone was there, he might clear off if he realised she was taking photos. Then, making her jump, the car engine started up again. The vehicle seemed to be reversing out the way it had come in, back towards the service road. Whatever had been causing the sounds had gone.

But Sally had had enough. Clearly, it hadn't been anything sinister, only some worker clearing debris. But she didn't want to linger. She'd taken a number of photos and one of them might offer the subject she was after. She turned her back on the path and set off on a different way back to the car park, negotiating a route through the undergrowth and the trees. Emerging into the open, she saw with relief that her bike was still there. It had been joined by a silver SUV. Could the owner of that have been responsible for the spooky noises? She wasn't going to hang around and find out. She hastened to unlock the chain and cycled off home, as if competing in a road race.

Tom, meanwhile, in another part of the wood, had been happily – or more or less happily – walking the red path. But now he had reached a point where the way split into two. A red arrow painted on a stubby post helpfully indicated the right-hand path. A blue arrow pointed to the left. Tom made an impulsive decision to abandon the red route and throw in his lot with the blue. Perhaps he'd only picked red in the first place because it reflected his anger. Setting aside thoughts of both Madison and the unknown driver, he turned left on to the blue path. From such impulses can dire consequences result.

The path broadened, wide enough now for emergency or work vehicles accessing it from the opposite direction. Traffic had been here recently. He had to pick his way through rutted tracks, crisscrossing, and including, possibly, those of a small tractor. Maintenance work had been going on. Overgrowing blackberry bushes had been cleared and a tree felled. The brambles and most of the tree had been taken away, presumably on a trailer pulled by the tractor. The main section of the trunk remained by the path and someone was sitting on the ground, propped against it with his legs stuck out straight in front of him. Why on earth was the idiot sitting on the ground when he could be sitting on the felled trunk or the stump? If he sat there, like he was doing, the damp must be seeping up into his clothing in a most unpleasant way.

There was something wrong about the position of the body and particularly the angle of the man's head, tilted back; something wrong with the face. A prickle of unease ran up Tom's spine.

Drawing nearer, he could see that much of the lower part of the face simply wasn't there, not in an intact form. It was a mess of ruined, bloody flesh through which, incongruously, broken teeth stumps protruded. Tom turned aside and gagged, inured though he was to gruesome sights. Back in control, he stepped cautiously towards the seated figure. The man wore corduroy slacks and a scruffy old Barbour. On his feet were strong boots not unlike the ones Tom himself was wearing. A shotgun had fallen to one side and lay partly across his outstretched legs. The man's hands had released their grip and lay uselessly by his sides, his fingers stiffening into claws. Above the ruin of the lower face, the brow and the eyes, the very top of the bridge of the nose, were relatively undamaged. He had long blond hair. Perhaps he'd been proud of it. Now the small vanity seemed pathetic.

Why did the poor beggars try to kill themselves that way? Tom asked himself. 'Blowing your brains out', as it was usually called, wasn't so easy. Horrible wounds resulted, but not necessarily death. A millimetre or two would have made the difference, leaving the victim a wrecked gargoyle but alive. Possibly, the autopsy would show that pellets, taking an upward course through the roof of his mouth, had entered the brain.

Tom stepped over the cropped brambles, worked his way to the rear of the body, and studied it from that angle. He then squinted at the tree trunk against which the poor fellow was propped. Lastly, his gaze moved to the collar of the Barbour.

Tom returned to where he'd first stood, stooped and gently

took hold of the man's wrist. He didn't expect to find a pulse. He wanted to establish how far rigor mortis had got. The cool conditions would delay its progress; the seated figure was barely beginning to stiffen. A layman would have noticed nothing at all. Tom made an ad hoc judgement and decided the man had been dead under an hour, possibly forty minutes. He remembered the wise words of one of his more experienced colleagues. Beware of being too inflexible over times of death. When was the victim last seen alive? When was he found? Between the two events, he died. That is the only definite piece of knowledge you've got.

He straightened up and took out his phone, relieved that he could get a signal out here. The ordinary citizen would call 999. But Tom was part of the system, he thought wryly, as he scrolled down the list of stored numbers. He rang Jess Campbell.

'What do you mean, you're out and about in the woods?' her voice squawked in his ear. 'You're sick and supposed to be at home!'

'I've found a body.'

'What do you mean, a body? What sort of body?'

'Bloke shot himself.'

A pause. 'Stay right there. Keep anyone else away. I'll be right out.'

Duty done, he crossed the path and leaned against a tree with his arms folded, waiting for the cavalry to arrive. It was very quiet now. The birds seemed to have fled the branches above his head and nothing scuttled through the undergrowth. He kept a sharp eye and ear out for the approach of anyone else. Those were Jess's orders and, in any case, Tom didn't want more walkers stumbling on the grisly sight. If he had continued down the red route, he thought ruefully, and not made the spur-of-the-moment decision to switch to the blue, he wouldn't have seen it himself.

The sense of feeling better that he had begun to experience had vanished as a result of events. His symptoms had returned. His nose and throat itched. His head was beginning to ache again. He could feel a sneeze building up and managed to scrabble in his pocket for a paper handkerchief before it erupted, making a noise not unlike a gunshot.

Thinking of gunshots, had no one heard a shot earlier? More thoughts struck him. He'd like to go back to the body, but he'd mess up the mud around it even more than he had done. You should keep away from a scene of – not crime. Poor devil had probably just decided to end it all. Tom scowled. He squinted at the seated figure a few feet away. Something about the way it sat there wasn't quite right. Heedless of the sodden mulch beneath his feet, Tom dropped down to sit with his back propped against the tree and re-enacted what might have occurred, using a thick stick lying nearby as a shotgun. The poor chap had probably pointed the barrel of the gun at his own face, contrived to fire it and fallen back as shot peppered his lower face and neck. The weapon had dropped from his hands. Tom released the stick. He let his hands fall to his sides as the dead man's were at his. The stick gun fell on to his lap and rolled off on to the ground.

He got up, wiped his trousers clean of wet vegetation and peered across at the corpse. He recalled his first thought on seeing the man; how stupid it was to sit on the wet ground. Just sitting for a few minutes had left the seat of Tom's trousers uncomfortably wet. The material of the dead man's trousers should be soaked.

'Not wet enough!' said Tom aloud. He went back to his tree,

propped himself against it, arms folded, and continued to contemplate his silent companion.

'Something not right about you, mate,' he said after a moment or two. 'You haven't been sitting there more than fifteen to twenty minutes. You didn't die there, in my view. Some blighter's moved you.'

Eventually, when Tom was beginning to think he'd be here, getting steadily colder and iller, until whatever he'd got turned to pneumonia, he heard the distant sound of motor vehicles, then of voices approaching.

A couple of uniformed men appeared first and, recognising Tom, called 'Morning, Doc!' before they began to look into the undergrowth around the spot. Two more figures came into view, one of them female, of medium height, with short red hair. Tom raised an arm and waved at Jess Campbell.

'Nasty,' she said when she reached the scene and had briefly studied the seated figure and the shotgun. She had moved away and joined Tom by his tree. For all her professional composure, her blue-grey eyes held deep shock.

'You'll want a print of my boots,' said Tom. 'I tried not to mess up the ground but I did take a close look at him.'

'We didn't request the police doctor. We thought you could certify that he's dead.' She crossed her arms and tucked her bare hands under her armpits to warm them. 'We'll get some screens up around him and cordon off the area. Photographer and mortuary van are on their way.'

The man with her – Tom identified the bulky form and morose expression of Sergeant Phil Morton – said, 'Poor devil. Wonder what made him do it?'

'How long do you think he's been dead, Tom?' Jess asked next.

Tom told her and added, holding Morton's gaze, 'But he didn't die there – or I don't think so.'

They both looked at him.

Morton, always a contrary sort of bloke, as Tom recalled, objected. 'He couldn't have moved far with the lower half of his face blown away.'

'Clothes are too dry,' said Tom. 'Back of his trousers, where his legs rest on the mud, should be wet right through. They're only fairly damp, despite the fact he's as good as sitting in a puddle. Also, although there is blood on his coat, there are no fragments of bone or flesh on that tree trunk behind him; it's as clean as a whistle. Nor are any pellets that might have missed his face embedded in the tree trunk or in the trees around. I'm not a firearms man, so I could be wrong, but would the gun have fallen like that? And then there's the nature of the injuries. I've seen a few shotgun deaths in my time. To me, that pattern of damage suggests that someone else blasted him in the face from a distance of, oh, a couple of metres away? Only a suggestion, mind you,' he finished, on an apologetic note. 'Check with Ballistics.'

Morton swore softly.

'In fact,' added Tom, warming to his theory, 'victims can survive that sort of blast, from that distance. This poor devil didn't. My guess is that pellets entered the brain.' He paused. 'I suppose I can't do the examination?'

Jess asked, her voice suddenly sharp, 'Of course you can't! You're ill! You're supposed to be at home, keeping warm and nursing that cold, not roaming around out here finding corpses.'

'Can't keep away from them,' said Tom weakly, almost managing to summon up a rueful smile before another sneeze caught him unawares and shattered the silence again.

'Oy!' protested Morton crossly. 'Don't give us all your blooming germs!'

'You haven't seen or heard anyone else around, I suppose?' Jess asked him.

Tom, his face smothered in his handkerchief, shook his head. When he could speak he croaked, 'Not a soul. I don't know what happened to that cyclist.'

'Which cyclist?' she asked abruptly.

'The one who left a bike chained to the fence post, back there in the car park.'

Morton muttered something under his breath and stalked away down the path. A few minutes later he was back.

'No bike there now,' he informed them.

'Then it looks like we've lost a witness!' Jess grumbled. 'Phil.' She turned to Morton. 'Better arrange for SOCO to come out here. We may have a scene of crime, after all. Hello! What's this?'

A sable and white rough collie had appeared, bounding down the track towards him. A voice yelled, 'Fred! Come back here!'

The dog skidded to a halt before the trio by the tree and panted happily at them, its bright eyes, above its long, pointed nose, fixed on them as if it expected something of them. The owner of the voice came running around the bend in the path and was revealed as a tall, strongly built woman in her forties with a weather-beaten complexion and wild, curling, grey hair. She wore a heavy knitted sweater under a shabby padded gilet and cord slacks tucked into gumboots. She staggered to a stop before them, saw the body, and exclaimed, 'What the hell's that?'

The collie had seen the body also, abandoned the group and rushed across to examine it. Morton darted after it and, having failed to catch its collar, tried to shoo the animal away.

'I'll get him!' shouted the woman, and ran across the muddy ground around the body to grab the dog's collar. Her animal secured, she remained staring down at the grisly sight.

'Madam!' shouted the exasperated Morton. 'Please take your dog and keep away from the area!'

'Decided to end it all!' said the woman with remarkable objectivity. She leaned towards the corpse and asked it, 'Why do it, you silly beggar? Giving everyone trouble!'

'Just go away!' snapped Morton. 'Take the dog with you and keep him on a lead. Look, you don't want to be here . . .'

She took no notice of him. She pursed her lips and considered the dead man. 'I'm not squeamish, officer, I won't faint or throw up.'

'I'm not worried about you!' snarled Morton. 'I'm worried about a crime scene.'

'Crime?' She looked up at last. 'What crime? Suicide isn't an offence these days, is it?'

Morton took a deep breath.

Before he could speak, Jess joined them. She had been listening to and watching the woman carefully.

'Can we have your name and address? We'll need prints of your footwear to eliminate them from the scene.'

The woman looked startled and transferred her attention from the body and Morton to Jess. 'Briggs. Mrs Tessa Briggs at the

Old Farmhouse. Down there.' She pointed into the distance back the way she'd approached, though nothing could be seen for the trees. 'I walk my dog here nearly every day,' she said defiantly.

Morton muttered something that, fortunately, was indistinguishable. The collie was pulling against the grip the owner had on its collar. It whined and writhed in obvious distress, trying to reach the body.

'Stop that, Fred!' snapped the owner. 'Nothing to do with you!'

But Fred had a mind of his own on that. He raised his nose into the air and let out an eerie howl.

Jess said gently, 'Looks as if your dog knows him.'

Morton asked, squinting at the woman because a winter sunbeam had broken through the cloud and dazzled him, 'Do you by any chance recognise the deceased, Mrs Briggs?'

The woman looked even more startled. 'Not much left to recognise, is there?'

'You didn't, for example, see anyone around earlier, anyone dressed like this man?' Morton moved to avoid the sun and peered at her again.

His scrutiny troubled Mrs Briggs. In fairness, Jess thought that Morton's glum face scowling at you was enough to unnerve anyone. She'd seen perfectly honest citizens get the jitters after a few minutes of it. The woman chose to get defensive.

'If I had, I'd have paid no attention. Around here every other walker is dressed much like that.' She indicated the body with an irritable gesture of her hand but did not look down again at the grisly scene. The collie, however, kept its eyes fixed on the dead man, and distressed whines sounded in its throat.

'You live not far away from these woods, you say. Did you hear a shot?' Jess prompted.

'Hear shots all the time. Don't take any notice of them,' she snapped. 'There's a place not far from here that's set up for clay-pigeon shooting. It's on land that used to belong to Crooked Farm. When the wind's in a certain direction, I hear *bang*, *bang*, *bang* all ruddy day. All kinds of people go there. Companies set up days out for their employees. Team building, they call it, don't they? Girls turn up in high heels, I've been told.'

As she listened to this, Jess was thinking that the woman was talking too much. Waffle, she judged it. It was probably the result of shock. The collie had now slumped dejectedly on the ground, his nose pressed on his outstretched front paws, keeping a mournful watch on the body. Jess felt frustration mounting in her, but there was no point in expressing it. She thought, *I wish Fred could give a statement.*

Chapter 4

'Hello, Tess,' said Guy Kingsley in mild surprise. 'Looking for Hattie? She's not out here. As far as I know, she's in the house.' Before she could answer, he went on, 'What do you think?' He waved proudly at the building work that had transformed the former stables.

Tessa Briggs, standing with her hands in her gilet pockets and her boots planted firmly in the muddy yard, glanced dismissively at Guy's pet project. 'Will be OK, I suppose. Hope you don't lose money on this brainwave, like the others!'

'You always show such confidence in me, Tess.'

'Don't call me Tess! I don't like it and you know it.'

'I don't like you dissing all my ideas, but I put up with it. So you can put up with me calling you Tess,' he retorted.

Tessa drew a deep breath. 'I haven't got time for a stupid argument with you. But it's you I want to see, not Hattie.'

Guy looked genuinely surprised. 'Good grief! I thought I was right off your list of favourite people, together with Carl. I don't blame you for not liking Carl. I don't care for the blighter myself. But I—'

'Oh, do shut up, Guy!' burst out Tessa. 'This is very important! And I've got to tell you quickly before Hattie comes out here.'

A wary look entered Guy's eyes. 'OK, come inside. It's quite safe. Derek's gone off for his lunch.' He brushed ineffectively at his wood-shaving-speckled sweater. It had holes at both elbows and rivalled Tessa's gilet for 'scruffy'.

Tessa followed him into the stable block, where, despite her urgent need to speak to him, she was briefly distracted by the freshly plastered walls, the half-installed plumbing, the stacked planks and the carpet of sawdust.

'Hell!' she said. 'What a mess!' She got back immediately to her errand. 'Listen up, Guy, it's Carl I've got to talk to you about.'

'He's not around, is he?' snapped Guy. 'I told him to stay away! He upsets Hattie. He's always broke and he's always moaning about John Hemmings's will!'

'He won't be bothering her again about that, or anything else. He's dead,' said Tessa bluntly. 'Or I think he is.'

'What on earth do you mean? You think he's dead? Who says so?'

'Will you shut up for a minute? I'm telling you, or trying to!' Tessa drew a deep breath. 'I took Fred down to Crooked Man Woods to walk him. We were going down one of the tracks and turned a bend to find coppers all over the place. They'd had a report of a body. And there was a body, right enough. It was propped up against a felled tree trunk. Fred went dashing up to it straight away and I went after him to try and catch him. The copper floundering around trying to seize his collar couldn't do it. I'm pretty sure it was Carl – the dead'un, I mean.'

'You know Carl as well as I do,' said Guy suspiciously. 'How can you only be "pretty sure"? You must know. How did he die?'

'Shotgun blast in the face. That's why I've got some reservations.

But the face – what was left of it – looked like Carl. And it was his hair; long enough for a girl, like he wore it – daft hairstyle at his age, in my opinion. But Fred knew him, no doubt about it; he started howling. Carl didn't have many qualities that recommended him to me, but he was good with animals, I'll say that. He made a fuss of Fred on the rare occasions we met up with him and Fred never forgets a friend.

'There was a woman police officer there, in ordinary clothes, not uniform, a sharp-looking number with red hair, and not the type to miss a trick. She and the fellow with her, a lynx-eyed blighter with a face like a wet week, also in civvies, asked me if I recognised the dead man, because they thought my dog did. I didn't let on, but there was Fred, tugging like mad, trying to get to the body, whining and telling the world he knew him. It was clear neither of them believed me. They then asked if I'd heard a shot earlier, and I mumbled about the clay-pigeon range and said I never took any notice of shots.'

'That, Tess, old girl,' said Guy evenly, 'was bloody stupid, if I may say so. You wouldn't pay attention to shots coming from the clay-pigeon set-up, but you'd pay attention to one coming from the woods. Shooting isn't allowed there. You should have been on the phone to the police, reporting it. Especially if it was a single shot, not like the shooting range, where they blast off quick fire.'

'To be honest, I had heard something earlier but wasn't sure enough. I waited for another and there wasn't one, so I left it. I didn't mention that to the police in the woods. I panicked, I suppose.'

Guy frowned. 'The officers you spoke to sound like plainclothes

– CID. What were they doing there? Got there pretty quickly, didn't they, for a suicide?'

Tessa looked at the ground. 'That's just it. There were uniformed guys poking about in the trees, and I got the impression the other two didn't think it was suicide. Don't ask me why they were so suspicious. He was sitting there, half his face gone, and a shotgun lying across his legs. How could it be anything else?'

There was a pause, then Guy said firmly, 'Listen, Tess. Perhaps Fred was howling like the hound of the Baskervilles, but that doesn't mean he knew it was Carl. It may be that he just knew the person was dead, and that freaked him out. You think Fred's a super-intelligent dog, but he's not a human, is he? You can't say that he has a human's thought processes.'

'Fred knew the bloke,' said Tessa stubbornly. 'Even the cops could see it.'

'Well, I'm not going to frighten Hattie into hysterics just because of Fred's behaviour. I don't think we should tell her about this right now. We can wait until—'

'Until what?' Tessa broke in angrily. 'Until the police arrive with the news? Who would you rather told her? Them or us?'

'If it wasn't – isn't – Carl, then they won't come, will they?' he pointed out.

'It *was* Carl,' said Tessa bluntly.

Guy said nothing and they stood in the shadowy stable amongst the debris, staring one another out. Finally, Guy took off his tweed cap, put up a hand to sweep an errant fringe of hair off his forehead, and replaced the cap with a military precision. 'All right, I respect your judgement, Tess, even if I'm not sure about Fred's. You reckon it was Carl, we'll take it that it *was* the silly bugger.

What was he doing in Crooked Man Woods? He lives in London. If he was in the area at all, he'd have been coming here to bend Hattie's ear about money.'

'I don't know, do I?' retorted Tessa.

For a moment, a wry smile touched Guy's lips. 'Oh, I'm never sure what you know, Tess.'

Her complexion turned a beetroot red. 'Look here, I didn't ask to find him!'

'No, no, of course you didn't,' he soothed her. 'All right, it *was* Carl you found – or someone else had found earlier and called the cops. If not, the police wouldn't have turned up so fast. Any sign of another civilian hanging around? Some innocent walker looking green or throwing up in the trees?'

She frowned. 'There was a youngish fellow, leaning against a tree a little way off. He did look a bit pale. He wasn't being violently ill or anything like that; he was pretty calm, in fact.'

'OK, Tess, then this is what we'll do. I'll go into the house and find Hattie, tell her you're here and that, possibly, you've got some bad news. I'll explain it all, and then call you in if Hattie wants to hear more. I've never wished the fellow dead. But in one way I hope you're right and I'm not about to frighten my wife into hysterics just because Fred threw a hissy fit in the woods.'

Harriet was huddled in a big old leather chair with side wings in the style sometimes called 'Queen Anne'. It had been her father's favourite seat. She ran a hand over the warm, smooth surface of the padded armrest, sensing his hand making the same gesture and, before his, an earlier generation doing the same thing. This room had been his study and escaped alteration through the years.

As a small child, she had liked to climb into the chair and curl up. It had always made her feel safe. It was failing to work its magic now. With a long wool cardigan wrapped around her and her fingers gripping a mug of lemon tea, she was waiting for Tessa to arrive with Guy.

The tea made her hands hot and the rest of her feel colder. She had drawn up her legs under her and knew that she had adopted the stance of that long-ago little girl. When her mother died, she had spent a lot of time in this chair. Then Nancy had arrived in her life as her father's new wife and someone Dad had optimistically hoped would be a new mother for her.

Harriet could see Nancy in her mind's eye: her floating skirts, ethnic waistcoats and multicoloured strings of beads, her long, mermaid-like, russet hair. She had cut an incongruous figure in the setting of the old house, fluttering through its rooms like some exotic butterfly that had flown in through a window and become trapped. Nancy had done her best, but she was far from the traditional notion of a mother. She never encouraged Harriet to eat her greens or suggested they spend a wet afternoon baking and decorating little cakes. But she did spend a whole hour one summer afternoon braiding daisies into her stepdaughter's hair. Harriet hadn't minded Nancy's arrival, because she sensed a return of happiness in her father. The problem had been that Nancy had trailed Carl in her wake, a truculent, difficult small boy.

Harriet remembered the first time she and he had met. He had stood in the middle of this room, staring round at everything and judging every stick of furniture and china vase. She had gazed at him fascinated because he was so beautiful, with his thick bob of blond hair and bright blue eyes. Then he had turned those blue eyes on her and assessed her in the same way he'd been judging the room. She had known then, with a child's unerring intuition, that she would never be free of him. He had arrived determined to take over everything: her father as replacement for the father who had deserted him, her home, her life and, ultimately, her.

Yet, in a curious way, they'd got along well together during their shared childhood. She'd felt that Carl had been proud to have her as his sister, even if she hadn't really been that, not a blood relative at all. He'd protected and championed her as loyally as a real brother would. She had sensed how vulnerable he was, deep down, particularly when Nancy died from a tumour on the brain diagnosed far too late. Harriet, not quite fourteen, had run to throw her arms around lanky, just-sixteen-year-old Carl and had promised to look after him.

'He took me at my word,' she murmured into the steam rising from her lemon tea. 'Poor Carl.'

Everything had been all right until Guy arrived in her life. Carl had recognised someone who would make a stronger claim on her and couldn't contain his jealousy. Guy, she was sure, had identified how dangerous Carl could be.

And now Carl was dead; gone, but never to be forgotten. She had heard the crunch of wheels earlier and knew that Tessa had arrived and that, true to the scenario she had sketched out to Harriet earlier, she would be talking to Guy, telling him what had happened. Soon they'd appear to break the dreadful news. Or perhaps Guy would come alone. One or both, they would tell her; and all she had to do was look shocked. Wasn't that what Tessa had said?

'I'm an idiot,' Harriet whispered. Her tea was cooling rapidly and the steam had almost evaporated. 'If I'd been thinking even a little clearly, I'd have refused to go along with Tessa's game plan. It's barmy. We won't get away with it. I should have picked up the phone, called the police to report that I'd found a body as soon as I got back here, then gone and told Guy. We'd have waited here together for them to come. But I called Tessa instead. Now I've got to get through this shameful piece of play-acting. Guy's not a fool. He'll know that something's wrong. Eventually, I'll have to tell him that Carl was coming down here to see me, because what other reason could there be for his presence but a plea for money? Guy will ask why Carl was in the wood. It will all come out. Guy will be upset that I've misled him. And then, what about the police? Isn't deliberately misleading them an offence? Tessa and I will look a pair of real idiots because of her stupid plan to "find" Carl.'

Maybe she could phone the police before Guy and Tessa got here? But it was too late. Footsteps were approaching.

She heard Guy ask, 'Hattie?' She looked up and saw him gazing down at her with concern. Tessa stood a little behind him. She looked worried. She thinks I can't go through with it, Hattie thought. Probably, she's right.

There was no need to act out any pretend shock. She was stunned by Tessa's news. A wild card had been thrown on to the table. Tess had not 'found' Carl. Her friend had driven to the woods and set off down the blue path, only to find the police already there. Harriet could hardly believe her ears. How could the police have got there so soon? She gazed from Guy to Tessa and back again, unable to speak. Guy interpreted that as distress. He spoke of calling their doctor. Tessa intervened.

'We don't need a doctor. We just need to put her to bed, keep her warm and let things take their course.'

They guided her upstairs. Tessa undressed her and tucked her up like an infant. But as soon as they left her, Harriet slid out of bed and – still like a small child – crept out on to the landing. She leaned over to try to catch what they were saying. Their voices were muffled. They'd closed the drawing-room door. Harriet ventured down the stairs, almost to the very bottom, where she sat down, face pressed against the uprights of the banister, listening.

Guy's voice was loud and angry. She could hear what he was saying clearly. 'What the hell is going on, Tess?'

'How do I know?' from Tessa.

She sounds too defensive, thought the eavesdropping Harriet.

'I know my wife.' Guy's voice faded then grew louder again. There was a bump, as if he'd collided with something. He must be striding up and down the room. 'You should have told the police you thought the dead man was Carl.'

'Well, I didn't!' snapped Tessa.

'And I'm going to!' he retorted.

'Suppose it isn't Carl?'

Guy's voice grew angry. 'You told me you were sure it was! Or that ruddy dog of yours was sure! You persuaded me to tell Hattie he was dead on the basis of it. For pity's sake, are you now changing your mind?!'

'No!' Tessa exploded. 'I'm not. But Hattie's in no state to have the house filled with police.'

'Think straight, Tess, can't you? You have – we have – information, and it should be given to the police. I'll phone them now.

53

I'll say you've discussed it with me. That's true. You have. You were doubtful, when you saw the body, whether it could be Carl, and you didn't want to mislead them. But you've had time to think it over and now you're sure. You came here because you were distressed and felt the family should know of the possibility.'

'That's true, too!' said Tessa sourly.

'Right! So we've decided to tell them.' Guy was now sounding very crisp and military, even though it was a good while since he'd left the army. 'It's a requirement, Tess!'

'Hattie can't cope with the police now!' Tessa was digging her heels in. She's trying to protect me, thought Harriet. They both want to protect me but they have different ideas how to do it, always have had.

'And when they do find out his identity, they will come here! What then? They'll soon suss out we already know.' His voice was growing aggressive. Guy didn't lose his temper often, even when arguing with Tessa. But when he did there was something ruthless about him.

Tessa had heard it, and there was a silence. Sounding grumpy in defeat, she said, 'All right. But wait until tomorrow. First thing in the morning, I'll call the police. I'll tell them I've been thinking about it all night. That I decided I had to tell them I think it's Carl.'

'No, Tess, we tell them *now*! We've already told Hattie. How can we tell the police tomorrow? Tell them you weren't sure in the woods, but you've thought it over and you are now!' A short pause, then Guy spoke again. 'Harriet's my wife and it's my decision. Since you won't pick up that phone, Tess, I bloody well will!'

'All right!' Tessa was angry because she knew Guy meant it. 'Just let me go upstairs and warn Hattie that the police may turn up at any moment.'

Harriet hurried back to her bed.

Moments later, Tessa appeared, with a face like thunder. 'Your husband is impossible!' She made a visible effort to control her ire. 'How are you doing, sweetie?' She sat down on the edge of the bed. 'Listen, love, Guy says we must tell the cops I have identified Carl. He's right, of course. But the' – Tessa glanced over her shoulder towards the closed door and lowered her voice – 'but the rest of our plan still stands.'

'Our plan?' Harriet muttered. 'My plan was to meet Carl in a nice, quiet place, without Guy knowing, and make him accept that there would be no more money. Not this nightmare.'

Tessa drew in a deep breath and then released it with a hiss. 'Then you agreed to my plan. Look, the main thing is, *you weren't there. You* didn't find him. Guy can wonder all he likes what Carl was doing in Crooked Man Woods, but there is absolutely no reason for him to know you'd arranged to meet him there. Nor that you found Carl before I did.'

Harriet said: 'You didn't, did you, find him? When you and Guy told me about it just now, you said that the police were already there when you got to the woods.'

'Yes, I hadn't expected that. I don't know how the cops got there so quickly.' Tessa scowled, then took her friend's hand. 'Keep your nerve, Hattie. It will be all right. No one need know you were in the woods this morning. You're doing fine now. Guy accepts you're shocked. The cops will accept you're shocked. They'll come and talk to you, sure. But then they will go away and – and whatever happens, you won't be involved.'

'Is Inspector Campbell in the building?' Ian Carter asked, stepping from his office into the corridor to intercept Tracy Bennison, who was marching briskly past, the soles of her shoes squeaking discordantly on the freshly cleaned floor tiles.

Bennison skidded to a halt with a noise like the skirl of bagpipes as his voice sounded behind her. She backed up a few steps. 'I saw her earlier, sir. I think she's still here.'

'See if you can find her and tell her I'd like a word, would you?'

He went back into his office and, as the squeal of Bennison's rubber soles receded, wandered over to the window and stared down into the car park, his hands resting on the windowsill. It was just over three years since he'd worn a wedding band. Yet, whenever he caught a glimpse of the back of his left hand, he fancied he could still see the faint impression in the skin of the ring finger. Imagination, of course. Trees fringing the parking area were bending and swaying before the stiff wind that swept across the area and sent the clouds above scudding across the sky. 'Driving away the rain', he'd heard people say of a wind like that.

Christmas and New Year had receded into memory. It seemed ages since he had returned his daughter, Millie, to her boarding school for the spring term. It was Millie's first school year as a boarder, having begun the previous September at the beginning of the winter term. The decision to send her to board had been largely that of Sophie, his former wife, who had now moved to live in France with her second husband, Rodney. Ian hadn't been happy about it at first. But he'd realised that at least it meant that

Millie was still in the country. He was able to see her more often than he'd done when Sophie and that smug blighter Rodney had been living here. Moreover, Millie had settled in well and seemed happy.

'All for the best,' said Ian aloud. 'Or as much as can be.'

'What is, sir?' asked a voice behind him, and he spun round to find that Jess had arrived and was standing by his desk.

'Thinking aloud!' he said quickly. 'We need a chat about this shotgun case. Sit down.'

When they had seated themselves, he indicated a scuffed leather wallet and a plastic envelope holding a paper driving licence of the type being phased out lying on the desk. 'According to these items, found in the deceased's inner coat pocket, our body is that of someone called Carl Finch.'

'Yes, we're assuming that to be his identity,' Jess said. She paused. 'Tom Palmer, who found him, thinks he was killed elsewhere and the body moved to the woods. We are looking for a cyclist who may have been in the area and seen something. Tom's certain there was a bike in the parking area of the woods when he got there. It was gone by the time we arrived. Unless he or she comes forward, we may never trace the rider.'

Carter made a muffled sound that mixed suspicion with derision. 'What was Palmer doing in the woods? I understood he was sick and off work. Sounds to me as if he was making one of those hiking trips he's so keen on!'

Jess hastened to defend Tom. 'He really is off sick. He's got a very bad cold. But he wanted some fresh air, he says, and thought a stroll in the woods might clear his head. Now he's sorry he didn't stay home.'

'That'll teach him!' commented Carter with satisfaction. 'So what was Mr Finch – if our dead man really is Finch – doing in the middle of the countryside, dead in a wood? His driving licence gives an address in north London.' Carter tilted forward over his desk so that Jess was looking at his thick, iron-grey hair. He touched the items on the desk gently and then looked up. 'You remember children's parties when you were young?' he asked unexpectedly.

Startled not only by the question, but by being caught in the sharp gaze of those hazel eyes, which sometimes, as now, took on a greenish shade, Jess heard herself blurt, 'I'm a twin, as you know. My brother and I had a joint birthday party and two sets of guests make a big crowd. There were balloons and cakes with coloured icing on them, lots of screaming and yelling and nearly always someone being sick. It was great.'

'Millie enjoyed birthday parties,' Carter said, leaning back in his chair again. 'I suppose she still does. But after Sophie and I parted, and since Rodney came into the equation, I haven't been there. Rodney has.' He had been unable to keep the bitterness from his voice. He paused, and resumed more briskly. 'I remember there was one game she liked, because she was good at it. There was a tray with various objects on it, lots of them. The kids had three minutes or so to study them and commit them to memory. Then the tray was taken away and they had to write down all the objects they could remember. Millie had – still has – a memory like the proverbial elephant. She could usually remember every one.'

'I remember that game,' Jess said.

He pointed at the desk. 'This time, it's easy. There are only two objects here to remember. Where are the rest? Where's his smartphone? He must have had one. Where are his car keys and, come to that, where's his car? He either drove to the woods himself, or he died elsewhere – and Tom Palmer believes there is a possibility he did. In that case, his body was transported to the woods in another vehicle. But he'd come down from London so his own car must be somewhere.'

'He could have travelled from London by train,' Jess suggested, 'and someone else drove him, alive or dead, to the woods. We'll know more about that when Maurice Melton has given his findings.'

'Fortunately,' said Carter, 'Melton doesn't disappear every time he gets a cold. I understand he's coming in later this evening, especially to do the post mortem.' He picked up the wallet. 'If Finch came by train, it would be to Gloucester railway station. To get from there to Crooked Man Woods, way out in the country, he'd need a car. Or someone must have given him a lift. There's no return train ticket in this wallet, by the way. Where are his house keys? He might have left his car keys at home if they weren't required. But he would need his front-door key to get back inside when he returned home.' Carter uttered a sort of discontented growl. 'There aren't enough items in that wallet.'

'There are credit cards and some cash! Oh, and we have the driving licence!' Jess protested.

'Yes, I know. But where are all the other bits and pieces that find their way into a wallet? No photo of a loved one or a pet. No receipts for fuel or the last time he used his Visa or credit card. My wallet's stuffed full of odd bits of paper and photos of Millie.'

'Perhaps Finch didn't have a loved one, or a child, or a pet.'

A quick succession of agonised squeaks from outside in the corridor was growing louder.

'Can't someone do something about that floor?' Carter complained. 'I know it's been given a facelift and a special polish, but surely—'

He broke off as someone rapped at the door. Sergeant Phil Morton's unmistakable outline filled the space.

'Thought you'd both like to know, sir, we've had a phone call from a Captain Guy Kingsley who lives at a place called the Old Nunnery. He reckons the dead man in the woods could be his brother-in-law.'

Both Ian Carter and Jess stared at him. 'How does he know about a body in the woods?' Jess asked.

Morton gave a rare smile. 'You recall that woman with the dog, the one who came along and marched all over the scene? Well, it seems that she got to thinking after she left us there and she decided she did know the deceased, after all. She is now pretty certain it is Carl Finch, as that driving licence shows.' Morton pointed at the desk. 'So she went to the house, this Old Nunnery, because that's where Finch's sister – actually, stepsister – and her husband live, and told them.'

'Why the dickens didn't she come here and tell us – or phone?' demanded Carter, pushing back his chair with a noisy scrape as he got to his feet.

'She thought a friend ought to break the news of Finch's death to the family, not the police,' explained Morton. 'She told this Captain Kingsley – he's no longer a serving officer, by the way – and together they broke the news to Mrs Harriet Kingsley. Then

Captain Kingsley' – Morton rolled the title off his tongue with a malicious relish – 'phoned us.' Morton's smile became positively demonic. 'He thought it was the correct thing to do.'

There was a silence. Then the expression in the hazel eyes hardened and Carter said quietly, 'Jess – and you, Phil – I do so hope this isn't going to be a case of someone playing silly games.'

Chapter 5

Ian Carter outlined their strategy as Phil Morton drove him with Jess to the Old Nunnery. 'You talk to Finch's sister, Harriet Kingsley, Jess. I'll take the husband outside, or into another room, and ask him what he can tell us about Finch and if he has any objection to viewing the body with regard to making a positive identification. It's unreasonable to ask the sister to look at the remains. But Guy Kingsley was in the army at some point, so he ought to be up to it.'

'What about Mrs Briggs, the woman with the dog?'

'Your job, Phil!' said Carter.

Morton, glowering through the windscreen, said, 'If she'd spoken up back there in the woods and identified the dead man, we would have come here directly, without Mrs Briggs making herself a go-between. I can't get on with people like her, the old county type. They used to run things, and think they still do – or should do! She's a law unto herself. She can't be trusted to tell us everything, even now. She thinks we're a bunch of clod-hopping peasants. We've got no business poking our noses into the private business of our betters!'

'She was trying to protect a friend,' Carter returned mildly. 'She says she wanted to break the news to the family. She didn't want it left to us. There's logic in that. OK, she should have come

63

to us first. But you know as well as I do, Sergeant, that people put family loyalties and friendship first. So you can put away the red flag!'

'But we are treating this as a suspicious death, sir?' Morton persisted.

'Yes, but I don't want the family alarmed. It's bad enough that they have to cope with a shocking death. They don't yet need to know we think the body may have been moved. Or that some other person fired the fatal shot. Until the post mortem's been completed, we can't be sure of that ourselves.'

'Tom wouldn't have suggested it, if he wasn't sure,' Jess said.

'We need the coroner's go-ahead, even so. So, kid gloves on, right? We are sympathetic, but we try to find out everything we can about the family. Something is wrong. Someone, possibly Finch himself, filleted the contents of his wallet. What is it he, or someone else, didn't want us to see?'

They had reached the Old Nunnery and turned into the drive.

'Nice place,' muttered Morton.

A muddy jeep was already parked before the house and, as they climbed out of their car, muffled barking sounded from it. A hairy canine face bobbed up and down at a window, bright, round eyes either side of a long, white muzzle in a thick mane of golden tan hair.

'Fred!' said Jess. 'That means Mrs Briggs is still here!'

'Ruddy woman,' muttered Morton from the rear. 'Is she going to be under our feet every minute?'

'Relax, Phil,' advised Jess.

Morton remained unmollified. 'We are taking her word for it, ma'am. I mean, Mrs Briggs *now* says it was Finch back there in the woods this morning. But she wasn't sure enough to say so at the time. Suppose she's wrong? Half the bloke's face was gone. The items found in his pocket could have been planted there. We could all be charging off down the wrong path.'

A faint whine came from the jeep followed by a frantic scrabbling at the windows as Fred tried to persuade them to release him.

'That's why we're here,' said Morton, answering his own question. 'The ruddy dog identified him.'

The three people they'd come to see were gathered in a large, comfortable room. The walls were painted jade green below a white plaster frieze. Against the wall facing the windows, oak bookcases had been built in at least a hundred years ago. They were in three adjacent sets of shelves. Two of the shelves were filled with modern books but the remaining third, on the right of the group, held very old books, with cracked and peeling dark leather spines, packed closely together. Another frieze of oak leaves and animal forms ran along the top of the wide stone hearth, in which a log fire crackled and spat. This room, thought Jess, must be one of the oldest parts of the house and had survived pretty well intact.

Harriet Kingsley was a pale figure in a blue wool sweater and jeans, snuggled into a leather-covered, Queen Anne-style chair. Jess judged her to be an attractive thirty-nine or forty. It was hard to tell because she had that girlish look some fair-skinned, fair-haired women keep long after girlhood. A blue-and-pink silk scarf was wound round her neck and fell in two crumpled ribbons down the front of the sweater. Her fingers played nervously with the trailing ends. Her long hair had been brushed back and tied with another scarf at the nape of her neck. The sweater and jeans looked very clean, as if they had just been taken from a drawer. Her hair looked freshly arranged. Jess thought, *someone has tidied her ready to see us, got her to change into clean clothes and brush her hair, probably got her to wash her face.* Why? What was wrong with the clothes she had been wearing?

Her husband, Guy Kingsley, hovered protectively at the side of the chair, with one arm along the back of it, above his wife's head. Otherwise, he stood very straight, staring at the visitors, as if about to deliver a report to a senior officer.

Mrs Briggs looked much as she had done in the woods earlier. She stood in front of the fireplace with her hands thrust into the pockets of her well-worn gilet. With more time to study her, Jess noted her wide-set hazel eyes, snub nose and lack of lipstick. Her untidy, greying hair suggested that she'd chopped it off herself. Nevertheless, thought Jess, she's younger than I judged her to be back there in the woods. She and Harriet are much the same age. Tessa Briggs doesn't bother about how she looks and probably never has. No one has mentioned a Mr Briggs. Is he dead? Divorced? Decamped? Away on business? With luck, Phil Morton will find out.

After expressing an apology for troubling them all at such a distressing moment, Carter turned his attention to Guy Kingsley.

'Captain Kingsley, perhaps you and I could have a word in private?'

Kingsley hesitated and looked down at his wife. She reached

up a hand to pat his arm. 'Go ahead, Guy, I'll be all right. Tessa is here.'

'Well,' Carter said mildly, 'I'd like Mrs Briggs to go and have another talk with Sergeant Morton. We saw your dog in your car, Mrs Briggs. He doesn't like being left out of things, I fancy. Perhaps you and Sergeant Morton could release him and take him for a walk in the grounds, if that's all right with you, Captain Kingsley?'

'Someone should stay with Harriet!' Tessa Briggs said belligerently.

'Inspector Campbell has a lot of experience talking to the recently bereaved,' said Carter.

Kingsley, recognising an order, however gently expressed, said, 'Come along, Tess.'

'I'm all right,' Harriet said, when she and Jess were at last alone. 'They wanted to call a doctor to me, but I don't need one. I'm upset, of course I am. Carl and I – I was very fond of Carl.'

'The body has yet to be identified officially,' Jess said quietly.

Harriet twitched. 'I can't do it, look at him. Too horrible.' Her hands tightened on the silk scarf ends. 'Horrible,' she repeated.

The disjointed response wasn't unexpected. Jess assured her: 'We weren't going to suggest you did. Superintendent Carter is asking your husband if he'll take a look at the body.'

Harriet didn't reply for a few moments, staring past Jess towards the bookcases on the far wall. Then she whispered, 'He did shoot himself, didn't he?'

'We're not sure.'

'No one else would shoot him!' Harriet now looked Jess full in the face. 'No one else would shoot Carl,' she repeated firmly. 'It's impossible.'

'Why don't you tell me about your brother?' Jess suggested. 'Did he have a partner, wife or ex-wife? Because she'll have to be told.'

'No, no wife. I don't know about his love life. It wasn't something he ever mentioned. There are things about Carl I don't know, because he never told me. He wasn't my blood brother. He was my stepbrother, not related at all, strictly speaking. Dad took him on when he married Carl's mother. But we grew up here together, for the larger part of our childhood.' Harriet shifted in the wide depths of the big leather chair into which she seemed to have retreated like a sea creature into its shell.

That chair, thought Jess, is a place of safety for her. She's afraid to leave it because she might fall apart. They are all hiding something. Or she is – and that woman Briggs. Not sure about the husband. But he'll be a much tougher nut to crack if he is.

The far wall still seemed to hold Harriet's attention. Now she raised her arm and pointed towards it. Jess turned her head, looked across the room and saw, to the right of the bookcases, a portrait in oils of a pretty woman in a blue dress.

'Your mother?' she guessed.

'Yes. She was driving home alone one dark evening. A gate had been left open to a field and horses had got out into the lane. She drove straight into one of them. She and the horse were both killed. I was four years old.'

'I'm very sorry,' said Jess quietly.

'After she died I would come in here and stand in front of that painting. I'd imagine she was smiling at me.' Harriet gave a brief, sad smile.

'That must have been hard for your father, to be left with a very young child.'

Harriet nodded. 'Dad was shattered by it, but he was determined to create a happy family life for me. It wasn't easy, of course. He had to be away a lot. I had a succession of nannies. Most of them were young and they didn't stay long. The Old Nunnery was too remote, more so back then than it is now. Being on their own here with me, when Dad was away, really spooked them. We had a daily cleaner, Mrs Walsh, but she went home early, just after lunch. Sometimes Dad was away for two or three days at a time, so you can understand why the nannies soon decided they'd had enough. There's quite a lot of old wood in the rafters and wainscoting. At night it moves, creaking and squeaking. Perhaps the squeaking was mice. Mrs Walsh didn't take too much trouble over the cleaning. Then Dad remarried. He wanted me to have a mother, or at least a permanent female figure in my life.' Quickly, she added, 'Of course, that's not the only reason he married Nancy. I mean, he was lonely, too.'

'Was Nancy someone you already knew?'

'Oh no, she was a woman he met on a train.' Harriet looked up and pulled a wry expression. 'I don't mean an exotic transcontinental luxury train; and she wasn't a mysterious beauty wrapped in furs – you know, like in an old film. It was a regular workhorse of a train, bringing Dad back from London, and it broke down. They were stuck on the line in the middle of nowhere for two hours. Sitting opposite him was an attractive, fairly young woman wearing a rather odd mix of clothes and lace-up boots. The clothes caught his interest first, he always said. She had a little boy with her. He was nine, actually, not that little.'

Harriet stopped speaking and Jess prompted gently, 'Carl?'

Harriet blinked and stared at her with a startled expression, as if she really had forgotten she was talking to a stranger. 'Yes, Carl. Dad and Nancy, the woman with the boots, got talking during the two hours. They found out they were both single parents. Carl's father had been a session musician, dependent on work being offered and travelling to wherever he might find it. Nancy hadn't seen him since Carl was two. I think she fascinated Dad. He'd never met anyone quite like her. I liked her, too, when I finally met her. So Dad got the bright idea that it would be a good thing all round if he and Nancy got together, made a new little nuclear family: Dad, Mum, two kids – national average.'

'And it worked out well, you say?'

'Oh, yes, while we were children it worked fine.'

'Tell me,' Jess asked her. 'Did your father formally adopt Carl?'

Harriet shook her head. 'No, and when Nancy died Carl had just turned sixteen. She'd been having really bad headaches for a while and had been treating them with herbal brews from plants she gathered herself. The cause was much too serious for that to do any good, but she didn't consult a doctor until far too late.

'There was no problem about Carl remaining here. He wanted to stay and there was nowhere else for him to go. Not being legally adopted didn't worry him. Of course, later, when Dad's will was read and almost everything, including the house and land, came to me, it was a shock to Carl. I don't mean Dad didn't leave him *anything*. He was quite generous in his bequest. But Carl . . . I realise now that Carl had persuaded himself that the estate would be divided between us, him and me, including the house. He made a bit of a fuss. I sometimes wonder if, for Carl, it was as if a second father had turned his back on him.'

'Like the deserting musician?'

'Yes, a bit like that.' Harriet hesitated. 'But that wasn't it! Dad saw to it that Carl had a good education and, yes, behaved like a father to him. But generations of our family have lived here at the Old Nunnery. Dad wanted me to pass the house on to my children; he made that quite clear. That's why I think that not adopting Carl, when he was a child, was deliberate on Dad's part. Trouble is, Guy and I don't have any children.

'Guy was still in the army at the time of our wedding, but when his last tour in Afghanistan was over, he quit. He said it wasn't fair to me for him to be away and, anyway, he had plans for this house – and Dad was very ill. Guy and I moved in to take care of him.'

'And Carl moved out?' Jess asked shrewdly.

Harriet flushed. 'He'd already done that. He was living in London. He had a job there and seemed settled at the time. Later, he turned out to be not so good at keeping jobs. When Dad died, it turned out there wasn't quite as much money— Well, Guy and I have been trying to make a profitable business out of the house ever since.'

'Why do you think Carl was in the area today? Had he come down from London to see you?'

'He must have done, I suppose.' Harriet began to look distressed. 'I don't know.'

'Any idea why he would have gone to those woods, not come here to the house?'

'He'd stopped doing that, coming here. He and Guy, well, they don't – didn't – get along.' Suddenly, Harriet swung her feet to the ground and sat up straight. 'I'm sorry, I can't go on with this conversation. I feel as if someone has kicked the feet from under me. So can we stop this now? I can't go on talking about my brother as if he – he was still alive, about to walk in. Surely you understand? I can't tell you why he was in Crooked Man Woods today. I haven't the slightest idea.'

'I do understand how upsetting this is for you,' Jess said sympathetically. 'I'll come back another time.'

'Oh?' said Harriet, sinking back into the chair and staring at her in dismay. 'Will you?'

Meanwhile, Phil Morton was having an even less productive talk with Tessa Briggs. With Fred trotting happily ahead of them, his tail waving gently, they had crossed the cultivated part of the garden. They were now descending a grassy slope. The light was fading fast and it wasn't possible to appreciate fully the view before them but, even so, it impressed. In summer, thought Morton, it must be spectacular. The land rolled away like a carpet down to a fringe of trees and a glittering ribbon that sparkled in the evening sun like tinsel. A stream, thought Morton. To think of owning this perfect place!

The conversation had so far been monosyllabic. Now he was offering a new opening.

'Nice place,' he said enviously. 'Big, too. Perhaps, if I win the lottery, I'll buy a hideaway like this.' He gestured at the open grassland around them. 'They don't plan to do anything with this?'

'They used to keep horses,' said Tessa briefly.

'Who rode? Both Mrs Kingsley and her husband?'

'Hattie had a pony when she was a kid, like we all did.'

Well, thought Morton, you might have done. It wasn't the usual thing where I come from. The best I could hope for was a second-hand bike, and I had to wait for that until my brother outgrew it.

Tessa added, in a burst of speech, 'Carl had a pony, too, because John Hemmings didn't want him to feel left out, and I suppose he thought Nancy would expect it. But it was one of the many things John did out of kindness that put the wrong ideas into Carl's head.'

'Wrong ideas?' Morton probed.

Tessa refused to expand and went on brusquely: 'It was a waste of time, because Carl wasn't interested; the wretched animal was sold after a short time. Hattie was devoted to Pip, her pony, and even after she outgrew him they kept him on to spend his retirement here, in this field.'

'Carl wasn't a countryman?' suggested Morton.

'How could he be? Until he came here he'd lived in a tower block. Fast cars, that's what he liked, and he got himself one as soon as he was old enough to hold a licence.'

'Pity there are no horses here now.' Morton swept a hand across the view.

'Well, they ran a riding stables for a bit,' said Tessa.

'The Kingsleys?'

Tessa turned her head to look at him. 'Of course. Who else?'

'I meant' – Morton feared he was floundering – 'had Mrs Kingsley's family run a riding stables here? This is her family home, I understand.'

'Yes, it's that all right.' Tessa nodded. 'But John Hemmings wasn't the sort to run a set-up like a riding stables. He was a businessman, had a finger in a lot of pies, but property development, mostly.'

'So all this, and the house, belong to Mrs Kingsley?'

Tessa Briggs scowled at him and replied simply, 'Yes.'

'Nice place to inherit,' said Morton, determined to get something out of this battleaxe of a woman.

Perhaps Tessa realised he wasn't going to give up and that she would have to provide some information. 'I understand,' she added grudgingly, 'that Hattie's grandfather, Charlie Hemmings, started out as a builder turned developer. He married well. That's how he got this house. His wife had inherited it following the death of an aunt. Charlie went on to buy land. In those far-off days, it was cheap. His son, John Hemmings, set about developing it. He put golf courses, or housing estates, all over the place, whatever suited the local market. Even developed a few abroad – Spain, Portugal. Don't ask me for details. I don't know.'

'But you sound like an old friend of the family?'

'Hattie and I went to school together.'

'And you farm near here, I gather? You and your husband?'

'He's gone,' she retorted. 'And it's only a farm in name now. Most of the land was sold off. There's just the farmhouse left, and a couple of fields.'

Her mouth snapped shut and Morton guessed he wasn't going to get any more. But he had one last try.

'So you knew the dead man, Carl Finch, well?'

'Of course I knew Carl.' Tessa stopped and faced him. 'He lived here from when he was a kid until he left to go off to London. He was away at school, of course, in term time, as were Hattie and I. But in the holidays we were all here and hung out together – until we got a bit older and Carl made other friends.'

'What friends?' Morton gazed blandly at the nearest tree.

'Oh, local lads. He played for the cricket team and drank in local pubs. Whatever young men do! Look here, I didn't tell you it was him in the woods when we were there because I'd had a shock, and I couldn't believe it was possible. We all thought he was in London. Afterwards, I realised it must be Carl, the silly sod. So I thought I'd better come up here and tell – tell Guy and Hattie.'

'You didn't like Carl Finch?' Morton suggested gently, turning his gaze back on her.

'Couldn't stand him!' replied Mrs Briggs, and for the first time the words burst out spontaneously. Seeing that Morton was waiting for some explanation, she went on, 'There are givers and takers in this life, and Carl Finch was a taker. He could be fun, but I never felt quite at ease with him. He was a watcher. Do you know what I mean?'

'Not exactly,' said Morton cautiously.

Tessa drew a deep breath. 'Well, he was always sizing the situation up and looking to see if it could be made to work for him. Really, that's all you need to know about Carl Finch.'

They turned back towards the house. 'Those buildings over

there, behind the house, they're the stables?' asked Morton, pointing. 'Where the riding school was?'

'Yes.' Tessa's voice suggested that, as far as she was concerned, any further conversation with Morton was superfluous.

'They're all in a bit of a mess now,' observed Morton cheerfully. 'They seem to be doing renovations.'

'They're being converted into holiday accommodation,' she told him grudgingly.

'Quite the thing now, I suppose, if you've got a big place like this.' Morton nodded sagely. 'Who does the Range Rover belong to – the black one parked over there?'

'Guy.'

'Mrs Kingsley got a car of her own?'

'Look here,' snarled Tessa. 'Do you need to know bally everything? Hattie had a little runabout but it kept breaking down so she sold it in a part-exchange deal for a new vehicle. She's waiting on delivery for that.'

'I'm just interested in cars,' said Morton.

'It strikes me, Sergeant,' said Mrs Briggs, 'that you're interested in a lot of things.'

'Can't be helped,' said Morton with a sigh. 'It's partly my nature and partly training.'

'Look here!' She wheeled round and forced him to halt. 'Out with it! Do you think Carl's death is fishy?'

'Why would we think that?' he asked her.

'Because you've all raced up here mob-handed to interview us all!'

'Superintendent Carter is here to ask Captain Kingsley if he will go to identify the body, and to explain to him just what a mess his brother-in-law's face is, so that he is prepared for it.'

'Don't envy him that!' she muttered.

'Inspector Campbell is talking to Mrs Kingsley. She's good at talking to people who are very shocked.'

'And you?' Tessa fixed a gimlet eye on him.

'Oh, me,' said Morton mildly, 'I'm just the driver.'

'Piffle!' retorted Mrs Briggs.

'What a bloody mess,' said Guy Kingsley softly.

The attendant had pulled out the drawer with its burden of a sheeted form and turned back the cloth covering the head. Kingsley and Carter stood by the side of it. Carter had already seen the corpse once and Kingsley must have seen similar sights during his army time, but neither of them had quite been able to control their instinctive revulsion.

'Sorry to bring you to see it,' Carter replied. 'But so far we've only got Mrs Briggs's word for it being Carl Finch.'

'What? Oh, it's Carl, all right. And don't apologise for bringing me down here to identify the poor bloke. You couldn't bring Harriet.'

'The features are partly destroyed,' Carter said. 'Would you know if there are any identifying marks on the body? Just to confirm we have the right man.'

Kingsley nodded. 'Yes, there should be a long scar across the palm of his left hand. He slashed it with a Stanley knife when he was a kid, making a model plane or something. He had to be rushed into A&E, get it stitched.'

Carter nodded at the attendant, who drew back the sheet from the left arm.

'That's it,' Kingsley confirmed. 'He was lucky not to lose the use of any of his fingers. It's Carl. Oh, and I believe he broke his left arm, also when he was a kid, about twelve. That was falling out of a tree. That should show up on an X-ray.'

'Fair enough.' Carter nodded at the attendant. 'You can put him away.'

Outside the building, Kingsley said, 'I've seen some gruesome injuries. But out there, in Afghanistan, you expected it. You knew it could happen to you, if it was your day to step on some home-made explosive device. But this is different – and you saw how upset my wife is already. She's probably still clinging to a faint hope that it's not Carl, and I'm going to have to destroy that. Do you mind? I could do with a drink.'

'There's a pub around the corner,' Carter told him. 'I'm on duty, so I'll be drinking something non-alcoholic. But I understand you wanting something stronger.'

When they were settled, Kingsley said, 'I knew Tess Briggs wouldn't have come haring up to the house with the news if she hadn't been sure, but—'

'It's a pity she didn't tell the officers at the scene that she recognised the deceased. She was certain enough to come imme-diately to tell you and your wife.' Carter sipped his tomato juice, wondering why he'd ordered it. He didn't care for it.

'Don't blame Tess. She wanted to be the one to tell Hattie, not some copper suddenly on the doorstep – no offence.'

Carter set down his tomato juice. 'Tell me about your wife's stepbrother. Did you look on him as a brother-in-law?'

'Not really. We weren't pals. He claimed I'd influenced John Hemmings, Hattie's father, into cutting him out of a share in the property. I didn't, by the way.'

'And that was the reason you didn't get on?'

Kingsley frowned at a crowd of young men who had gathered at the bar and were noisily demanding service. 'That and the fact that I'd married Hattie and taken her attention away from him. He was a selfish blighter. It seems a rotten thing to do, speak ill of him when he's not far from us here, cold in a mortuary drawer. But – what the hell – he was.'

Fortunately, the young men were moving away into a further room off the main bar. The pub was an old one, and rambling. The group was now completely out of sight, around a corner, and only the occasional burst of laughter indicated their presence.

'Did you know he owned a shotgun?'

'Carl? No, I didn't. I can't imagine why he needed one. He didn't live in the country.'

'Do you shoot?'

'Do I have a shotgun? Yes, I do, as it happens. It's locked in a gun cabinet, as it should be, and I have a licence. I can show you both gun and licence when we get back.'

'I will need to see the gun, as a matter of routine. Another thing – do you happen to know what kind of car Finch drove?'

Kingsley nodded. 'Yes, he was driving a Renault these days, a Megane. He bought it fairly recently, I believe. There should have been no way he could have afforded a new car. He may have been paying it off monthly. But knowing Carl, it's the sort of thing he'd do if he had a big win, say, at cards. He used to play with the high rollers, at private clubs and casinos. I know he occasionally did have a big win. But instead of using it to clear a backlog of debt, he'd go out and buy a new car, or he'd make some other big lifestyle statement, I suppose you'd call it. I'd say it was important to him to look as if he had money, not only for vanity's sake but because if some of the people he played cards with suspected he'd never be able to honour his losses, the roof would fall in on him.'

'So far, we've found no abandoned car at the woods. At least now you've told us we're looking for a Renault.'

'Tell me something,' Kingsley said suddenly. 'You've been a police officer a good few years, I imagine. You've made superintendent. You must have pretty well seen it all.'

'I've seen a lot,' Carter admitted cautiously, 'but there's always something surprising.'

'Fair enough. What I want to ask is, do you believe that some kinds of behaviour can be passed on through the genes?'

'Like selfishness? Or fecklessness? Is that what you mean?'

'If you like.'

'I can only say,' Carter said carefully, 'that children do pick up the behavioural patterns of those around them. I don't think that is quite what you mean, but it's nearest I'm prepared to go.'

Guy nodded. 'OK, let me tell you something about Carl's childhood. That colleague of yours – Inspector Campbell? Right, if she's talking to Hattie about Carl, Hattie may tell her how her father met Nancy, Carl's mother, on a train. I never knew Nancy but, from I've learned about her, she was a real flake. Apparently, she had hung around with rock musicians, and one of them had fathered Carl. He'd subsequently taken off, never sent any money for his child's support, and it would have been no good chasing him for any, because he never had any. He wasn't someone famous.

'I don't think Hattie knows the reason Nancy was on that train, with her child. I can tell you, because my father-in-law told me the tale, one Christmas Eve when we were sitting up late in his den having a nightcap. That's the room you were in earlier, with the log fire, only he called it a study. We turned it into a drawing room. He'd started reminiscing; you know how it is. Carl hadn't joined us for Christmas, ostensibly because he'd gone skiing. The real reason was because I would be there and he couldn't stand me. The feeling was mutual.

'Anyhow, the way things went, it seems Nancy had been on her way to visit some old auntie who had a few pounds put by. She was hoping the old lady would take a shine to young Carl and help out with a generous donation. She confessed that freely to John Hemmings. As I said, John, with a few whiskies inside him, had got sentimental about Nancy that Christmas Eve. "She was always open and truthful, never hid anything," he told me. I thought, though didn't say, *If you believe that, old chap, you'll believe anything*.

'I suspected that Nancy had summed up John very quickly. Old auntie had a few quid, but this lonely man on a train had a lot more. But John was getting maudlin, so I listened to it all without comment, then chivvied him off up to bed.'

Kingsley picked up his empty glass and contemplated it thoughtfully, as if it might turn into a crystal ball. 'Talk about a fateful encounter!'

He put the glass down. 'You know, John Hemmings did leave Carl a respectable sum. He got through it in no time. Lived well beyond his means. Liked hanging out with free-spending City traders, liked going to the races, casinos, any place where wads of cash changed hands. He couldn't keep up, of course, and was always looking for a handout. He used to turn up at the Old Nunnery with tales of financial woe. He could talk Hattie into subbing him, but not me. It was getting to be a habit, so I took him aside eventually and told him to stay away. I made it clear I would enforce that physically, if necessary – chuck him out.'

'And you think that's why he'd come down from London this time, to borrow money from your wife?'

Kingsley glowered at the glass. 'Sure of it.'

'So,' Carter said carefully, 'do you think that he had arranged to meet your wife in Crooked Man Woods?'

Kingsley looked up with a fierce expression on his face. 'Hattie had nothing to do with his death!'

'I'm not suggesting that. But you had forbidden him to come to the house. He may have been desperate to borrow some money—'

'I don't want Hattie badgered about this!' Kingsley snapped.

'It's called police enquiries, Captain Kingsley,' Carter reminded him, 'being made into a suspicious death.'

'I know, I know!' Kingsley drew a deep breath. 'Look, just let me ask her, OK? I will, as soon as it's – a suitable moment. That's not today, or tomorrow, but soon.'

Carter shook his head. 'I'm sorry. I understand you want to protect your wife. But you can't set the schedule of our enquiries, you know. Inspector Campbell will probably call and see Mrs Kingsley again tomorrow morning.'

Kingsley said softly, 'Damn!'

'Well, there it is,' Carter told him. He abandoned the unfinished tomato juice, pushing the glass away from him. It looked like blood. 'Finch must have had a reason for being in the area.'

Kingsley said nothing. Out of their sight, the group of young men were toasting someone noisily. Perhaps it was a birthday.

Looking at his companion, Ian Carter thought: *You and I are thinking the same thing, aren't we? Mrs Briggs and your wife have been less than frank.*

Chapter 6

'I brought takeaway,' announced Jess as Tom let her into the flat that evening. She held up a bulging carrier bag. 'Indian – you can probably smell it. Maurice Melton is going to do the post mortem this evening. He's coming in specially because you're on sick leave. Even if you do spend it looking for bodies. Also because, as you found the body, you're a witness.'

'Old Maurice is welcome to the job,' retorted Tom. 'I didn't go looking for that poor devil, you know, I just came across him, sitting there with his legs stuck out and half his face gone. Anyone walking down that path could've found him. That woman with the dog would've done so if I hadn't. She was next along. And I don't particularly want to see him again. Thanks for bringing the curry. What is it?'

Jess was unpacking the foil boxes in Tom's kitchenette. 'I brought chicken madras and lamb rogan josh. I thought the spices might clear out your cold. Then there are onion bhajis and vegetable pakoras, pilau rice . . . and I picked up a couple of cans of beer. I forgot the naan bread, but we can probably manage without it.'

'I'll settle up with you later for my half,' said Tom gratefully.

'Don't worry. You can buy me a curry some time and we'll be quits. I said I'd call in and see how you were this evening, anyway.'

'I feel a bit better. I knew a walk in the fresh air would do it.'

'Glad to hear you're feeling cheerier, but you still sound pretty nasal. And your walk in the fresh air didn't turn out to be much fun, did it?'

As they settled down with their meal Tom asked, 'How did Superintendent Carter take the glad tidings of a new murder?'

'Officially, as you well know, we don't know if it's a new murder until we get Dr Melton's report and the coroner's ruling. But there's been plenty happening. Tom, are you sure you didn't see or hear anything at all? Other than a bike whose owner had ridden off by the time we got there.'

'Nothing that suggested anyone was nearby. I just heard the usual rustling and so on in the undergrowth: birds, rabbits, small rodents – I don't know. I wasn't paying that much attention. If I was thinking of anything, it was Madison.'

'Oh, Tom,' said Jess, putting down her fork. 'I thought you were over that.'

'I am – was! But she's coming back to the UK. I got a cheery text message. I suspect she thinks we're going to pick up where we left off.'

'And how do you feel about that?' Jess asked cautiously.

Tom considered his answer. 'Not keen on the idea, frankly. I admit I was a bit upset when she took off like that. She hadn't let me know the Australia thing was even in the offing. She just presented me with a whatsit – a fait accompli. I found it a bit too casual – rather an insult, actually. In just the same way, she now tells me she's coming back.'

'Try not to brood about it. Until she gets here, you won't know exactly what she intends to do.'

'*She* intends?' snapped Tom. 'What about me?'

Jess took a deep breath. 'Wait till she gets here anyway. Wandering the countryside brooding on it won't help.'

'I wasn't,' said Tom with dignity, 'walking in the woods, dwelling on my lost love, like some clinically depressed Romantic poet. There were other things, too. I had quite a lot on my mind, in fact. For example, I was thinking about that crazy woman.'

'Mrs Briggs? She'd pretty comprehensively churned up the scene before we got her and her dog away. Phil Morton is fuming about it.'

Tom shook his head and swallowed. 'No, not her. She hadn't got there yet, had she? I mean the other woman, earlier.'

There was a pause. Then Jess asked with ominous calm, putting down her fork, 'Other woman?'

'Yep,' said Tom indistinctly, swallowing. 'She wasn't in the woods. I'd met her earlier. She was driving a Range Rover like she had a pack of wolves on her tail. She came belting towards me just before I got to the woods and nearly forced me into a stone wall. The road is pretty narrow there, and she must have seen me.'

'A Range Rover? What colour? What did the driver look like?'

'The vehicle was black – and before you ask me about the licence plate, I didn't notice it. It was all very quick. She appeared, I swerved, and whoosh! She was gone.'

'But you noticed the driver was a woman?' Jess asked eagerly.

'Yes, and she had long, light-coloured hair and a grim expression. That's all the description I can give you. I think her hair was tied back with a scarf. What's up? You look thunderstruck.'

'I am.' Jess sat back. 'I suspect I know who that was and, if I'm right, it really puts the cat among the pigeons. Ian Carter has been suspicious from the beginning about the whole set-up. I do wish, Tom, you'd mentioned this before. We'd have taken a totally different approach when we went to the house.'

'Well, nobody asked . . .' Tom said defensively.

'But when you found the body and suspected it had been moved, you must have realised *anything* could be important! Tom, for goodness' sake, during the whole conversation I had with Harriet Kingsley today, she was pulling the wool over my eyes. She claimed to have been nowhere near the woods! Both her husband and her close friend, Tessa Briggs, back her up. But Phil Morton saw a black Range Rover parked behind the house. He found out that both Guy and Harriet Kingsley are driving it at the moment, because Harriet is waiting for a new car to be delivered. Phil reckons that woman Briggs is very defensive and that she's hiding something. But don't you see? Perhaps they all are!'

Jess fell back in her chair and groaned. 'When I tell Ian that, quite possibly, Harriet Kingsley was travelling along the road past the woods much earlier, driving badly and apparently upset – and you saw her – he'll hit the roof,' she hissed. 'Phil is right to mistrust the whole bunch of them up at the Old Nunnery.' She pushed away her unfinished food. 'Oh, damn,' she said.

'Well,' said Tom. 'I apologise, of course, if you would have liked to know about that woman in the Range Rover. Put it down to my distress at finding a body sitting on the ground with only half a face. Anyway, I've told you now – and I did tell you about the bicycle in the car park.'

'We won't find that possible witness unless the cyclist comes forward,' Jess said gloomily. 'I don't know whether to wait until tomorrow to call Ian Carter about the driver who might well have been Harriet, or call him tonight.'

'What's he going to do tonight if you do tell him? Don't look so devastated. You can bounce in bright-eyed tomorrow morning and tell the man you have discovered a new lead! That should start the day off well. Finish your curry.'

'Don't you understand?' Jess demanded. 'This has turned everything we were told today upside down. You seem to think that doesn't matter. Well, it does!'

'Sorry, and all that,' returned Tom sturdily. 'But you and Carter and that sergeant, Morton, will work it out, with help from old Maurice's report.' He leaned back and pushed away his empty plate. 'I am off sick,' he said. 'I am out of the loop.'

'No, you're not! You found him. You're a witness. You saw the bicycle, and a woman driving a Range Rover. And if that woman was Harriet Kingsley, she's got some explaining to do. And you, Dr Palmer, can't just shrug it all off.'

'Sure I can. I've told you about it: now it's your problem.' Tom smiled serenely at her. 'I'm taking a week's leave, remember?'

'I just think,' said Sally Grove obstinately, 'that we ought not to call our exhibition "Palette and Brush". It sounds like a rather twee sort of pub.'

She'd often wished she were taller. Being short put you automatically at a disadvantage when arguing with men. She and Debbie were the only female members of their group, and Debbie always backed Mike, her husband. The men tended to band together in a dispute and so Sally was frequently left fighting her corner alone. But she wasn't going to let this one go unchallenged. 'Palette and Brush', indeed!

Support came from an unexpected quarter.

'I agree!' pronounced Gordon Ferris. 'Why can we not call it "Countryside Artists", because that's who we are.' He stroked his bushy beard in a self-conscious sort of way. 'I, for one, am proud of our little society.'

Sally had seen old family photos with Gordon in them. Last Christmas, Gordon had invited them all to his bungalow for 'festive drinks' in the form of red or white plonk from the village's one and only supermarket. His living-room walls, where not bedecked with Gordon's art, were plastered with photos of the man himself from infancy onwards. 'Mother put them up there!' he'd muttered with a touch of embarrassment, seeing Sally scrutinising them. He'd inherited the bungalow from his late parents. The photos had attracted Sally's attention mainly because, when young, Gordon had had a remarkable shock of thick red curls. Now he was as bald as the proverbial coot. Sally supposed he had grown the beard in compensation. That wasn't red. It was silvery grey, with a pinkish glow to it.

'Silly old duffer is striking attitudes again,' Mike Wilson muttered to his wife.

'Shh!' Debbie returned. More loudly, she added, 'I wouldn't go so far as to claim to be an artist, not a proper one! We are only hobbyists, after all, aren't we?'

Gordon's beard bristled.

'But I – Mike and I both – take great care to produce the best work we can. To find a subject for his wildlife paintings, Mike spent ages lying in wet bracken. I haven't got Mike's dedication when it comes to staking out badgers and foxes. I stick to flowers, and some of my studies haven't been too bad, even if I say so myself.'

There was a polite mutter of support from everyone.

'Some of Mike's wildlife studies have been brilliant,' she added hastily.

Another general mumble of support.

Debbie was a slightly built, pale woman with thin brown hair, yet she was pretty in a wispy sort of way and had a trick of staring at you – well, staring at men – with wide-open eyes. Sally suspected that, behind that mousy exterior and her vociferous support of everything Mike said or did, there lurked in Debbie a will of iron. As for Debbie's floral studies, well, to Sally's mind, Debbie had a good eye for detail, but the flowers she depicted so painstakingly lacked life. She didn't see her subject as Sally saw trees, as living things with infinite variety.

'We're all experienced. Debbie is right, we can't claim to be professionals,' Mike chimed in. Debbie smiled fondly at him. 'But we've all produced some very good work,' he went on. 'We mean to put only the best of what we've done on display. More to the point, that is how our exhibition is being advertised in the library, as work by local artists.'

Gordon, who had overheard Mike's original comment, looked mollified. They all looked at the person who had suggested the title 'Palette and Brush'.

'Oh, all right,' said Ron Purcell, with a lift of the eyebrows that might have meant anything. 'Just trying to think up something catchy as a name for the exhibition. Something to intrigue the public.'

Ron was losing his hair, too, thought Sally. He was going thin on top, and he was conscious of it, constantly putting up a hand to smooth flat what was left. She hoped Ron didn't grow a beard. He was one of those naturally thin people full of suppressed energy, suggesting one of those hurrying matchstick figures in a Lowry painting. A beard wouldn't suit him one bit. Gordon's beard at least looked right on him. She thought she'd understood the twitch of the eyebrows that had accompanied Ron's last words. There was an unspoken rivalry between him and Gordon.

'What public?' grumbled a new voice. 'It's a selection of our work stuck up on a wall in the local library. And it's run by volunteers now, and only open four days a week. How many people do you imagine will see it?'

They all chimed together in protest. 'Lots of people use the library, Desmond! You'd be surprised.' (From Ron.) 'Mike and I are in there all the time.' (From Debbie.) 'I use the library, too!' (From Sally.)

Desmond Mitchell gave way before the united onslaught. 'Oh, all right,' he said sulkily.

Ron got back to the title. 'So, then, what *are* we going to call it?' There was a note of challenge in the question. He'd not taken kindly to his suggestion being rejected. Sally wished she'd phrased her own comment more tactfully. She sensed a vulnerability in Ron that he hid well, and he was always nice to her. Born and bred in Weston St Ambrose, he had left in his twenties to work in various West Country banks, finishing as a bank manager. He chose that moment to take early retirement; and his wife chose the same moment to announce she was leaving him. The comfortable house in Cheltenham was sold and Ron found himself back in his native Weston, living in a cottage purchased from the estate of an elderly aunt. Having, as it were, come full circle, Ron was given to moments of moody introspection.

They were at the Wilsons' home, gathered before a selection of their work, which was propped up for the purpose of picking the best for the proposed display. It was a cluttered room, full of bric-a-brac, mostly in the form of china horses. It was difficult to move without knocking against something, and that always made the china animal atop wobble. Sally dreaded that one day she would be responsible for a breakage.

'"Winter in our Countryside",' suggested Mike, gesturing widely at the show of work. 'It is nearly all winter subjects.'

'The subjects I've put forward for selection are all autumnal!' snapped Ron, fighting back. 'And we need a title with more pulling power. Now, "Palette and Brush" . . .'

Sally was encouraged by finding herself on the winning side for once. But, since she anticipated that Ron's nose had been put out of joint by the rejection of his title, she threw out an olive branch.

'We need something to tempt people in, as Ron correctly says. "The Countryside about Us" – how about that? That's positive, and a bit intriguing. It indicates our subjects are local and that visitors to our show might recognise them.'

There was a confused murmur. But even Ron was nodding. Sally pressed on, success going to her head. 'After all, being local is a strong point, as, um, Gordon and Desmond say. We ought to stress it. People *will* recognise many of our subjects. For instance, I bike over to Crooked Man Woods quite often and my subjects were found in the woods. I was there this morning, as it happens.'

'Any luck?' asked Mike. Debbie gave Sally a funny look.

'Well.' Sally hadn't missed the look. 'Actually, something really odd happened. I was just about to photograph a really atmospheric group of trees, with twisted, bare branches, you know.'

'What sort of odd? Did you manage a good shot of it?' Ron asked with interest.

'No, because something interfered with my concentration and spoiled the shot I was trying for. It unsettled me, actually. There was something eerie about the woods today. I kept hearing things. In the end, I abandoned the whole idea—'

'Never mind the subjects we didn't find,' interrupted Desmond impatiently. 'What about this display of the ones we did?'

'I ought to have—' said Sally, her mind still on her experience that morning.

'An artist's life is full of missed opportunities,' pronounced Desmond, cutting her off. He sounded sad but did not explain just what opportunity he'd missed. Debbie gave Sally a little smile that could have meant anything.

'Trust old Dismal Des to come up with that!' muttered Mike.

They continued to wrangle over a title for the upcoming show of their work, with the exception of Sally, who, on the outside once again, remained silent and thoughtful.

'It was strange,' she said quietly. 'Perhaps I ought to have reported it to someone.'

But they had now taken up her title of 'The Countryside about Us' and were congratulating one another, as if they had all come up with it together. So no one was listening to her now.

Chapter 7

Phil Morton was pleased to be able to avoid the boredom of the inquest the following morning, since it would inevitably be adjourned to allow the police to complete their enquiries. Instead he had, in his opinion, a much more important job. He had to go and interview that battleaxe Tessa Briggs again. The news that Tom Palmer had seen a woman answering Harriet Kingsley's description and driving a black Range Rover near the woods before the discovery of the body had cast a whole new light on things.

'I knew it,' said Morton to himself as he drove towards the Old Farmhouse. 'I knew that lot have been messing us around. They're in cahoots, it's obvious! Let's see what Mrs B has to say this morning.'

'So, you're back.' Tessa Briggs greeted him. She had come out to meet him at the sound of his car. The collie stood at her side watching him with its bright eyes.

'You must have been expecting us,' Morton replied.

She raised her eyebrows and leaned sideways, looking past him. 'I can see only the one of you today, so who is "us"? The royal plural?'

'No, madam, the police, as a body.'

Unexpectedly, she gave a chuckle. 'Body, eh? Well-chosen word.'

They were standing in what must once have been the farmyard

in the days when Crooked Farm had been a working business. The house was over to the right, a substantial building that had withstood everything that weather and the passage of time could throw at it. Today it was bathed in a pale sunshine that brought out the honey tones of the stones and the mottled brown of the old roof. But of the remaining farm buildings, which must once have formed a square around the yard, only one large barn remained, its double doors standing open. Alongside it, a modern brick stable block consisted of three adjacent loose boxes. These appeared to be unoccupied at the moment, but in a large field behind the house Morton had noticed three horses grazing, all wearing waterproof coats against inclement weather. There were a couple of sets of parallel bars constructed in one corner of the field. A rusting corrugated-iron shed with slatted air vents stood in the far corner, probably also a leftover from farming days, perhaps used for sheep.

Tessa had been watching him in grim amusement as he studied the pastoral scene. Fred came over to him, sniffed at his feet and waved his frond of a tail in belated greeting.

'You take part in gymkhanas or eventing, that sort of thing?' Morton asked, returning Fred's welcome by scratching the dog's ear. 'I mean, you've got those jumps over there.'

'I don't compete any longer, haven't done since I was a teenager,' she told him. 'A couple of local young riders come over here and practise taking their ponies over the bars there.'

'So those horses belong to them?'

'Two of them do. One of them is mine, the grey, Misty. He's an old fellow, but he suits me for a gentle hack round the fields. The kids stable their animals here, and I look after them. It gives me something to do.'

'What do you keep in that big barn?' Morton asked, pointing at it.

'Nosy blighter, aren't you? You can take a look if you want. I garage my car in it and there's a workshop in there that my husband used. He tinkered with things.'

'You're a widow, Mrs Briggs? I'm sorry.'

'No, you're not, and I'm not – not a widow, I mean. I'm divorced. Don't ask me where Hal Briggs is, because I don't know and don't care. Are you coming into the house, or do you want to stay out here?'

An internal wall must have been knocked out to create the ample sitting room in which Morton found himself a few minutes later. Oak beams ran across the ceiling; original, he guessed. It was still possible to see the tool marks gouged in their blackened surfaces. Logs crackled in a wide stone hearth, sending up a resinous scent, some smoke and sudden tongues of flame. They gave out a comforting heat. Very nice, thought Morton enviously. This place must be worth a fortune, almost as much as the Old Nunnery.

'I understand the inquest was held this morning,' Tessa said, indicating a cosy armchair. 'I didn't go. Guy rang through about ten minutes ago and told me it was all over in a few minutes and then adjourned so that the police could work out exactly what happened. He didn't say any more; we didn't have time to chat. He was on his mobile.'

'It was a formality, at this stage,' Morton told her. 'To establish that it was an unlawful death.'

'Guy said the post-mortem examination showed that fragments of Carl's upper jaw had been forced up through the roof of his mouth into his brain. Is that right?'

'Yes,' Morton agreed, 'I've read the examiner's report. But for that, and some pellets that had taken the same route, he might have survived in a terribly injured state. Not very likely, though.'

She hunched her shoulders. 'Better he didn't, then.' She heaved a sigh. 'So, someone shot Carl. I can't say I'm overly surprised. Sorry if that shocks you, Sergeant Morton, but it's a simple fact. Carl had a knack of annoying people.'

'It takes a bit more than annoyance to inspire someone to blast another person away,' Morton pointed out.

'All right, all right,' agreed Tessa crossly. 'But, look here, it wasn't anyone round here who shot him.'

'So who was it?' Morton asked.

Tessa looked at him with exasperation. 'Someone who followed him down from London, of course! Who knows what sort of mischief he'd got into there. You can bet your bottom dollar he was up to his ears in something dodgy. Carl always was.'

'Mrs Briggs,' Morton said, 'before we go any further, I should warn you that it is an offence wilfully to mislead the police or interfere with their enquiries.'

'Who's done that?' she retorted. 'Not me. I told you I thought the body was Carl Finch, and it was.'

'We think it's possible that you knew, before you arrived at the scene, that you'd find Finch dead there.'

'How do you work that out?' she challenged, a glint in her eyes.

'For a start, because a witness has placed Mrs Harriet Kingsley near the woods earlier that morning, driving erratically and appearing distressed. Did she contact you, Mrs Briggs? Is that why you went to the woods? To try and find out what had happened?'

'Damn!' muttered Tessa. She leaned forward and glared at him. 'Harriet wouldn't hurt a fly! Don't try and pin this on her!'

'We don't pin things on people, Mrs Briggs,' Morton returned patiently. 'Just tell me whether Mrs Harriet Kingsley contacted you and told you that Finch's body was in the woods.'

Her face set mulishly. 'You'll have to ask Harriet that.'

'Oh, someone is, even as we speak.'

'You mean that red-haired woman inspector, I suppose? I hope she's being tactful. Harriet could break down completely, you know! She's – she's quite a fragile person.'

'I don't think *you're* easily rattled, Mrs Briggs. So I'm asking you whether you knew, when you went to the woods, that you'd find a body. I'd appreciate a straight answer.' Morton paused. 'And I'm a simple sort of bloke. I go on asking a question until I get some sort of answer, so don't waste both our time.'

'Oh, fancy yourself as the Grand Inquisitor, do you? Well, I'd like to speak to Harriet first, so you'll just have to wait,' Tessa told him.

'I'm good at waiting,' Morton told her, settling back in his chair. 'Of course, we could continue this conversation in official surroundings. It's entirely up to you.'

Tessa Briggs's face was a picture of thwarted fury as she surveyed her visitor: solid, implacable and very firmly wedged in that chair. Fred, sensing the increase of tension in the air, got up from where he'd been stretched out near the fire and padded over to his mistress. He pushed his long nose into her hand.

'You see, Mrs Briggs,' Morton went on, 'it seemed to us that your dog knew the dead man. So did you, because, although you didn't say so to us at the scene, you ran off straight away to inform the Kingsleys that it was Carl Finch in the woods with the lower half of his face missing.'

Tessa stroked the collie's head. 'You tell people too much, don't you, old chap?' she said to the dog. 'You're a real snitch, old fellow.' She looked up. 'All right, Fred spilled the beans. You saw how he came to greet you today, because he'd met you before. He'll never forget you.

'But, look here! Don't go reading more into this than there is, right? Harriet did go down there to meet Carl. When she got there, he was already dead. She panicked – of course she did! She didn't know what to do. She rang me. I told her to hold fast, and especially not to say anything to Guy until I'd had a chance to go down there and see for myself. I really thought it couldn't be Carl down there, and that Harriet had got it wrong.'

She gave an exasperated sigh. 'I just hoped no one else would have stumbled over him, if it turned out really to be Carl. Of course, whether it proved to be Carl or some other poor sod, I would still have contacted the police! I just wanted to know if it could be Carl, so that I could put Harriet's mind at rest if it wasn't. But when I arrived you lot were crawling all over the place. Harriet and I were not trying to mislead the *police*, Sergeant Morton. You've got to understand that. We were trying to hide from *Guy Kingsley* that Harriet had been going to meet Carl.'

'He'd have objected to his wife meeting her stepbrother? Why is that?'

'He wouldn't have liked it at all,' replied Tessa brusquely. 'And he wouldn't have wanted her to go alone. It's an old story, and a family matter. It's about money. That's all you need to know.'

'Unfortunately, we need to know everything,' Morton told her.

'And you don't mind asking, do you? Outright impertinence, half of it. All right, all right, you're doing your job. But Harriet didn't kill him!'

At that moment, to Morton's considerable alarm, a volley of gunshots rang out from not too far away. 'What the hell?' he exclaimed, jumping to his feet. Fred barked at his sudden movement but appeared unmoved by the gunfire.

A smile of satisfaction crossed Mrs Briggs's face. 'Don't be alarmed, Sergeant! It happens all the time. It's just paying customers over at the clay-pigeon shooting range. I told you about it, remember?'

On impulse, Morton asked, 'You don't mind living out here alone? You *do* live here on your own, I suppose?'

'I do. I don't have a secret lover hidden away. Yes, I do like living here. I was determined, when Hal and I divorced, and the land was sold, that nothing was going to shift me out of this house. I must say, Hal was very decent about that. He knew how much the house meant to me. Besides, he didn't want to stay around. Farming wasn't paying the way it had done and he wanted to try his hand at something else, somewhere else. Our principal business was raising animals for the beef market. That took a long time to recover from the foot-and-mouth disaster, and, in lots of ways, it never did.'

'You bred the cattle here?'

'Oh, no, we'd given that up. We bought in calves, fattened them up and, when they were the right size and weight, off they went.'

Morton found himself slightly shocked by her practical tone. 'No use getting attached to any of them, the calves, I mean.'

101

Tessa stared at him in genuine surprise. 'Attached? Good grief, no! Farming is a business.'

Another volley of shots rattled in the near-distance.

'It would get on my nerves,' said Morton crossly.

'Farming, or those paying punters over at the clay-pigeon range?' A rare smile touched Tessa's mouth.

'Ruddy guns going off all the time. Do you own a gun, Mrs Briggs?'

'Yes, I do. It belonged to Hal and he left it here with me. I've got a licence for it, in my name, and I can show you both the gun and the licence.'

'I would like to see it,' Morton told her.

She got to her feet. 'Come this way, Sergeant!'

She led him into a small, cluttered room that seemed to serve as an office. A computer stood on a purpose-built unit and there were a couple of old-fashioned metal filing cabinets. In one corner, bolted securely to the wall, was the gun cabinet. 'I'll fetch the key,' Tessa said.

She was gone only a couple of minutes. She unlocked the cabinet and indicated a gun-shaped canvas case resting upright inside. Tessa reached in and took it out. She opened it and slid out the weapon. 'OK?'

'Where do you keep the key to the cabinet?' Morton asked her.

'Ah! My secret, Sergeant Morton!'

'At least you have the sense not to keep it in the same room as the cabinet,' he told her. To himself, he was thinking, *but it's very nearby, only in the next room.*

Tessa returned the gun to its place and they made their way back to the large living room. There, she remained standing, so that Morton, too, had to stay on his feet. He knew this signalled that his visit was over.

'Just one last question,' he said. 'You didn't like Carl Finch. But you mentioned he made friends around here when he was younger. Are there still any of his friends living in the area?'

She shook her mop of untidy curls. 'Doubt it. He pushed off to London in his early twenties. I don't know of any close mates, no one who was likely to have kept in touch with him. I doubt there's anyone living here now who knew what Carl got up to after he moved away. Hattie and Guy didn't know, and they're the ones who would, if anyone. There was a rift, you understand, between him and the family.

'As for anyone else, he just played a bit of cricket locally when he was a teenager and had some drinking cronies from the team, like I told you. He had a couple of jobs in London, when he first left, neither of which lasted very long. John Hemmings used to grumble about that. Carl's mother, Nancy, had been dead several years and John didn't want Carl still on his hands as a grown man! In the end, I suppose Carl lived pretty well on his wits.'

Unexpectedly, she smiled in a reminiscent way. 'You only saw him with half his face missing. But when he was a young man, believe me, he was a very handsome chap. People were attracted to him. I dare say he was good company.'

She caught Morton's quizzical expression. 'Not that I ever fancied him!' she said firmly. 'Told you: never could stand him.'

Morton drove slowly down the narrow road from the Old Farmhouse, aware that Mrs Briggs stood in the yard and watched him leave. At the end of the farm road he turned on to the B road and began to drive towards Weston St Ambrose. The land was rising in a gentle slope and, when he crested the top of it, he saw Crooked Man Woods to his left. This was the edge of the woodland, he calculated, not far from the access road used by the workers. It was a peaceful view, timeless, he thought. Having got the better of Mrs Briggs and made her admit the plan she and Harriet had hatched, he was now feeling pleased, and in an unusually poetic frame of mind.

He wasn't the only one to think the view special. Just ahead of him, on the side of the road, stood a lone figure staring out across the landscape towards the woods. Morton frowned and slowed.

'Now, where did you come from?' he muttered. He couldn't see a parked car, or even a bicycle. The man must have walked here. He wore, Morton could now see, a thick jacket and a woollen hat. Fair enough, the wind cut across this higher part of the terrain with a knife-edge force. The watcher, as Morton was now thinking of him, took no notice of the approaching vehicle. He stood on a patch of muddy verge, off the road itself, and his interest seemed entirely taken up with the view. He was a very thin fellow, underneath that thick coat, thought Morton. Not thin in the sense of poor health, but one of those naturally slim people. Morton, who had to watch his waistline, and whose Czech wife made a point of watching it for him, felt envious. Curious, he pulled into the side of the road and got out of his car.

'Everything all right?' he asked sociably.

'Yes, thank you,' said the thin man. He turned his head briefly to glance at the questioner. He had finely drawn features, matching the rest of his build, and sharp, grey eyes. It was hard to put an age to him, especially with that knitted hat covering the top of his head. Morton guessed mid- to late fifties. The voice was educated and confident.

'Looking at something in particular?' prompted Morton.

'The view,' returned the thin man simply.

Morton persevered. 'Are you a visitor to the area?'

The man turned to look at him again, appearing faintly shocked. 'Good heavens, no! I live in Weston St Ambrose.' After a moment, during which he assessed Morton as Phil had him, he added, 'My name is Purcell. If I may ask you a question in turn, are you by any chance connected with the police?'

'Yes,' admitted Morton. He fumbled in his jacket for his ID. Purcell looked at it and nodded but made no comment.

'How did you guess?' asked Morton, irked.

'Stranger,' said Purcell briefly. 'Not a tourist.' He pointed towards the line of trees in the distance. 'Something to do with that business, I'm guessing.'

'Correct, Mr Purcell. You weren't out here the day it happened, by any chance? Didn't hear a shot, perhaps? Or see anything unusual?'

'Sorry,' returned Purcell. 'I wasn't here that morning.'

Morton, whose ear was attuned to witnesses making statements, fancied a very slight hesitation on the other's part. But it would be no use pressing the point. Purcell had returned to studying the view.

'I've painted this scene many times,' he said unexpectedly. 'Always from this viewpoint and at all seasons of the year.'

'Ah, you're an artist, Mr Purcell?' asked Morton, surprised.

'Only an amateur,' confessed Purcell a touch sheepishly. 'I belong to a group. "Countryside Artists", we call ourselves. All amateurs, but keen, you know.'

'Nice to have the talent,' said Morton.

'Well,' said Purcell, squinting at the view, 'I was thinking of having another go at it, this landscape, but I'm not so sure I can improve on what I've done before.' He took off his woollen hat, smoothed his thinning hair and pulled down the hat. 'Nice to have chatted to you, Sergeant Morton,' he said.

'Likewise,' said Morton. He watched the thin man step out briskly along the edge of the road.

Morton returned to his car and, as he drove past Purcell, raised a hand in farewell.

Purcell raised his hand in acknowledgement but did not slow his pace.

'Rum lot around here,' murmured Morton. 'And cautious, too.'

'Unlawful killing!' Ian Carter had said to Jess earlier, as they left the coroner's courtroom that morning. 'What we expected, but it does now free us up to do what's needed. Come on. I'll buy you lunch and we'll talk over where to take our investigation next.'

'There's a place about five miles down the road, The Crown,' suggested Jess. 'They do bar lunches but, honestly, I ate rather a lot last night with Tom. I took in a curry for us both.'

'Ah, Dr Palmer,' said Carter. 'The man with the intermittent memory, who now remembers a mysterious blonde driving a black Range Rover who may well have been Mrs Kingsley. A great pity he didn't think to mention it at the scene of the crime, before you interviewed that lady.'

'He wouldn't have forgotten to mention it at the scene, but for his cold and feeling muzzy,' said Jess, in Tom's defence.

'Those symptoms didn't put him off his food, though, did they? Neither did the grisly sight in the woods. Curry, indeed! Weren't *you* put off your chicken madras?'

'No,' said Jess. 'I just put Carl Finch out of my mind. If I brooded on every grim sight I saw in the course of a working day, I'd never eat.'

'Point taken. But Palmer should have told you about the driver. You heard it all at the inquest. Someone blasted Mr Finch out of this world and then dumped him, artistically arranged, in Crooked Man Woods. So all we have to do now is find out who.'

'Phil Morton's gone out to talk to Mrs Briggs again. As soon as I hear from him, I'm going back to see Harriet, before she thinks up another version of events.'

She sounded so fierce that Carter cast her a quizzical look. 'Well, here we are at the pub. Any idea what you'd like?'

A little later, when they had both settled for the ploughman's platter, Jess said, 'He was in the coroner's court this morning. Captain Kingsley, I mean.'

'I saw him. He scuttled out before we could speak. He'd call it making a strategic withdrawal.' Carter gave a grunt of disapproval. 'Gone home to confer with his wife. I'm afraid they may have had time to cook up a new story, as you suggested they will.'

'Are we considering either of them as suspects?'

'We have to put them at the top of the list. After all, Carl was being a nuisance, and had been one, it seems, since they married. There is that business of the will. Finch thought he was entitled to money – more money than he received. Kingsley was frank about the bad feeling between him and Finch and the trouble Finch caused them. He was so vehement about it I don't know

107

whether he realised that he was providing himself with an excellent motive for Finch's murder!'

'Double bluff?' Jess speculated. 'He's so open and upfront about it all that we think he can't possibly be guilty?'

Carter's normally stern expression melted into a sudden grin, making him look much younger. 'What a suspicious mind you have, Inspector Campbell! We know Kingsley's own gun wasn't the murder weapon, because we have that. We've checked out Kingsley's shotgun, by the way, as a matter of routine. All licensed and nicely locked away in a good gun cupboard.'

'He might have been able to get hold of another gun – the murder weapon – from somewhere,' Jess suggested.

She was thinking: *it's the grey hair that makes Ian look older than he is. Makes him look more strait-laced, too. He's really quite easy to get on with, but people who don't know him very well are made nervous.*

'Certainly, but where, when, and from whom? The answers to that could be hard to find.' The smile had gone, and he looked now, if anything, irritated. 'The murder weapon appears to have been unlicensed, and I'm told it might be pretty old. The trouble is that, in the countryside, there are quite a few old weapons like that lying around, passed on from father to son, together with the general goods and chattels of the family home.'

'So it could even have been a gun belonging to John Hemmings, Harriet's father?' Jess said excitedly. 'Finch could have got hold of that!'

'It's a possibility. Listen.' Carter sat back and pushed away his plate. 'I'm going to get in touch with the Met today and make a trip up to London in the morning. You'd better come with me.

We need to get a look inside the dead man's home. We don't have his keys, but we can now legally force an entry, or the Metropolitan Police can on our behalf. But I want to be there.

'For now, you concentrate on the Kingsleys. Get the truth out of the pair of them and make them sign statements. They'll soon realise it's a mistake to try and make fools of the police!'

At the Old Nunnery, Guy Kingsley was making an identical announcement to his wife. 'Unlawful killing!' he announced. He pulled off his coat and threw it in the general direction of a sofa.

Harriet, from the depths of her father's Queen Anne chair, whispered, 'That means they believe it's murder, don't they?'

'Yes, my sweet, it does.' Guy dragged another chair nearer to his wife and sat down, leaning forward, with his forearms resting on his knees and his hands loosely clasped. 'Look here, Hattie, I don't know what you're playing at, but I don't like being made a fool of!'

'I haven't tried to make a fool of you . . .' His wife's voice wobbled.

Kingsley drew a deep breath. 'All right, all right. For pity's sake, don't cry!' He reached out and took her hand in reassurance, but when he spoke his voice was still brisk.

'Listen up, Hattie, you've got to tell me *everything*! Please don't repeat any of that little drama you and Tessa put on for my benefit. I admit I was taken in. But now I know it was a load of cods-wallop. I don't know what you and Tess are playing at, but it's a mistake. This is murder! It would be bad enough if Carl had shot himself, but he didn't. Someone else did. The police will be back here sooner rather than later, and this time they will want the truth. What's more, they won't be very happy at being given the runaround the last time they came. Any more than I am. So you've got to get up out of that chair and start acting sensibly.'

'I didn't kill him,' Harriet said, still in a whisper.

'My dear girl, I am not suggesting for one minute you blasted the poor blighter with a shotgun! I know *you* didn't kill him. Come to that, neither did I, in case you're wondering.' Guy paused. 'Did you think I might have done?'

'No!' Harriet sat up straight. 'If you want to know, I was sure the coroner would rule suicide. Not that it wouldn't still be an awful thing, as you said, and I'd feel responsible for not doing something to stop it. I do feel wretched about refusing to share out the money in the first place, years ago, when Dad died. I don't mean that I'd have sold up and given Carl half. Just given him a bit more than Dad left him.'

'Why, for pity's sake? If your father had wanted him to have more, he'd have put that in the will!'

'Carl thinks – Carl thought – Dad would have done, but for us persuading him not to.'

Guy said quietly, 'Harriet, you can never buy off someone like Carl. No matter how much you'd given him at the time, he'd still have come back for more, as he did.'

'I know.' Harriet sounded resigned. 'But knowing it doesn't help. Anyway, I couldn't have given him any more. I have, I admit, given him money in the past. But these projects of yours have cost us such a lot over the years that, when I told Carl this time we had none to spare, I was speaking the truth!'

Guy reddened. 'This holiday accommodation plan – it's going to work, Hattie.'

'Yes, yes! Listen, Guy,' Harriet said earnestly. 'We mustn't start squabbling over things like that. You're right. I shouldn't have misled you yesterday and I do need to tell you exactly what happened. But I can't tell you who killed Carl because I can't imagine that *anyone* would want to do that.' Harriet put up a hand to tuck back an errant lock of fair hair. 'Do you mind if I have a very small brandy first?'

'Yes, of course. I could do with one, too!' Guy got up and went to fetch two glasses.

'Was it very unpleasant, at the inquest?' Harriet asked when he came back.

'Routine stuff, and it wasn't a proper inquest, just a brief hearing. The police presented their evidence to date, the coroner agreed it was a case of – they don't call it murder at this stage, just unlawful killing. The police have been given time to complete their enquiries. Investigate, in other words. When it's all over, the coroner will rule finally. Now then, Hattie, let's have it. Had you arranged to meet up with Carl that morning, in the woods?'

She nodded and sipped her brandy. 'Before that, I need to explain why. I'd been having quite an exchange of emails with Carl. I didn't tell you, because you'd have hit the roof.'

'He wanted money again, I suppose?'

'Yes, and he was sounding increasingly desperate. I do now realise there was some special reason for it, though he didn't say what it was. I think he was afraid. At the time, I thought he was being extra difficult.'

'You should have told me, sweetheart.'

'What good would that have done? Sorry, Guy, it would just have been another row with Carl and, frankly, I was afraid you'd do something violent. I don't mean shoot him, for pity's sake! But you had threatened to throw him out of the house, using force if necessary. So I couldn't let him come here.'

She paused before adding, 'You know, Guy, that upset Carl very much, when you said you'd throw him out. This had been his home from the age of nine until – well, until we married, you and I. I know he had his place in London. But he'd always felt he had the right to come here, if he wanted. You can see his point of view, can't you?'

'I can see it, but I don't agree with it. He had no right at all!' Guy got up and went to pour himself another tot of brandy. He looked at her questioningly, holding up the bottle.

Harriet shook her head. 'No, thanks. I'm all right now. I had to keep the two of you apart, Guy. To tell you the truth, I was afraid that Carl might turn violent. Not towards me. And I don't mean using a weapon. I thought he might take a swing at you, and you'd have a real fight.'

'So you fixed up to meet him somewhere else? Was it in Crooked Man Woods?'

He was doing his best, Harriet knew, to sound understanding, but he couldn't help it. It was that military training. She still felt as if she'd been hauled up to face some sort of court martial. 'Yes, I knew I had to have a meeting. I wanted to tell him, once and for all, to leave us alone. That we don't have money to spare. I hoped finally to get him to understand that. But when I got there – to the woods – he was dead. I just – I just couldn't believe it. He was sitting there, Guy, his face was half gone and—'

Her voice had begun to tremble again. She tossed back the remainder of the brandy. 'Who would kill him, Guy? Why?'

'We're not the only people he was in dispute with, is my guess. For heaven's sake, Hattie! Why did you call Tess, when you came rushing home? Why couldn't you tell *me*?'

'You were outside arguing with Derek Davies. I wanted tell someone – but I didn't want to tell you I'd arranged to meet Carl behind your back. Of course I didn't!'

'All right.' Guy made a placatory gesture. 'I understand. I still wish – but if you didn't, it's my fault, I suppose. Yes, I would have gone with you and it would have been unpleasant.'

'So I rang Tessa. She came at once and she – suggested I stay here and say nothing to you at all. She'd go back to the woods and "find" Carl.' Harriet raised her hands and made quotation marks with her fingers. 'She'd report it to the police and I wouldn't be involved. It was a crazy plan, and it didn't work because, when she got there, the police were already all over the place. She'd taken Fred along with her and he knew it was Carl. He ran over to – to the body, and starting howling.'

'It was a crackpot plan,' Guy agreed emphatically. 'You wouldn't have gone along with it if I'd had the slightest inkling what the pair of you were about! Blast Tess! Why couldn't she mind her own business?'

'Don't be cross with Tessa, Guy. She was trying to help me.'

'All right. We've got more important things to worry about now than Tess.'

'Who – who did find him, Guy? How did the police get there so quickly? Tessa said she nearly fainted when she saw them all round the body.'

'I somehow don't imagine Tess fainting!' Guy managed a brief grin. 'It was a bit of – well, I won't say bad luck. It was one of those quirks of fate that you can't factor in when you're planning something, as you and Tess found out. A chap called Dr Palmer was just walking in the woods and came across the body. Apparently, this Palmer sometimes does work for the police, so he knew the drill. That's how they got there so quickly. He'd also decided, by the time they arrived, that Carl's body had been moved. He hadn't examined it. It was just something to do with Carl sitting on very wet ground and his clothing being too dry. Anyway, then there was a post mortem. Another doctor did that, and he found there was other evidence of the body being moved. They also called in firearms experts, who judged the fatal shot to have been fired from a couple of metres away. It had been fired from the shotgun found with the body. That had been wiped clean of prints and the murderer had tried to stick Carl's prints on it – but that's not easy and it was too clumsy a job to fool anyone. The coroner inevitably returned a verdict of unlawful killing.'

Harriet stood up. 'I'd better ring Tessa and tell her.'

'I've done that. I rang her from my mobile with the coroner's ruling.'

'I'll call her anyway. The police will want her to make another statement, won't they?' Harriet scrambled from the chair. 'I must speak to her first, tell her I've spoken to you and explained it all.'

'Oh, my, yes!' Guy sounded almost satisfied. 'The cops will want to speak to Tess.'

But when Harriet returned after calling Tessa, she looked so dismayed that he jumped up. 'What's happened now?'

'They've been to see Tessa already,' she said miserably.

'Both Superintendent Carter and Inspector Campbell were in

court this morning!' Guy scowled. 'How did they get over to Tessa's place so fast?'

'It was that sergeant of theirs, the big chap with the sour expression. The one who talked to Tessa here, out in the garden. He's been again. The police *know*, Guy! They know I was at the woods and found Carl. Oh, Guy, whatever are we going to do?'

There was the sound of a vehicle drawing up outside. Guy went to the window.

'No time to discuss it any more now, love, the law is back here already. It's that woman with the red hair.'

Chapter 8

'I feel a fool,' Harriet said to Jess Campbell. 'I can only plead circumstances. I was very shocked when I found my brother. It knocked commonsense out of my head. I would never have agreed to Tessa's plan otherwise.' She drew a deep breath. 'I really am very, very sorry.'

Strike while the iron is hot. Jess was following this excellent principle. She'd driven out to the Old Nunnery after hearing from Phil Morton that Tessa Briggs had admitted originally learning of the body in the woods from Harriet. Phil had been cock-a-hoop about getting Tessa to own up, and rightly so, thought Jess. Now, she had every intention of forestalling any attempt by the Kingsleys to cook up another plan of action of their own. They hadn't been pleased to see her, but they hadn't been surprised, either.

Jess began, 'I hope, Mrs Kingsley—' But she got no further.

'If there is any blame, it should be put at my door,' Guy Kingsley interrupted loudly. 'I did not at first know that Hattie and Tessa Briggs had invented any story to put me off. My wife did not want me to know she'd arranged to meet Carl. She thought I would be angry, and I would have been. We've told you why. Carl was a bloody nuisance and always after money. He and I had several heated exchanges about it. I had told him to stay away from the house. But Hattie has told me all about it now, and if

117

anyone, other than myself, is to blame, it's Tessa, although even she had the best of motives, I'm sure.'

'Well,' said Jess, 'that all sounds very noble, Captain Kingsley, and it is good of you to shoulder the blame. However, had a witness not seen your wife driving away from the woods earlier, she and Mrs Briggs would have successfully put a spoke in the wheel of police investigations into what now we know to be a murder. That's a very serious matter.'

'I was worried about that driver, the one I nearly forced off the road,' Harriet admitted. 'I thought he might remember me.'

'He certainly did,' Jess told her. 'He also went on to find the body.'

Harriet looked briefly at her hands, clasped in her lap. 'I didn't go to the inquest this morning. It wasn't because I was afraid of seeing that driver there, and of his seeing and recognising me. It was because I was afraid they'd describe Carl's injuries in some horrible post-mortem report. I apologise again for being so silly and not admitting I'd been to the woods when you first came here.'

'All right,' Jess said. 'We'll leave that for the moment. We need to move on. But you must tell me everything, Mrs Kingsley. When there is a family tragedy of this kind, our enquiries inevitably dig up the dirt, to put it bluntly. There are always details families want to hide: things that are embarrassing or may cause more trouble. But I'm afraid that kind of privacy goes right out of the window when we, the police, become involved. Now then, is there anything else you could tell me that might give us a lead to finding your stepbrother's killer? Who else knew you were going to meet him in Crooked Man Woods? That's a vital missing piece of the jigsaw.'

'No one!' Harriet burst out. 'I hadn't told Guy, as I explained, and I didn't tell Tessa. She is the only one I might have told. I didn't because, like Guy, she would have made a big fuss and told me not to go. She'd have insisted I get in touch with Carl and cancel the arrangement. Or else, she would have insisted on coming with me, which would have been even worse. So I told no one.'

'Could someone have found out? For example, did he write to you? Send a text message, or an email someone might have seen on screen?'

'No! I mean, he didn't write letters. He did send emails and he did ring my mobile occasionally, until I told him to stop, after he rang once when Guy was with me and –' She broke off and glanced at her husband. 'Guy was upset.'

'Yes, I was!' snapped Kingsley. 'But I had no idea he was going to come down from London and meet Hattie that morning, in the woods. If he sent emails, I didn't see them and my wife didn't tell me!'

Harriet got up and went to the nearby desk. She slid open a drawer and returned carrying a closed laptop computer. 'I send and get emails on it and, yes, I corresponded with my brother – stepbrother – via this. But I always deleted them afterwards. Anyway, you don't know my password to get into my email account, do you, Guy?'

'No!' said Guy. He was looking very angry and clearly suppressing a desire to burst out in a torrent of speech.

Oh, dear, thought Jess. I'm afraid there's going to be a serious row about all this between the Kingsleys when I've gone. Perhaps there already has been. She felt sorry for Harriet, who had clearly been living for some time with an impossible situation. Her stepbrother had been feckless and a leech, but she must have loved him as a brother. Her husband couldn't stand Carl Finch. There must have been massive arguments, probably threats. Harriet's intention first and foremost had been to keep Carl and Guy apart, a wretched tug of war for her to be in the middle of.

Aloud, she said, 'Have you any idea at all why your brother needed money urgently?'

Kingsley answered. 'He gambled. He also invested in hare-brained get-rich-quick schemes. Of course, he lost his money, at cards and in business. He'd probably borrowed money. He must have been up to his eyes in debt.'

Jess nodded but turned back to Harriet. 'Mrs Kingsley?'

'As Guy says, Carl gambled and risked money on stupid ventures. I don't know exactly how he got through so much money. He didn't confide in me to that extent. If you want honesty, then I can tell I didn't really want to know the details of how Carl got into such difficulties. I used to tell him that, whatever kind of life he was leading, he ought to stop it. But the more details I knew, the more I'd have to worry about.'

'Did you feel that, this time, he was more than usually worried about being in need of a bail-out?'

'Yes,' Harriet admitted. 'He was very worried, scared. I don't know whom or what he was frightened of. But he'd got himself into a really bad situation and he couldn't get out of it. That much I could tell from the tone of the emails, and the occasional call he did make to my mobile.'

'Did your father own a shotgun, Mrs Kingsley?' Jess introduced the new subject deliberately, not giving Harriet time to control her reaction.

But Harriet looked genuinely bewildered. 'No, why would he? He didn't go in for country sports. Nancy wouldn't have allowed it. She was all about being at one with nature, you know. She would stand out in the countryside with her arms outspread and eyes shut, absorbing the Earth's force. She looked rather beautiful when she did that.'

'Barking mad!' said Guy tersely. 'At least she didn't do it in the nude, I hope!'

'Well,' confessed Harriet, blushing, 'when she first came, she did. But Dad really put his foot down and said, no way!'

Kingsley rolled his eyes. 'Well, I never saw a gun about the place, other than my own. That's kept locked away, and your superintendent inspected it. We never found so much as an old air pistol when we were going through stuff up in the attics, and we hunted through pretty thoroughly.'

Harriet said in explanation, 'Guy and I had a go at running an antiques business. Because this house has never been really cleared out in a couple of hundred years, things have accumulated and, as they became unneeded, they were put up in the attics, as Guy says. I can confirm we didn't find a weapon of any kind up there when we were antique hunting, just a lot of furniture and some musty old clothes and books. We soon found out the furniture wasn't worth anything.'

Kingsley slapped his palms on the arms of his chair and made a decisive statement. 'Clearly, Carl's trouble was in London. Someone either followed him down here or, more likely, someone there had learned of his proposed meeting with Harriet in the woods. He might have told someone. Or someone saw the emails he sent her, or her replies. Whoever killed Carl, you need to look in London.'

'Mrs Kingsley.' Jess turned to Harriet. 'Can we borrow this computer? You may have deleted Carl's emails, but our expert might be able to retrieve them. There could be some clue in them. We will return the machine to you in good order, of course.'

'All right,' said Harriet meekly.

'One other thing. Have you any photos of your stepbrother? The more recent, the better. We – er – need to have a photograph we can show potential witnesses.'

'Yes, of course, I'll bring you what I have.' Harriet stood up and walked out of the room.

When they were alone, Guy Kingsley said, 'Look here, Inspector Campbell, you may be thinking I'm some kind of a monster whose wife is afraid of him. But I'm not, and she isn't. But you can have no idea what a powerful personality Carl was. That was the reason I banned him from the house. I knew he could always persuade Harriet to do what he wanted. He was a big chap, as you've seen, and in life he looked pretty impressive. I've seen the effect all that long blond hair and those film-star looks had when he walked into a room, especially on people who didn't know him from Adam.' Guy gave a kind of growl. 'Also, he had a pretty good opinion of himself. He thought he was the "bee's knees", as they say. Most of all, he knew how to bear a grudge. Oh, yes, he knew that!'

'You never got along with him? Not at first, even?'

'Never!' said Kingsley firmly. 'When Harriet brought me here and I met him – in this room, as it happens – we took one look at each other, and that was it. Mutual dislike. We were rivals, you see. He wanted to dominate Harriet, be the only other man in her life, other than her father.'

'Her husband, perhaps? There wouldn't have been a legal impediment, would there?' It was a question that had to be asked. Jess wasn't surprised to see Kingsley's face turn first white and then red.

'For God's sake,' he said thickly, 'never mention anything like that to Harriet!'

There was a footstep outside in the hallway and Harriet returned, holding an envelope. 'I've put some snaps of Carl in here, but they were taken a few years ago. There is one taken here, with my father, not long before Dad died. That would be the most recent one I have.'

She held out the envelope. She looked very pale.

I wonder, thought Jess, if she overheard my question?

'I do understand Harriet's problem,' Jess told Carter later. 'I have a brother. We're very close. If he came and asked me for money, I'd do my best to give him what he needed, even if I was angry with him. But I'm not married. I don't have to consider anyone else.'

'Would you go on giving your brother money, if he kept coming back, as Carl Finch did?' Carter beat a rapid tattoo with his fingertips on the desk.

'I wouldn't be able to, because I don't have it, and Simon would know that. Nor would Simon just turn up and ask for funds without explaining exactly why he needed them so urgently. I'd expect him to have a serious reason, one he could tell me. To be honest, I can't imagine a situation arising with me and Simon that would be anything like the wretched tangle Harriet Kingsley was in.'

Carter grunted and began to roll a ballpoint back and forth across the top of his desk. 'Finch thought he was entitled to money, that was the top and bottom of it. He had misunderstood his position in the family. He had persuaded himself that John Hemmings saw him in the same light as he saw his daughter by blood. He was wrong. Hemmings had no intention that the family home and the bulk of his wealth should go anywhere but to his blood child. As to the other thing – the situation you mentioned to Kingsley and which he didn't like one bit.'

'About there being no impediment in law to Carl and Harriet marrying?' Jess grimaced. 'Kingsley didn't like that idea at all!'

'You can't be surprised! We have no reason to suppose that was ever Finch's intention. In any case, it couldn't have been in Harriet's mind, because she married someone else.'

He replaced the pen tidily in a tray. 'Tessa Briggs wanted to protect Harriet; she seems very fond of her. Hence the theatre about pretending Harriet hadn't found the body. The explanation is plausible.

'While Phil was at the Briggs' place, he heard firing from the clay-pigeon range. If you recall, Mrs Briggs said in her original statement that she wouldn't have noticed a shot if there had been one in the woods. Phil disagrees. She would have done so, because such a shot would have come from the other direction. So let's assume she didn't hear a shot. We now know for certain that the body was moved, but we don't know how far. Not a great distance, because he hadn't been dead that long. So, where the devil was he killed? And where is that Renault he was driving?'

'There's a lot of open countryside around there,' said Jess. 'Could be anywhere.'

The following morning, Carter and Jess set off for London. They might strike lucky, said Carter to her. There could be something of interest in Finch's home and, in any case, removing oneself physically from the scene of the crime could help.

'Clears the mind,' he said. 'Puts things in perspective.'

Finch had lived in a pretty mews. The former stables had been converted into cottages on the townhouse principle. The main residential part was upstairs, over the street-level garage and front door. There were two cars parked in the mews when Carter and Jess arrived, and a reception party consisting of two men, standing together and engaged in desultory conversation.

The younger one was slightly built and of mild appearance. Perhaps for that reason, he sported a distinctive hairstyle. The hair was clipped close to both sides of his skull, but on the top it had been allowed to grow longer and been teased into flame-shapes, pointing in varying directions. The general effect was of a palm tree in a tropical storm. Incongruously, given the unconventional nature of his coiffure, he was wearing a suit and carried a briefcase.

The other man was sturdily built and wearing a leather jacket. He had close-cropped hair, an alert expression and, Carter had to admit, had 'POLICE' written all over him.

'Sergeant Mullins, sir,' said the latter, adding with a nod towards Jess, 'Ma'am. Good journey up from Gloucestershire?' He gestured at his companion with the wild haircut. 'This is Mr Loveday. He represents the letting agency. He's got the keys.'

'That's helpful,' said Carter, shaking the hand Mr Loveday nervously held out. 'We won't have to break in.'

Mr Loveday's nervousness increased and his expression became as distraught as his hair. 'The last thing we want is damage! That's why the agency keeps a set of all the keys to all properties. Tenants go on holiday, you see, and there's an emergency: a burst pipe, a flood coming through the ceiling from the property above, that sort of thing. Or there's an' – he swallowed – 'an accident,' he said, 'like, er, this time.'

'Quite,' said Carter. 'Lead on, then, Mr Loveday.'

Loveday glanced at Sergeant Mullins, who urged, not unkindly, 'Get on with it, the superintendent hasn't got all day.'

'Oh, er, yes,' stammered Loveday, and produced a set of keys with a paper label attached. His letting agent's training kicked in and he announced with some assurance that they would find an entry hall and stairwell, with a downstairs toilet.

'We'll take a look in the garage first,' ordered Mullins.

Loveday's fragile confidence shattered. 'Er, yes, of course . . .'

Under Loveday's mournful eye, they checked the garage to be sure Finch's Renault wasn't there. It wasn't, and neither was anything else, except a small collection of the usual handy tools and a stepladder. They then all four squeezed into the minuscule downstairs lobby. They glanced into what Loveday now described as the 'downstairs facilities'. That proved to be an icy-cold, oddly shaped cubbyhole with a child-sized lavatory bowl at one end and a tiny hand-basin fixed to the wall.

'You've got to be joking,' observed Mullins.

Perhaps because of the Munchkin-sized proportions of the property, or because of the temperature, Finch had stored his wine bottles here, installing a tall rack in what little space remained. The visitors stuck their head through the door, but no one attempted to enter. Finally, they clattered noisily up the narrow stairs to the flat itself. At last they were in Carl Finch's home.

'These are compact properties, as you see,' said Loveday, unnecessarily, to Carter and Jess, as if they were a pair of prospective tenants. 'But not cramped, and there is plenty of light and access to a roof garden.' He pointed to a hatch in the ceiling.

Mullins, behind the group, was heard to mutter something about the impossibility of swinging cats.

Loveday defended the agency's interests energetically. 'I can assure you a property like this is eagerly sought after in this part of London. Having a garage is rare, and so is not having neighbours above or beneath. The party walls to the properties on either side are solid. The properties are very quiet. Only residential traffic uses the road below. Now that the flat is, or about to become, vacant and on the market again, the agency will let it overnight, believe me! We have a list of people wanting something like this.'

'I'm sure,' said Carter politely.

Loveday, encouraged, went on: 'Could you give me any idea when the property will be cleared of Mr Finch's effects? This is a furnished let, but all clothes, personal items, electrical goods belonging to the late tenant, and so on, will have to be removed very soon. The agency cannot act as a storage facility. We also need to turn off and drain the remaining heating and inform the utility suppliers. The owner will want us to get this property available for relet—'

'This is a murder investigation, old son,' said Mullins, in his kindly way, which did not, second time round, sound quite so kindly as it had at first.

Loveday flushed brick red. 'I know, the agency is aware . . . Dreadful thing, of course. The murder didn't take place here, on the property, I understand? Is that right? We hope not, because it would put some people off.'

Jess began: 'This isn't the scene of the crime, Mr Loveday, as far as we know. We might, of course, find evidence suggesting it was – traces of blood, something like that.' (Loveday looked as if he might faint.) 'We need to take a good look round and, if there is nothing here for us, the flat should—'

'*Who the hell are you?*'

The voice, crisp and female, came from the door. It caused all four of them to spin round, to see a tall, slim woman in her thirties glaring at them. She was dressed in a figure-hugging red jacket and a short, tight skirt. The outfit was completed, Jess noted with some envy, with a chunky necklace of natural stones in silver settings. Her long, curling, tawny hair was brushed back and secured with a band. She had a large and very expensive-looking bag slung over her shoulder.

Carter, for his part, and with memory of Sophie once admiring a similar bag on the shoulder of some celebrity, dredged up the name 'Birkin'. Well, well, Mr Finch, he thought, if this lady is your girlfriend, no wonder you never had any money!

So taken aback had they all been by her sudden appearance, no one answered her for a moment, allowing her to steam on while they gawped.

'What are you doing in Carl's flat? Are you bailiffs? If you are, you can clear off! This is a furnished flat, very little here belongs to Carl, but you need him here to identify which items. I want to see your authority!'

Sergeant Mullins regained confidence and stepped forward, warrant card held up for her to see. The other two police officers scrabbled to produce their police IDs. Loveday shuffled to one side, out of range of her accusatory glare, dissociating himself from the forces of law and order.

'Police, ma'am, not bailiffs,' said Mullins in his genial way. 'We are here on official business.'

She walked right up to them, scrutinised their photographs and checked each against the officers' faces. Carter suddenly felt himself in the office of the headmistress of his primary school, hauled up with fellow offenders for making an icy slide in the school playground one winter. He could even remember Miss Duckworth's lecture, particularly the bit about broken legs and cracked skulls. They'd all been interested in that aspect and had discussed it eagerly afterwards. They even went back to their slide to see if anyone had come a cropper and was lying there with broken limbs. But all they found was the janitor with a bucket of salt.

Perhaps because he was studying her with interest, she honed in on him. 'You're a bit senior to be doing this sort of snooping, aren't you, Superintendent?'

'I'm in charge of this investigation. May I know your name?' he asked politely. He hoped he didn't sound defensive. 'What are you doing here?'

She flushed. 'Natalie Adam,' she said. 'I'm a friend of Carl's, and I called by to see him on spec. Where is he? Why are you all here? What investigation? And why Gloucestershire police?' Her assurance had been slipping as she piled up her questions. 'Something's happened. What?'

'I'm very sorry, Ms Adam, but I have to tell you that Carl Finch is dead,' he said gently.

'He can't be!' she challenged. 'What did he die of? Was he in a car crash?'

'No, I am afraid Mr Finch has been murdered.'

'*Here?*' she yelled, full force.

Loveday scuttled past them all. 'I'll wait downstairs in my car,' he told them, and fled.

'Perhaps you'd better sit down, love,' suggested Mullins, ushering her to a nearby chair. She had suddenly turned grey-white, even her lips emptying of colour.

She sat down with a bump. 'Here?' she repeated, and looked wildly round the room.

'No, Ms Adam. He was away from home in Gloucestershire at the time the incident occurred,' Jess told her. 'Would you like a glass of water?'

Natalie gestured away the offer. 'Of course,' she murmured. 'You two belong to the Gloucestershire police, I should have known.' Colour flooded back into her face and, as quickly as she had folded, she rallied. 'Don't tell me!' she snapped. 'He went down to that wretched house, that Old Nunnery, to see his tight-fisted sister and her scheming husband! What happened?'

'Mr Finch's body was discovered in some woodland, a few miles from the house you mention. He had been shot.'

Her voice crackled with emotion. 'Did one of them shoot him? Did they finally decide to get rid of him once and for all? I wouldn't put it past them, either of them. Poor Carl . . .'

She clenched her fists. There were tears in her eyes, but Jess knew she wouldn't weep, not in front of them. She'd wait until she was alone, then it would all pour out, together with screams and imprecations and probably some breakages.

'I told him not to go,' she muttered. 'I warned him he couldn't trust that couple.'

'He told you he had planned this trip?' Carter asked quickly.

'I knew it was in his mind. He talked about going. We even argued a bit about it. Perhaps that's why he didn't tell me the exact date. That's why I came here today, expecting to find him. I've been trying to get in touch with him, but he doesn't – didn't – answer his mobile or reply to any text messages or emails. I've been getting worried.' She suddenly scrabbled in the Birkin handbag and pulled out a small mirror and a tissue. She inspected her face, dabbed away a film of moisture on her lower eyelids, put tissue and mirror away and was outwardly calm again.

'Did he have a particular reason, that you know of, for visiting his stepsister at this time?' Carter added, 'We already understand he was in the habit of asking Mrs Kingsley for money.'

'He only wanted what was rightfully his!' she retorted. 'You needn't make it sound as if he was scrounging or begging, because he wasn't! His stepfather would have left him far more than he did, if the other two hadn't persuaded the old man to change his will when he was very ill and vulnerable. The poor old chap didn't understand what he was doing.'

'Finch told you this?' Carter asked.

'Yes, of course he did! Look, are you going to try and tell me Carl lied to me? Because I know him better . . .' She bit off her words and her facial muscles twitched as she fought to control them. 'I knew him better. He wouldn't tell me an untruth.'

'But you have no other evidence for it? No one else corroborated the story, about the influence?' Carter said gently.

She flung back her head and her mane of hair and fixed him defiantly with her eyes. 'Who else was there? It was a dirty, sneaky business, and you can't expect everyone to know! But Carl knew.'

Carter suggested, 'The solicitor who drew up the will would have known if he were suddenly called in to make a major change.'

'The solicitor?' Natalie gave a snort of derision. 'He was an old family friend and Harriet's godfather, for crying out loud! Of course he was in league with Harriet and her husband, Guy – have you met Guy?'

'I have,' said Carter. 'Am I to understand you've met him, too?'

'Yes!' Her mouth twisted into an angry sneer. 'He turned up here, out of the blue, early one evening. Carl and I were celebrating. I'd brought off a successful deal at work – I'm in investment banking. So I brought over a bottle of champagne and we were discussing where to go out to dinner when, suddenly, the doorbell rang. It gave us both quite a start because we – he – wasn't expecting anyone. Carl went to the intercom. There was the usual distant squawk as the caller identified himself. Then Carl shouted into it, "*What's happened to Harriet?*"

'My heart sank, because I knew the score, and I thought, if she's had a serious accident or worse, Carl would lose any chance of getting what he was owed. But when he came back he said it was his sister's husband. He hadn't expected him. The man had never come before. He was sure something serious must have happened to Harriet, so he released the downstairs catch to let Guy come up.

'I'd never met any of the family, although Carl had told me all about them, so I was really curious. Then in strode Guy Kingsley himself, very much the ex-officer and gentleman, cavalry twill trousers and green tweed jacket. Doesn't time ever move on for those people? He was really put out at finding me here. Or he was at first. He said he'd been in town on business and had decided to take the opportunity to call. He assured Carl that Harriet was fine, but he wanted to discuss what he called a family matter.

'Guy gave me a look when he said this. I should take the hint and go, it meant. I didn't trust him, so I said I wanted to stay. Carl said that was fine by him. I ought to hear for myself what he was up against. Then Guy gave a really nasty smirk and said perhaps I should hear it. He started telling Carl that he would have to stand on his own feet. He wouldn't allow Harriet to give Carl any money and, as for the old man changing his will, that was utter rubbish, and just hadn't happened. Carl must be cracked if he thought it had. The old chap had been perfectly clear in his mind until the last breath.

'After that, he, Guy, turned to me and said, "He's penniless, my dear, and he always will be. So, unless you're prepared to support him for the rest of your days, now is the time to cut and run." How dare he?'

Natalie reddened at the memory. 'Talking to me as if I was some dimwit. I know – knew – Carl had financial troubles. Everyone does, from time to time. If he could have got help from his sister, he could have got everything sorted out.'

She stopped speaking. Carter prompted, 'And what happened then?'

'There was a bit of a scrap,' she said. 'Nothing much. No blood, just a tussle and a chair or two knocked over, a bit of shouting. Carl is – was – a big chap and, although Guy looked fit and, obviously, the army had taught him to look after himself, Carl did manage to push him out of the door. I thought they might both fall down the stairs. That did worry me, I admit. I ran after them. But they got to the bottom of the stairs somehow intact, and Carl pushed Guy outside. That was that. We tidied up the flat and went out to dinner.'

'Who threw the first punch?'

She frowned. 'I'm not sure. I think they just sort of went for each other at the same time. Honestly, I nearly took a swing at Guy myself! He was so arrogant, so superior . . . You couldn't expect Carl to put up with that!'

'What date was this? Can you remember?' Carter asked her.

'It was last September. We didn't talk of it again, Carl and I, because he knew I understood how it was. I told him he'd never have to explain things to me, because I'd seen for myself that Guy Kingsley was a shit.'

'You never met Harriet?'

She shook her head. 'But I imagine she and Kingsley are well matched. If you want to know who killed Carl, go and arrest them. Either one of them did it, or arranged for someone else to do it.'

'Ms Adam,' Carter said seriously, 'was Finch in any other trouble or dispute, other than with his stepsister and her husband?'

She hesitated. 'I probably shouldn't tell you, but you'll find out anyway. Don't ask me for details. I don't have them. There was, still is, a plan to create a luxury holiday complex on an island in the Caribbean, a top-of-the-market, exclusive place. The island, Carl said, is mostly privately owned by one family, whose spokesperson is a formidable widow. Carl was sort of acting as her agent, getting people to invest. But there have been problems. Carl never wanted to discuss the details with me, but I know he was worried at the delays. He'd been really optimistic at first, excited about the possibilities. These projects often run into problems, don't they? I told Carl not to worry, things would sort themselves out.'

She stopped speaking to stare at them thoughtfully, as if assessing their worthiness of any further confidence. When she began to speak again it was rapidly, in staccato bursts. 'I don't know if this is anything to do with that, or something else entirely. But I know he went to Oxford recently, to see an old chap called Alcott – Edgar Alcott. He's some sort of an antiques collector, Carl told me. He'd known him quite a while. I . . .'

She swivelled on her heel and took a short turn up and down the room. 'Look,' she went on, coming to a halt before them. 'I never really understood that friendship. I don't think Carl really liked Alcott. He used to go and see him from time to time, but he didn't like being pressed for too much explanation. I got the feeling that he felt some kind of an obligation towards Alcott. Or that Alcott had some sort of hold on him. I suspected it might have to do with the island development plan. Perhaps he'd persuaded Alcott to invest. But I really don't know.

'But it was after Carl came back from his last visit to Oxford that he began talking about visiting his sister again. I thought it would be a serious waste of time, having met Guy. But since his return from Oxford, Carl had been quite tetchy and nervy, so I didn't say too much. I should have said more,' Natalie added suddenly. 'I should have talked him out of it. He might be alive now!'

She began to scrabble in the depths of her designer bag, shielding her face from them. Then she withdrew her business card and scribbled her private phone number on the reverse. She handed it to Carter. 'I want to know the minute you've got him!' she ordered.

Carter appreciated her confidence that they would get Finch's murderer soon. He hoped so, too, but wished he could feel more sure of it. Finch probably had a network of acquaintances he had talked into supporting this island project. Possibly, he'd done the same sort of thing before, with some other 'can't fail' project. Some investors would never get their money back. Plenty of people might have borne him a grudge. Natalie Adam probably didn't know half of it.

Finch's flat yielded up little more information, and they left, taking with them the victim's computer. Mr Loveday was visibly relieved on being told there was no indication it was a scene of crime, and that he could switch off the heating and lock the place up again.

'When—?' he began.

'We can't release the flat yet, I'm afraid, Mr Loveday,' Carter told him.

Loveday's features twisted in misery. 'When I get back to the office, they'll demand—'

'We'll let you know!' said Jess.

It had started to rain, so they took a brisk farewell of Sergeant Mullins, expressing their thanks, and set out for Paddington station and home.

'Half an hour to wait,' observed Carter, staring up at the departures screen. 'I'll get us a coffee, or would you prefer tea?'

'Coffee would be fine. I'll park myself on that bench over there before someone else does.'

On his return, carrying two plastic tubs and handing one of them to her, Carter said, 'That young woman, Natalie, she's a tough cookie. You wouldn't think she'd be gullible, would you?' He seated himself as he spoke.

'I'd like to think I wouldn't have been taken in by Finch's stories,' Jess told him. 'Gosh, this is hot! Thanks.' She prised the lid from the coffee tub with caution. 'But he obviously convinced Natalie of that load of tripe about his stepfather being persuaded to write him out of a larger share in the estate. What surprises me is that Natalie didn't disappear over the horizon after Guy's visit. Guy spelled it out to her. Whether or not Carl was right about the will, clearly he was unlikely to get his hands on any more money.'

Carter, sipping cautiously, suggested, 'Perhaps Guy went the wrong way about it, just telling her point-blank. In a head-on confrontation, I think Ms Adam's instinct is to stick to her guns.' He set down his coffee on the seat beside him. 'We're all capable of losing our grip on commonsense when we're in love, anyway. We all think we've met Mr or Miss Right, and it's a shock when it turns out we've met Mr or Miss Wrong.'

Jess cast him a startled look, but he was gazing at a bedraggled pigeon marching flat-footedly up and down in a search for scraps. Carter often spoke about his daughter but had never mentioned the trauma of the break-up of his marriage. 'So, where do we go next?' she asked.

'Oh, I think a trip to Oxford is next on the books, don't you? Tomorrow, if possible. I'm curious to meet Edgar Alcott, the antiques collector. But I'll take Phil Morton with me, if you don't mind. I have my suspicions about Finch's reasons for visiting Oxford, and I think a couple of heavyweights like myself and Phil might make Alcott realise we mean business. You could ask Guy Kingsley about that scrap in Finch's flat, by the way. I wonder if he's ever told his wife about it.'

He re-covered his coffee and went on: 'Since we haven't found Finch's car, we still don't know *where* he was killed. That flat will have to be searched for forensic traces. It looks neat and tidy now, no gunshot marks on the walls. But he could have died there. It's highly unlikely, mind you, because a blast from a shotgun would have peppered the walls and the noise wouldn't pass unnoticed in that mews. He was much more likely to have died in the woods, or in the general vicinity.'

'It is possible to sketch another scenario,' suggested Jess. 'One putting the murder at that flat. Didn't Loveday boast how thick the party walls are in those properties?'

Carter looked doubtful. 'It would mean dragging the body downstairs and into the garage, stuffing it into a car. Whose car?'

'Finch's car is missing.'

'So what happened to the murderer's car? Did he leave it parked up there all day while he drove Finch's Renault, with the body in the boot or under a blanket on the back seat, all the way to the West Country?'

'He parked it in Finch's garage and came back for it later,' was Jess's explanation. 'Dr Melton's report finds that the body was moved.'

Carter was shaking his head, unconvinced. 'There wouldn't be time, given the condition of the body, between the killing and the discovery, to drive the victim from that flat in London all the way to those woods. Rigor mortis would have been far more advanced. And where is the car now? If the killer left the Renault down in Gloucestershire, how did he get from the woods to, say, a railway station, miles away? He had to get back to base somehow.'

'Why? He might live in the general area of the woods. He could have arranged to meet Carl in London and made his way to that flat by public transport.' Jess's voice gained in enthusiasm as she warmed to her theory. 'He kills Finch, puts the body in the Renault, as we said, drives to the woods, leaves Finch there, hides the Renault away somewhere and leaves the scene. Perhaps he only has a reasonably short distance to go before he's home.' Jess grew even more enthusiastic. 'Didn't Tom see a bicycle chained up in the car park of the woods? It had gone by the time we looked for it.'

To her surprise, Carter burst into laughter. 'Sorry, Jess!' he apologised, 'I'm not laughing at you, or your theory. It's ingenious, I agree, although I still don't think anyone could have fired off a shotgun in that flat without attracting any attention. Or doing any damage to the surroundings, come to that. Where are the bloodstains, the damaged walls? What tickles me is the picture of the murderer, having done all that, pedalling sedately away on a bike! Going off home for a cup of tea and to put his feet up after all his exertions.'

'All right,' Jess conceded regretfully. 'But don't tell me stranger things haven't happened!'

'True, we've both known cases where the murderer has done the deed and then gone off to a family gathering, cool as a cucumber.' There was a silence while both drank their coffee. 'We have to find that Renault,' Carter muttered. 'If the killer drove it away somewhere, where is it? Give me your cup. I'll drop them in that bin over there.'

Chapter 9

'Dear me,' said Edgar Alcott, 'this is very distressing news, Superintendent Carter.' He tapped his fingertips together and for a moment seemed lost in thought.

Carter cleared his throat. 'It has been reported in the press and on television news programmes. I'm surprised you haven't seen it anywhere.'

Alcott looked up sharply at the sound of Carter's voice. 'I do not possess a television set!' The older man spoke as if the very idea was unacceptable. 'And I only ever read the financial press. Tabloid journalism, Superintendent, is not to my taste.'

Carter and Phil Morton were seated in Alcott's minuscule drawing room in an unwished proximity. There was nothing that could be done about that, due both to the size of the room and to Morton being a little over six foot tall and a rugby player. Carter, who was nearly the same height and solidly built, was aware that, even both seated, they dwarfed their host.

Alcott, however, appeared by no means intimidated by their presence. He sat neatly before them, his ankles crossed, so they could see he wore pale blue silk socks with his custom-made shoes. He appeared in every way as perfect as a doll freshly taken from its cellophane wrapping. But these were not a doll's blank eyes,

141

thought Carter. They gleamed with a malicious kind of intelligence. Their sharp scrutiny was disconcerting.

When Carter informed him of Finch's death, however, Alcott had cast his eyes down and, at the same time, raised manicured fingers to touch his mouth. Only when his expression was fully under his control had he looked up again.

'Poor Carl dead, you say?' he murmured now. He gripped his small white hands. 'No, no, I had not seen the news anywhere and I am very shocked. He was a young man and appeared very fit.'

'He was murdered, sir,' said Morton from the armchair in which he was uncomfortably wedged. 'Shot.'

Alcott had been ignoring Morton, but now turned his head to look straight at him. He considered the sergeant at leisure, studying him from top to toe, with the curiosity of a visitor to a zoo who has been presented with some previously never seen animal. But both Carter and Morton knew instinctively that Edgar Alcott had faced the police before; when and in what circumstances they did not yet know. But both of them sensed Alcott's underlying defensive wariness, despite the band-box appearance and old-maidish calm.

'Even more unbelievable,' he said. 'I am extremely sorry to hear that. Why?' He leaned forward on the last word, and raised his eyebrows.

With this simple question he successfully threw both his visitors momentarily off balance.

'We don't yet know why, Mr Alcott, or by whom or, indeed, exactly where. We only know where his body was discovered. That is why we are conducting these enquiries,' Carter managed.

'And they have brought you to me. Dear, dear . . .' murmured Alcott. 'I cannot imagine why. Or, indeed, how.'

Carter chose to ignore the invitation to explain their presence.

A slight expression of annoyance passed across Alcott's face and was gone almost at once. Carter thought of a wisp of cloud scudding across the face of the sun. 'I can tell you nothing!' Alcott said firmly.

'We understand Mr Finch recently visited you here, in Oxford.'

'Now, who told you that, I wonder?' Alcott's eyebrows twitched again. But he had himself well under control this time and no cloud appeared. His tone was almost benign.

You are a tricky old devil, thought Carter. And you are quick on your feet – or whatever the relevant expression for thought is.

'We are very anxious, you see, to trace Mr Finch's recent movements. We find ourselves rather in the dark, frankly, and we would be very grateful for any light you could shed on his state of mind.'

'Well, he did come to see me, yes. It was a social call. I have no idea about his *state of mind.*' Alcott waved both hands, palms outward. 'I can only say he seemed much as usual. I wish I could suggest some explanation for this awful event, but I'm afraid I can't. Was it a mistake, do you think? Or a dreadful accident? One hears of victims shot in error. Guns are such dangerous things. I simply can't imagine why anyone should *want* to kill that poor boy.' Alcott shook his head sorrowfully.

Carter resisted the urge to remind his host that Finch had been in his forties and not, by any description, a boy. But Alcott, he guessed, was really quite old, and being well preserved didn't quite disguise it. On the other hand, he had known enough ageing crooks in his time to be aware that drawing the old-age pension is not necessarily incompatible with a life of crime.

'We understand he owned a Renault Megane,' Carter said aloud. 'Did he drive it to Oxford, park it outside this house, perhaps?'

'He came by train,' said Alcott promptly. 'Parking is never easy in Oxford, even in residential streets. I have no idea what kind of car he drove. I myself do not drive. *He really was murdered*, you say? Forgive me if I continue to doubt your news, but it does sound extraordinary, so one has great difficulty in absorbing the fact. There is no chance he committed suicide?' For the first time, Alcott sounded less than confident.

'No, sir, someone definitely shot him,' said Morton.

Alcott threw up his white hands but not quickly enough to hide the relief in his eyes. 'Oh! Dreadful! I have no idea who could have done such a frightful thing, or why. What a world we live in! Can you wonder that I prefer to stay here with my books and other treasures?' He shook his head. 'It takes a lot to tempt me out of my little home.'

Carter had not come here to discuss the state of the world. 'Could you tell us how you came to know Mr Finch? And for how long?'

'I met him almost four years ago.'

'In Oxford?'

'Oh, no, at an auction house in London, in the saleroom. The sale was devoted to books and maps of the ancient world. I have an interest in the classical world, so I took courage and boarded a train, something I rarely do. One is sealed in with germs, awful. I had a sore throat for a week afterwards.' He must have noticed his visitors becoming restless and continued more briskly: 'There were a couple of items in the catalogue that interested me. I did not, however, buy either of them, in the end. I was outbid. It is important, Superintendent Carter, when one goes to auction sales, to have an idea in one's mind what one is willing to pay. Otherwise, you know, one can get quite carried away.'

'Are you, or were you, connected with the university?' Carter asked curiously.

Alcott sighed with what appeared a genuine regret. 'Alas, no, I have never had the scholarship to aspire to an academic career. It is a happy man who is able to combine his personal interest with the way he earns his living. I was never able to do that.'

'What did you do, sir?' asked Morton. 'For a living, I mean.'

Alcott clearly thought the question rather blunt. He frowned and cast a reproachful glance at Morton. When he replied, he addressed himself to Carter.

'In the course of a busy working life I had interests in various businesses. In the latter years I had a part interest in several health spas, in London and in Manchester. I am not, as you will have realised, a person who chooses to spend his day mixing with all and sundry. The spas were all run by managers, and all were above board, I assure you.'

If Morton had wanted revenge for being snubbed, he clearly thought the moment had come. He had acquired the look of a keen terrier that had just spotted a rat.

'These health spas, sir, would they be what some people might call massage parlours?'

'Some people might, Sergeant,' said Alcott coolly. 'You yourself might, I dare say. I cannot prevent you thinking whatever you wish. But I insist that nothing took place that was in the slightest improper on any of our premises. As the Romans put it, *mens sana in corpore sano*. That, Sergeant Morton, means "a healthy mind in a healthy body". It was our guiding principle. They were private clubs and used by respectable businessmen. We kept out riffraff and undesirables.'

'Never raided, sir?' enquired Morton, not releasing his grip on his prey.

Alcott reddened. 'Once or twice, Sergeant, but never resulting in any prosecutions. False accusations had been laid against us by business rivals.'

Carter glanced at Morton and took back control of the conversation. 'Was it a profitable line of business, sir?'

'Oh, yes, Superintendent. The stress of modern living is nowhere more apparent than in our great cities.'

'So, what brought you to Oxford?'

'Ah, now!' Alcott suddenly livened up. 'I was able to take a fairly early retirement from business. I wanted to move out of London. It is not a healthy place. I am asthmatic, you know. I had decided I would like to spend my declining years in one of our university cities. I finally found this little house in Oxford, and it suits me down to the ground. I now devote myself to my interest – hobby, you might call it – in classical history and culture.'

'And was Carl Finch interested in classical culture?' Carter asked incredulously.

'He knew nothing about it whatsoever!' was Alcott's prompt response.

'So, how did he come to be in that saleroom?'

Again, Alcott became more animated. It was as if anything to do with his hobby really was all that mattered to him. 'I arrived late at the sale and there wasn't a free seat. I stood at the back of the room at first, but it was inconvenient and I couldn't see well.

There was a man seated at the end of the back row, just in front of me. He was a well-built chap with rather long blond hair; so much I could see from where I stood. He must have noticed me enter and realised I had not found anywhere to sit. So he stood up and offered me his seat. I was very glad to accept it. After the sale, I offered to buy him a cup of tea by way of thanks. He appeared quite pleased to accept. I soon found out why. He had, he said, some old books on classical history. They had belonged to his late father. He had wondered if they had any value and he'd come to the saleroom that day to see what sort of prices old books on that subject fetched. He wanted to sell them, if they were worth anything.'

'And were they?'

'Oh, yes. When he told me what he had, I could scarcely believe my ears.' Alcott's pale cheeks flushed. His voice quivered with the remembered excitement of the moment. 'He had a complete early set of volumes of Edward Gibbon's *History of the Decline and Fall of the Roman Empire*. I couldn't believe my ears. Have you any idea, Superintendent, how rare such a find is? And complete! Occasionally, one or two volumes of the original or an early edition turn up, but to have a complete set, in good condition, had long been my dream. I told him I would need to view them, of course. But yes, I was most definitely interested!'

'Did you ask how his late father had come by them?'

'I certainly did. With antiques of any nature, provenance is important. It seems his family had lived in the same house for generations. The house was – still is – called the Old Nunnery and is in Gloucestershire. No one in the present family had any interest in old books. The Gibbon volumes had been removed to an attic some years before and left up there in a box with some other volumes, neglected and forgotten. People are such philistines.'

'And he did bring them to you, for you to examine them?'

'Yes, he brought them here to this house. They were in a very fair condition, considering they had been many years in an unheated attic. They had suffered a little from damp, but they were complete. I had no hesitation in offering him six thousand pounds on the spot.'

'Six thousand!' exclaimed Carter and Morton together.

For the first time, Alcott smiled, albeit briefly. 'You may think I took advantage of his ignorance and underpaid. But I assure you I was scrupulously fair in my discussion with him. I told him frankly that, should he take the books to the right auction, or even to another private buyer, he might get much more. The gamble would be that he might not, or that he would have to wait. For my part, I was prepared to give him six thousand that very day. He accepted.' Alcott paused. 'I had the impression he was in need of money rather urgently.'

Alcott waved a white hand gracefully at a glass-fronted walnut bookcase. 'The books are in there. You may see them yourself.' He smiled contentedly. '"Faithful mirrors that reflect the minds of sages and heroes." The words are Gibbon's.'

Morton cast his eyes up to the ceiling, but Carter needed no urging. He jumped to his feet and went to the bookcase. When he came back to his chair, he asked, 'Did he sell you any other books?'

'Just the one, and nowhere near as valuable. It is a sketchbook belonging to a naval officer, dating from the 1820s and '30s. Young gentlemen in those days, long before photography, very often sketched interesting sights on their travels. This particular officer had been in the Mediterranean and made watercolour sketches at various sites of classical antiquity. As amateur watercolours go, they have a naïve charm. I gave him a couple of hundred pounds for it. He was always in need of money, poor Carl.'

This gave Carter the entry he sought. 'Did you ever lend him any money, or have any other business dealings with him, apart from purchasing the books you've mentioned? Forgive me, Mr Alcott, but it puzzles me that you and Finch had anything in common, once the business with the books was done. But if you were in the habit of lending him sums of money when he was short of cash . . .'

Alcott hesitated for a moment. Then he appeared to decide that frankness was the best road to follow. 'Our friendship continued, even though no more old books were involved. But I did not lend him money, Mr Carter, in the way you suggested. Once or twice I made small investments at his suggestion and received a modest but welcome return on my money.' Alcott sighed. 'He was a dear boy. Foolish, of course, in pursuing a lifestyle he couldn't afford. You might say I took a benevolent interest in him.'

'If I could return to these investments, made, as you say, on Finch's recommendation, what is the situation now, at Finch's death?'

Again Alcott hesitated, but spoke firmly in answer. 'Am I out of pocket? Yes. That is to say, I followed his advice – not for the first time, as I mentioned – and invested some money in a consortium developing a luxury holiday complex on a small island in the Caribbean.'

'May I ask how much?' Carter sounded his politest, but Alcott was not misled.

His eyelids flickered. 'Eighty thousand pounds,' he said.

Morton whistled softly under his breath.

Alcott made a gesture with both hands, spreading them out to either side. 'Sadly, it turned out that the project had not been sufficiently thought through. Oh, the costs and the potential were all well researched. But there has been considerable local opposition, quite unexpectedly. You would think a boost to the depressed local economy would be welcome but, alas, it is apparently not so. To make things worse, it now appears there is some kind of rare turtle that lays its eggs on the principal stretch of beach . . .' Alcott waved his hands. 'Think of it, a turtle! The best-laid plans, Superintendent Carter, of mice and men, as the poet wrote, are apt to go wrong, and we have been undone by a turtle.'

'So,' Carter said, 'on his last visit to you here, Carl Finch and you must have discussed this failed—'

'Oh, not *failed*, not entirely!' protested Alcott. 'But things are held up and, when that happens, you know, investors get jittery and want to get their money out.'

'And you, sir, you wanted your money back?'

Alcott dusted an invisible blemish from his jacket lapel. 'It would have been nice. But I quite understood the situation. I did not blame Carl. Please believe me, in no way did I hold him responsible. Carl advised me to wait. Things could be sorted out.'

'And you believed this? You, a businessman of many years' experience?'

'I did not want to make things worse than they were for Carl, poor boy.'

Barely audibly, Morton murmured, 'You fancied him!'

But Alcott had heard and turned first scarlet and then white with rage. 'Can you not control your sergeant, Superintendent Carter?'

'I apologise for Sergeant Morton's remark. It was uncalled for.' Carter looked at Morton. 'Sergeant!'

'Yes, sir. Sorry, sir.'

'It was both uncalled for and untrue!' Alcott rose to his feet. Two red patches had appeared on his pale face, each glowing on a cheekbone, increasing his doll-like appearance. 'I think it is time for you both to leave!'

'I'm very sorry, sir,' said Morton abjectly when they were outside. 'I hadn't meant to say it aloud. It sort of slipped out. The old fraud gave me the creeps. Benevolent interest, be blowed!'

Carter laughed. 'Oh, that was nonsense, of course. But more importantly, Alcott is not the sort of man who overlooks bad advice in a business affair that costs him money. We'll pass on the enquiry into this investment project in the Caribbean to the boys who know more about that sort of thing.'

'Fraud squad? You think it was a scam?'

'Not necessarily. Alcott is a sharp old fellow and I don't think he would invest without making his own enquiries first. It could have been a legitimate project that's run into unforeseen difficulties. That detail about the turtle . . .'

'I don't believe it,' said Morton sapiently. 'I mean, strange or what?'

Carter smiled. 'Strange enough to be true, Phil. At any rate, Alcott made no attempt to deny his interest in the scheme, and he won't be the only one likely to have lost his investment.'

'So there must be quite a list of people with a grudge against Finch, all furious about losing their cash!' muttered Morton. 'Any one of them could have followed him to those woods and blasted him away.'

Carter looked unconvinced. 'We'll have to consider it but, remember, without Finch, who was their link with the company behind the deal to set up this millionaire's playground, the investors will all have lost their direct contact with the widowed lady who, we're told, is the moving force behind it.'

He paused. 'I suspect that Alcott made it clear to Carl that he wanted his money back. Back there at the house I got the distinct impression he was anxious to be reassured that Finch didn't commit suicide, which suggests he'd been pressing for his money.'

After a few minutes' silence, Morton asked, 'What was all that about getting acquainted with him over a book deal? Funny old way to meet someone, and I still can't believe Alcott let the acquaintance run on without some ulterior motive.'

'I accept that Alcott was keen to buy the books that brought them together in the first place. He is a genuine collector; and the volumes are there, *Decline and Fall*, in that bookcase,' Carter told him. 'I don't doubt he met Finch at that antiques auction, just as he says, and originally the subject of their conversation would have been entirely about those books. Finch not only wanted to sell, he wanted to sell fast, probably before their provenance came into question. Alcott may have suspected that and taken the opportunity to acquire a bargain.'

The idea of six thousand pounds being considered a bargain price for a set of old books rendered Morton speechless.

'But, collector's greed satisfied, Alcott didn't want to let Carl go,' Carter continued. 'We can only speculate as to his reasons. However, whatever they were, they wouldn't excuse Carl being the cause of Alcott losing a lot of money. Alcott must have kicked up a fuss. Moreover, some of Alcott's past business ventures may have led him into make acquaintance with, let's say, the fringes of the underworld.'

'So Carl Finch realised that he was likely to be visited by a couple of guys anxious to apply a little persuasion if he didn't find the cash? No wonder Finch was worried.' Morton shook his head sadly. 'Silly sod,' he said.

'Finch does seem to have lacked commonsense.'

As Carter spoke, they overtook a car with a family in it. Memory delivered him a sharp reminder, sending him images of long-ago outings when Millie was small, and wiping Alcott and Finch from his thoughts. They had been a family unit then, the three of them: himself, Sophie and their daughter. As that unit, they'd visited various theme parks. At the time, he'd invariably found them awful places, designed to part parents from their money as fast as possible. But Millie had loved anything like that. Even Sophie had appeared to enjoy them. Memories could be happy and painful. Perhaps he took refuge in police work, shutting out a personal world. Now he felt the pain quite physically.

Beside him, Morton muttered, 'I still think Alcott's interest was in more than the business project.'

'All right, then,' Carter replied. 'Perhaps Finch had the kind of male beauty the ancients admired and respected, and which would appeal to Alcott.'

Morton took the practical view. 'I don't know about ancient goings-on. From all I've ever seen in films it was pretty well non-stop orgies – with the Romans, anyway. It's a wonder they had time to build an empire.' He added, with unexpected shrewdness, 'Perhaps Alcott lives in *his* own dream world – you know, the one in which he's a respected authority on ancient history and all that. But really, he's just an old pimp and a dodgy businessman. Before he turned legit with those health spas, you can bet he ran a string of escort agencies and the like.'

While Carter was in Oxford, Jess had returned to the Old Nunnery. She had hoped to be able to find Guy alone. For once, circumstances played into her hands. No one was in the house, but the sounds of raised male voices guided her to the former stables. There she found Guy deep in conversation with a stocky man with bushy, greying hair and a pencil stub stuck behind his ear.

'It won't work!' declared this man, in the assured way of one who knows.

'You must be able to fit a small worktop in somehow, Derek,' argued Guy.

'Not if you want clear access to the en suite,' said the carpenter. 'I warned about that, didn't I? Now then, if you want a little table for a kettle and a tray with teacups, there's no problem. But a worktop, well, that's different, isn't it? That's got taps. That's got a little sink. It has to be plumbed in. You're talking kitchenette.'

'No, I'm not talking any sort of kitchen!' exclaimed the clearly exasperated Kingsley. 'I don't want somewhere the visitors can cook themselves a three-course meal! It's just somewhere they can make toast or—'

Neither man had seen Jess approach. 'Captain Kingsley?' she said loudly.

Both turned to face her, looking startled. Then Guy rallied. 'Oh, Inspector Campbell! Harriet's not here, she's gone off to have lunch with Tess Briggs at the Royal Oak in Weston St Ambrose.'

Derek, the carpenter, eyed Jess up and down as if assessing her dimensions with regard to fitting her into the ground plan of the holiday accommodation. She almost expected him to say it couldn't be done, not if anyone wanted to open a door. Then, unexpectedly, he asked, 'Got him yet, have you, the murderer?'

'Making slow progress,' Jess assured him. 'Captain Kingsley, can we talk somewhere?'

'Come into the kitchen,' he said. 'I could do with a coffee. We'll sort it out later, Derek.'

'Not if you want a kitchenette,' retorted Derek. 'It can't be done.'

Guy drew a deep breath and led Jess into the house at a brisk pace.

'He drives me round the bend!' he said to her as he filled the kettle. 'He just wants to do everything his way. You'd think I was asking him to fit out a four-star hotel. You can see for yourself the work is basically finished, all the big things. All I want from Derek is built-in wardrobes and little units for visitors to make a cup of tea and a basic snack. But Derek' – Guy drew a deep breath – 'Derek – in his judgement – is a master craftsman and a design genius.'

'It's all costing a lot of money, I suppose?' Jess remarked.

Guy, his attention on his coffee-making, grunted agreement. There are noisy kettles and quieter ones, Jess thought, amused. This one sounded as if a small but irritated dragon were trapped inside it. A muffled roar was building up and a column of steam began to escape from the spout in angry puffs. Abruptly, the kettle clicked itself off and the dragon fell silent. Guy set two mugs down on the table and sat down opposite her. Only now did he remember to take off his cap and toss it in the general direction of a coat rack. But he still wore his quilted body-warmer over his disreputable sweater. Jess reflected that kitchens are often the warmest room in a house. If so, the temperature of this one boded ill for the rest of the rooms.

'It's costing an arm and a leg,' he said now, in reply to her question. 'But if I can only hurry Derek up a bit, when he's done, Hattie and I can paint the walls and ceilings. Then we'll get in the carpet fitters and some furniture and, all being well, we'll be open for business by the summer.'

'I understand you've a lot on your mind,' she told him, 'quite apart from the murder. I'm sorry we have to keep bothering you, but our enquiries do mean we'll be taking up your time until we establish exactly what happened to your brother-in-law. Stepbrother-in-law,' she amended. 'We visited his mews cottage in London yesterday,' she went on. 'A nice little place.'

'Find anything?' Guy asked sharply. He looked taken aback at the idea they had been so thorough.

'Experts are examining his computer.' She paused for effect. 'While we were there, a friend of Finch's arrived, a Natalie Adam.'

Guy threw up his hands. 'Damn!' he said. 'Is that woman still hanging around? She told you, I suppose, about the visit I paid Carl?'

'She did.'

'Look.' Guy leaned forward. 'Harriet knows nothing about that.

I've never told her I went to see Carl, and I'd rather she didn't find out. She's always clung to the belief that she can handle Carl all by herself. But it was obvious to me from the start that she couldn't. Carl knew exactly how to use her affection for him, pull all the right strings: the shared childhood, the way his mother looked after her, all the sentimental stuff. But you've seen for yourself out there . . .' Guy gestured towards the building work. 'We haven't got money to spend on people like Carl Finch!'

'You and Finch had some sort of a brawl, I understand, while you were in London.'

'Brawl?' Guy was anxious to dismiss this image. 'Nothing like that, just a push-and-shove sort of encounter; no blood, no bruises, no black eyes. A chair might have fallen over. Otherwise, neither of us raised a sweat! Natalie being there stopped it being anything more. What was *she* doing there, anyway, yesterday?' he demanded of Jess.

'Trying to contact him. He hadn't been returning her calls or text messages, not even answering his mobile. We still haven't found his mobile, by the way, or his car keys, or his car.'

'Have you searched those woods? I suppose you have. His mobile and keys could have been pushed into any bit of under-growth.'

'Yes, we have, and we are as certain as we can be that they are not there. The car is less easy to hide, but we haven't found that either. Tell me, have you heard of a man called Edgar Alcott?'

'No.' Guy looked blank. 'Who is he?'

'We're not sure, but we believe Finch visited him recently, in Oxford.'

'I can't imagine why,' Guy told her. He frowned and shook his head. 'No, never heard of him. Hattie's certainly never mentioned anyone of that name. The truth is, Inspector Campbell, that we neither of us had any idea what Carl got up to in London. As for any reason for his going to Oxford . . . I can't offer you any explanation at all for his going there, I'm afraid.'

'We hope to find out soon. Superintendent Carter is driving to Oxford to interview Alcott today.'

'Whatever the reason is, I just hope it doesn't involve us – Hattie and me!' Guy snapped.

But, as things turned out, it had involved the Old Nunnery. On his return from Oxford, Carter brought Jess up to date on what they'd learned.

'Finch was removing items from the house and selling them!' Jess exclaimed incredulously. 'I must say, he didn't lack nerve. Guy and Harriet surely had no idea. I can't see Guy allowing it.'

'I suspect it had been going on for a long time. It probably started as soon as that will was read and Finch realised he wasn't going to get what he felt he was entitled to! He decided to put matters right by helping himself.'

Jess said thoughtfully, 'When he was a kid, he probably explored that house thoroughly. He knew where everything was. The attics must have fascinated him.'

'Probably. We'll go and tell the Kingsleys now, if you've got the time to spare,' Carter said. 'It's late, I know, but sometimes it pays to strike while the iron is hot. Your visit this morning telling Guy we know about his dust-up with Carl in London will have unsettled him. We might as well build on that.'

It had already grown dark when they reached the Old Nunnery.

The golden glow from a few windows dotted the massive black bulk of the old house like warning lanterns slung at night around a wooden man o' war at anchor. Clearly, neither Guy nor Harriet had expected them to return that day.

'Is it me you want to see?' asked Harriet unhappily. 'I know I wasn't here when you came this morning, Inspector Campbell. Tessa thought I needed a break and took me off to lunch.'

'We'd like to see you both,' said Carter. 'Because we've learned something that might be of interest to you.'

They received the news of the books Carl had sold in a stunned silence.

'Do you mean to tell us?' Guy asked, his face a picture of outraged disbelief. 'Do you seriously mean to say that Hattie and I were struggling to make a going concern of an antiques business, selling some of her old furniture and knick-knacks, which turned out to be worthless junk. Yet, all the time, up there in the attics, there was a set of valuable books . . . six thousand pounds' worth, at least – maybe more! That blighter Carl stole—'

'I won't have my stepbrother called a thief!' Harriet spoke loudly and firmly. Carter and her husband both looked at her in surprise. She was flushed with anger. 'If Carl recognised those books might be valuable and took the trouble to find out, then it's right he benefited. We didn't bother about them.'

Guy had been scowling in thought. 'Look here, I'm pretty sure they weren't up there in the attic when we were hunting around,' he said suddenly. 'I'd have seen them. Or you would, Hat! He must have pinched them before that. He must have sneaked up there and had a good look round for something portable. What else did he smuggle out of the house? I wonder. You told me,

Hattie, that when you were kids exploring up there you found boxes of china and other stuff. So where did all that go? Don't tell me to a jumble sale, because I don't buy it! Carl sneaked it all away a bit at a time. He was waltzing in and out of this house as if he owned the place—'

Guy broke off abruptly, perhaps struck by the accuracy of his last words. Carl had thought he should own half the house.

'I don't care,' his wife said obstinately.

'But Hattie, he *stole* them. We should try and get them back!'

Carter intervened. 'You could consult your solicitor, certainly. But you admit you don't actually know when the books were taken. As for any other items that might have been stored in the attics, you have no evidence he took any of them or, indeed, exactly what they were.

'You inherited both this house and its contents on your father's death, Mrs Kingsley. So if the books were still here, then Finch unlawfully helped himself to your property and sold it. But your husband says he's fairly sure they weren't there when he was searching the attics. That suggests that Finch may have taken them even before your father's death, when they were Mr Hemmings's property, or certainly very soon after his death. If later challenged, Finch might have claimed Mr Hemmings gave the books to him before he died. You may find getting them back a protracted wrangle. You think, Captain Kingsley, that Finch was coming here and searching about over a period of time, so how did he get in? Did he have his own key to the house?'

Harriet looked startled. 'Well, yes, he could have still had his key. He had one when he lived here, certainly. I don't know, is the answer. It's possible.'

'If he did, he didn't actually break in. He entered with his own key. He might have taken the view that the books were abandoned, up there in the attics. Consult a lawyer, by all means. But be prepared for a tussle. Finch sold the books on. Alcott bought them in good faith.'

'Carl still helped himself to the damn things without any authority!' Guy stormed. 'Why would John Hemmings give a set of old books to Carl? John himself had probably forgotten all about them!'

'I don't care!' Harriet shouted. 'They became my property when Dad died, if they were still here at that time. And I don't want to pursue the matter any further! Carl is dead. Things are bad enough. I repeat, I won't have him called a thief!'

As the echo of her voice died away and her listeners stared at her, startled, she added, 'I've had an awful day. Tessa kept trying to stuff food down me. I now know how those poor geese must feel.'

In Oxford that evening Edgar Alcott picked up the phone and, having first carefully cleaned it with an antiseptic wipe, called a number written on a notepad beside the instrument.

'Ah, yes, good evening. Edgar here. Oh, no, nothing very much. Just to let you know that they've been to see me. What? Superintendent Carter and an oafish sergeant. No, nobody called Campbell, no woman, red-haired or otherwise. Oh, it wasn't a problem at all, other than the sergeant treading mud into my hall carpet. I don't expect them back again, but I thought you'd like to know.'

The person at the other end of the line spoke at some length. Edgar listened, examining the nails on his left hand as he did. 'Yes, I would,' he replied at last. 'I'd be very interested.'

Chapter 10

Tom Palmer could have told Jess where Harriet Kingsley had been that day because, by chance, Tom had also lunched at the Royal Oak in Weston St Ambrose.

There comes a point when tinned soup and instant noodles no longer provide a satisfying diet. It must be a sign he was feeling better. For a few days, he hadn't really cared what he ate – although Jess's Indian takeaway had been a pleasant surprise. But this morning he had awoken feeling much better, and hungry. If he were to return to work next week, as he planned, he would have to take in some nourishment. He fancied a steak.

He knew the Royal Oak well because he and Madison had often ended up there in the old days, after a companionable walk. He must be getting over Madison, too, because, frankly, he had avoided that hotel restaurant for some months after she'd taken off for Australia. Now, it no longer seemed to matter that he'd been there with her.

He hadn't expected the place to be busy, not at this time of the year. In summer the Royal Oak did good business with tourists and its menu became more ambitious. Although the menu was more basic in the 'off' season, the restaurant had a good name for those seeking a quiet meal. Today it was certainly quiet, with just a party of four elderly diners at one table and, over there, by the window, two women.

It wasn't until Tom found a table himself and sat down that he identified the two women, and his heart sank. One was that female with the dog who'd turned up in Crooked Man Woods on the day he'd found the body. The other one, he was sure of it, was the demon driver who had nearly forced him off the road on his way to the woods. Jess had told him his description of that driver fitted Harriet Kingsley. *So* Mrs Kingsley and Mrs Briggs were old chums, were they? The plot thickens, Watson! *I wonder if Jess knows?* he thought. She probably did, by now.

He was anxious that Mrs Briggs might spot him; she'd probably recognise him. He hadn't spoken to her at the scene, only the police had done that, but she had probably noticed him leaning against a tree looking pale and wan and snuffling into a succession of handkerchiefs. Instinct told him she was the sort of woman who noticed everything and had an excellent memory. But he'd promised himself a steak at the Royal Oak and he wasn't going to be deprived of it by Mrs Briggs. All he needed to do was move to a more secluded table. There was one nearby, in the shelter of a large potted yucca. The Royal Oak was an old place, its dining room poorly lit during the day. Between the natural gloom and the yucca, he should be safe.

He could, however, see the women without too much trouble, just by leaning to one side and peering through the plant's long, thin leaves. To be honest, it wasn't Mrs Briggs he wanted to keep an eye on. He wanted a better look at Harriet. Yep! That was the woman in the Range Rover. She was attractive, if a bit stressed-looking. She was pushing her food around her plate as if her appetite was poor. Mrs Briggs leaned forward, obviously urging her to eat. Mrs Briggs's manner, Tom decided, was part protective and part possessive, like a domineering mother.

At this point, a girl with purple hair and heavily studded earlobes arrived at his table and held out a single sheet of paper on which was the menu for the day.

'We also got specials,' she said. 'And soup is parsnip and apple.'

Tom scanned the menu. Under 'Mains' it offered a traditional roast chicken and vegetables, battered cod with chips, and a vegetarian option in pasta form. 'What are the specials?' he demanded, unimpressed.

'Written up on the blackboard over there,' she said, pointing across the room to the wall just behind the two women diners.

He couldn't read the faintly chalked message on the blackboard from here, and he wasn't going to get up and walk over there because Mrs Briggs would see him.

'Can't see it from here, I'm afraid,' he said briskly to the purple-haired attendant. 'Can you tell me what are they?'

She gave him a look that suggested he was being difficult. 'Fishcakes or chicken teriyaki,' she said. 'Fishcakes are salmon.'

Probably tinned salmon at that. Chicken teriyaki, however, was an unexpected exotic visitor to the menu in winter. Perhaps the chef was trying it out. But Tom wasn't prepared to gamble on the teriyaki and certainly he wasn't going to be appeased by an offer of fishcakes. He knew what he wanted.

'No, thank you, I'd like a steak.'

She had now definitely decided he was being difficult. 'It's not on the menu today.' She indicated the printed sheet again.

Across the room, Harriet had pushed away her plate. She looked drawn and miserable. Tom wondered what she'd chosen to order;

he couldn't see. She didn't look as if she would have picked the roast today. Perhaps she'd gone for the vegetarian option. Madison had been vegetarian. She had watched him eating steak with an air of tolerance. but she'd liked things like mushroom risotto and cauliflower cheese. Tom had hated cauliflower cheese all his life. His grandmother had made him eat it. Why on earth had he and Madison ever been an item?

'Perhaps you'd ask,' he requested the purple-haired damsel.

'What?'

'Would you ask them in the kitchen,' he expanded his request, 'if they have a steak?'

Briefly, the girl looked as if she would join battle, but there was a resolve in Tom's voice that stopped her. She marched off, quivering with rage.

Across the room, Mrs Briggs suddenly stood up. Tom experienced a moment of panic. If she wanted to visit the ladies', those facilities were located outside the dining room, off the main entrance hall. She would need to walk past his table. She would see him. He got out his smartphone and began to study it intently, hoping to escape attention.

But she wasn't coming this way. She was going over to the specials board. Was she hoping to persuade Harriet to try a different dish, force-feed her with fishcakes?

'We haven't seen you here for a while, Dr Palmer!' declared a male voice above his head.

Tom looked up, startled, to see the middle-aged waiter who had supervised the restaurant for years.

'You used to come in a lot with your young lady,' said the waiter.

'Yes, she's – she's gone abroad.'

The waiter looked down with friendly sympathy. 'Oh, dear, I'm sorry to hear that. Stefanie says you asked for a steak.'

'No chance, I suppose?' asked Tom, hope fading.

But the waiter was not a man to pile further woes on the head of a deserted lover. 'I'll see if we can find one,' he said confidentially.

'Medium rare?' Tom felt absurdly grateful.

'Certainly!' The waiter made a majestic departure, ignoring the waving hand of Tessa Briggs.

'Hello, Tom, feeling better?' It was a different male voice. This time when Tom looked up he saw the plump, smiling face of Maurice Melton hovering over him with the enquiring expression it probably wore when Maurice was taking stock of a newly arrived cadaver.

What was this place? Waterloo station? How many more casual visitors were going to pass through? And what on earth was old Maurice doing here?

Aloud, Tom heard himself muttering an explanation about the need for solid food and his planned returned to work.

Maurice, as he feared, replied with a request to be allowed to join him. Stefanie appeared and handed the new arrival the same dog-eared menu sheet rejected by Tom. She managed, as she did this, to pass a surly message to Tom.

'Your steak's just coming.'

'Steak, eh?' boomed Maurice, scanning the menu. 'Where does it say that?'

'It doesn't,' said Stefanie. 'This gentleman made a special request. We haven't got enough steaks in the fridge to put it on the menu.

We had a run on them last night. Want me to go back and ask?'
She heaved a sigh.

'No, no, my dear, don't trouble yourself. I'll have the roast.'

His courtesy did not pass unappreciated. Stefanie gave him a dazzling smile, following it with a malicious glance at Tom.

'Not drinking, Tom?' Maurice sounded concerned.

'No, well, I've been taking medication for the cold.'

'Quite, very sensible. A half-bottle of red, then.'

'Of course, sir,' said Stefanie graciously, and set off. But it was not Stefanie's day. She had barely reached the door before a commanding voice echoed across the room.

'Young woman!' Mrs Briggs had already been ignored once and was not to be so twice. 'I have been trying to attract some attention for over five minutes!'

Stefanie trudged back and across to the window table.

'Interesting body you found in the woods, Tom,' said Maurice cheerfully, and loudly enough to be heard well beyond the yucca.

Tom repressed the instinct to lean across the table and stuff a napkin in Maurice's mouth. This was the very last thing he needed. At the moment, Mrs Briggs was taken up with telling Stefanie how poor the service was. But Maurice was not a man to speak quietly and, once Mrs Briggs had finished with Stefanie, it would only need her to catch just one key word. Luckily, the Polish barman had arrived with Maurice's half-bottle and conversation was diverted.

'What is this? Ah, a Merlot, very good. Pity you can't have a glass, Tom.'

The waiter reappeared, bearing Tom's steak. 'There you go, Dr Palmer.'

Rooted in Evil

'I've seen many shotgun injuries in my time,' announced Maurice, having savoured his Merlot.

'Maurice!' begged Tom. 'Not now! There's . . .' He tried frantically to indicate the table window without being obvious.

'Not while you're eating? Of course! We'll chat about it over coffee.'

Tom wondered how long he could make the steak last. But Mrs Briggs, having failed to entice Harriet to eat anything more, and told Stefanie in detail what was wrong with the Royal Oak, had asked for the bill. The two women passed by his table on their way out as Maurice's roast arrived. Neither of the women looked at them. Maurice's attention was diverted and, when he was ready to speak again, Harriet and her forceful companion had gone.

Tom was free now to enjoy his steak. Except that he had coffee to look forward to, during which Maurice would regale him with tales of shotgun injuries he had known. Tom didn't want to upset Maurice, who was a nice old boy and a skilled pathologist, so he would have to sit through it all. How did professional detectives, like Jess or Ian Carter, or any others, manage to conduct their enquiries without the world and his wife appearing and putting their oar in?

'I've started coming to this place for lunch,' said Maurice through a forkful of broccoli. 'It's nice and quiet.'

Stefanie would not have agreed with him. Two new diners had arrived at the entrance to the restaurant and she was explaining to them that the kitchen would be closing in ten minutes. They could, however, get a snack in the bar.

'But the kitchen isn't closed yet, you say?' The voice was female and challenging.

Maurice was deep in fond remembrance of some very interesting (to him) case. Tom's attention wandered to the doorway and the woman who had spoken. She was tall and ultra slim, dressed in skinny jeans and high, shiny lizard-skin-pattern boots. She also wore a fitted black leather jacket without a collar. Possibly, she thought this was country wear. She had long, tawny-blond hair, and dark glasses perched on top of her head, although the day wasn't particularly sunny. The fellow with her was tall, beefy, red-faced, ginger-haired and baggy-eyed. The front of his checked shirt bulged over the waistband of his chinos. He put the chap's age at around the same as his own and hoped, even with his cold, that he didn't look so out of condition.

'So we're not too late to order!' declared this man.

'It depends what you want!' returned Stefanie, undaunted.

Tom now found himself in sympathy with her. He also felt a little ashamed because earlier he'd made such a fuss demanding his steak. Poor kid was probably on minimum wage and for this pittance had to put up with a succession of awkward customers: Tom himself, Tessa Briggs, and now this pair.

Maurice had exhausted his stock of anecdotes about shotgun injuries and moved on, for some reason, to cases of possible misdiagnosis.

'Of course,' he said, carefully placing his knife and fork on a clean plate, 'we all of us remember the case of Sidney Fox and the Margate murder. Still a standard example for students, I dare say.'

'Yes,' said Tom absently.

'What is there?' demanded the ginger-haired bloke, loudly enough to cause even Maurice to pause and glance crossly in his direction.

'The roast today is chicken,' said Stefanie. 'Chef could still do that for you.'

'Yes,' said the woman nastily, 'because it was cooked mid-morning and has been hanging around ever since!'

'It's all that's left, unless you want fishcakes,' Stefanie told them. Unsurprisingly, this suggestion didn't help. 'Fishcakes!' the woman yelped.

'Look here,' said Ginger Hair. 'We've driven down from London and we have just booked into this hotel. The receptionist told us we were in time to get a meal.'

'I'm not eating fishcakes or left-over roast, Henry!' The slim woman turned back to Stephanie. The waitress was now looking the picture of purple-haired suppressed rage. At the end of the day she would probably hand in her notice.

'Is there anywhere else decent to eat nearby?' continued the woman.

'Not at the moment,' Stefanie told her. 'Usually, there would be the Fisherman's Rest at Lower Weston.' Maliciously, she added: 'But it got flooded out before Christmas and is still being refurbished.'

'And that's it? This is a tourist area. Surely there's somewhere else?'

'The Black Horse, down the street, does sandwiches and pizzas.'

'Oh, come along, Natalie!' said Henry. 'I saw a teashop. Perhaps they do something on toast.'

Stefanie watched them depart with the satisfied expression Boudicca might have worn on seeing Romans flee before her chariots. So much had triumph mellowed her that she suddenly wheeled round, swooped on their table and, smiling, announced, 'I hope you enjoyed your lunch?'

'Nice little girl, that,' said Maurice when she'd brought their coffees.

Tom eventually took farewell of Maurice in the hotel car park. Maurice told him how much he'd enjoyed his company. Tom replied in like manner. Maurice drove off in his Jaguar. Tom looked around at the remaining vehicles. The black Range Rover wasn't there and there was no sign of either of the two women. That wasn't surprising. There was, however, a gleaming, showroom-new Mercedes. Henry and Natalie, thought Tom.

He put his hands in his pockets and wandered back into the main street. He didn't particularly want to go home just yet. He began to stroll down the street in the general direction of the church. He paused before a newly opened antiques shop to study its window display of assorted knick-knacks and militaria. Nothing for him there. Oh, here was the teashop. Through the window he could see Henry and Natalie, glumly eating the something on toast. He moved on and came to a building with a placard outside. This, it told him, was the public library. It was run by volunteers and open only on specific days. Today was one of them. Tom, for want of anything else to do, went in.

It was bigger than he'd expected, and busier. A few people were studying the shelves of books. On the far wall a large display was being set up and a group of people were arguing in front of it. The display was of paintings executed by artists of a varying degree of competence. A man in his sixties, distinguished by the lack of hair on top of his head and the abundance of beard beneath his chin, seemed to be in charge of putting the individual pieces up, and then taking them down again. A banner above the display read 'The Countryside about Us'. Beneath it a smaller notice explained that the display was the work of local artists, members of the Weston St Ambrose Countryside Artists' club. Among the paintings was one of trees, and something about it looked familiar. Tom went to investigate.

'We have to change them around, Sally,' declared the bearded fellow. He wore a baggy pullover and baggy cord trousers to match, and he spoke in a booming voice. The sight and sound of him annoyed Tom. He had been taught chemistry at school by someone very similar.

'I liked mine where it was!' argued a small young woman with curling dark hair sticking out beneath a woollen hat.

'Well, Sally, yours is not the only work to be displayed here, you know, and you have to consider other people!' pronounced the bearded one.

'I have considered them, all of them!' retorted the small woman. 'I've moved my pictures twice to please people. I'm not moving them again!'

That's it! Tom cheered her on silently. Stand up for yourself.

'You're being difficult, you know,' Beardie reproved her. Even Tom could have told him that he was throwing extra coals on the fire.

'No, I'm not, Gordon, you are!' She stood only as high as the middle of the bearded man's chest and the effect was like a Jack Russell terrier holding its ground before a German shepherd. Her face was flushed, her eyes sparkled with the light of battle and the woollen hat had slipped backwards, revealing more dark curls. Tom was instantly smitten.

He inched closer under the excuse of looking at the pictures more closely, and got a surprise. It caused him to exclaim aloud, 'These trees are in Crooked Man Woods!'

Sally and the bearded man, Gordon, looked at him.

'Sorry,' Tom apologised. 'I was in those woods just the other day and I'm sure that's where that clump of trees in the picture is.'

'Yes, that's right!' said the small young woman, beaming at him.

'Excuse me, but we are rather busy!' Gordon squashed any budding discussion. 'I hope, when we have our display in place, you'll come back and look at *all* the exhibited work!'

That, Tom decided, was a way of telling him to push off. It was like being told to make do with fishcakes.

'Oh, I won't get in your way!' he declared with what he hoped was a disarming smile. 'I don't come to this village often and I might not see the finished exhibition. Don't mind if I take an unobtrusive peek, do you? I'll stand well back.'

The small girl, Sally, was trying not to grin. Fortunately, before this became a three-way argument, someone called out, 'Gordon!' The bearded man said stiffly, 'Excuse me a moment!' and moved off.

'He's all right really,' said Sally, sotto voce.

'Is he? I'll take your word for it.' Tom nodded at the board. 'I did recognise that clump of trees. You're talented.'

'Mm.' She appeared to assess the compliment as she might have sized up a potential subject. 'I couldn't really get it right, you know.' She was pointing at the painting. 'Are you an artist?'

'No, nothing like that, I'm afraid. I'm a walker. That's how I know the woods and the general countryside around.'

She seemed suddenly lost in thought, and not pleasant thoughts.

Her brow furrowed. 'They found a body in the woods very recently. Some poor man had shot himself.'

'I know,' Tom said. 'I found him. He didn't shoot himself. Someone else did that!'

Not surprisingly, she looked shocked. 'I hadn't heard that. How awful.' That furrowed brow was back. 'Then you and I were both in the woods that morning.'

'You were there!' Tom gasped.

'Yes, I paint trees, mostly. They're always fascinating – to me, anyway. I use my smartphone to snap anything that takes my eye. After I get home I work it up first as a sketch and then, if I'm satisfied, in paint. I know it's more traditional to go out with a sketchbook. Gordon does that quite a lot. I've just got into the habit of using my phone.'

'Sounds fair enough to me. Did you see or hear anything while you were there? Anything suspicious?'

'Well, I . . .' She appeared to make up her mind. 'Would you like a cup of tea?' she asked. 'I've got a Thermos in my bag, in the kitchen. I need a break from this lot, anyway.'

The kitchen was a cramped nook just off the main room. There was no door between the two and the sound of argument from the display drifted in. If libraries were supposed to be quiet places, this one certainly wasn't. On a rickety table were piled assorted mugs and cups, some of which wouldn't have looked out of place in the antiques shop down the road. There was also a carton of UHT milk, half a packet of sugar and an opened pack of digestive biscuits. Sally dragged a bag from beneath the table and extracted a Thermos flask.

'I bring my own tea because theirs – in that tin over there – is horrid, cheap stuff full of dust. There's no fresh milk, do you mind? The fridge here doesn't work. It's not a proper public library now, you see. It was. But now it's kept open by volunteers, and there's no money to replace the fridge. The biscuits are OK. Someone brought them in today.'

'Do you live here in Weston St Ambrose?' he asked.

'Yes. I can afford the rent on a small place here. The down side is that it means I have to travel some distance to work, so I have to run a car. Just around Weston, of course, I use my bike. Saves money. But I can't bike it to Stow, for example, and back.'

Tom, recalling the bicycle chained up in the car park at Crooked Man Woods, said, 'I think I saw your bike. I didn't see you in the woods, though.'

'Well, it wasn't a good day for me, too much distraction.' She paused. 'I wanted a subject interesting enough to go in this exhibition. I got there early because I hoped there wouldn't be anyone around. People have a knack of walking into shot.' She hesitated. 'Normally, I'm not nervous about being out on my own in the woods, but there was something really spooky about them that morning. I wasn't alone. I'm sure of it. Someone – or something – else was there. Well, now you tell me *you* were there, but this was – different.'

'How different?'

'That's it, you see. I could hear things but not see them.'

'Muntjak deer sometimes find their way into the woods,' Tom suggested.

Sally shook her head. 'I know the barking noises they make. But it wasn't deer. The sounds I heard were part human and part not. There was a panting and a muffled groaning. At one point it stopped, but then began again. Honestly, it really freaked me out. There was something despairing about it. You can bet I kept away from that spot. But I couldn't rid myself of the creepy feeling I had. I'd heard a vehicle just before. Visitors have to use the car park, but there is another way into the woods, from the further side.'

'I know it,' Tom said. 'It's a track used by forestry workers.'

'That's the one. The vehicle I heard must have taken that. I decided it was someone clearing rubbish. Anyway, then I heard it leave. I tried to concentrate after that, but I couldn't. I was looking over my shoulder every two minutes. After about another twenty minutes I decided to call it a day. I went back to the visitors' car park and there was a silver SUV there.'

'That was mine,' Tom told her.

'Oh? I didn't see you.'

'I went down the red path and then turned off on to the blue one. That's where I found – him.'

'I don't stick to the paths. I prowl about in the woods. I'm glad I didn't find the body! That would have been worse than my hearing things. Anyway, I cycled off home.'

'Did you, at any time, see a black Range Rover?'

'No.' She sounded quite decided.

'Listen,' Tom said urgently. 'You must tell the police all this. They've been looking for the owner of the bicycle. They're desperate for witnesses. You need to talk to Inspector Jessica Campbell. If you don't mind, I'll tell her about you. Where can she find you?'

'I'm a dental hygienist and I work out of different surgeries in the area on different days. Tomorrow I'll be in Stow on the Wold.' She scrabbled in her pocket and extracted a small notebook. 'This is the dental surgery's address in Stow. Of course, I'll be here at the library for the next hour or two. My name is Sally Grove,' she added belatedly.

It was confession time. Tom said: 'My name is Tom Palmer, and I'm a doctor. But I don't deal with live patients.' She looked understandably surprised but also curious. This was it. He had to tell her. 'I conduct post mortems.'

'Oh,' she said, 'then you'll be used to bodies. Finding one in the woods must have been a shock but, well, you will have seen nasty sights in the course of your work.'

'Yes,' said Tom.

'So have I!' she said with feeling. 'Looking into some people's mouths can really put you off your dinner.'

'Sally?' called a voice from the main room. 'Anyone seen Sally? She was here just now. Where's she gone?'

'I must go,' said Sally, 'or they'll take my work down and Gordon will put his up instead. He's after that spot, I know he is. Nice to meet you, Tom.'

'Likewise. You won't forget what I said about telling the police what you heard in the woods that morning?'

'I won't forget. Inspector Campbell, right?' She had now disappeared from sight. 'Oh, Gordon,' her voice drifted back, exasperation in it, 'you've moved all my exhibits!'

Though he had denied it to Jess, Tom had been rather embarrassed at forgetting to tell her at the scene about the woman driver who had nearly forced him off the road. Now he had a chance to make amends. Not only that, but he'd stolen a march on the professionals. He'd found the missing cyclist. He tried to phone Jess as he walked back to the car park. But he couldn't get through. He had to send a text message. 'Found missing cyclist. Sally Grove. Call me.'

But she didn't call him back until very late, just after ten that evening. Tom had watched the news headlines, found them all too depressing, switched off the television and, finding himself unexpectedly very tired, decided to go to bed. At that point, Jess rang. Briefly, he told her about Sally hearing odd sounds in the woods.

'It gave her the heebie-jeebies and I got the impression she's a pretty level-headed person.'

'But she didn't see anyone?'

'True. But I don't think she's the sort of person to imagine things.'

Jess was still sounding doubtful. 'Trees rustle and creak. As for the panting sound, it could have been the wind blowing through something. But I'll drive over to Stow on the Wold and seek her out tomorrow. Thanks, Tom.'

'Think nothing of it,' returned Tom magnanimously. 'Oh, I had lunch at the Royal Oak, and so did Mrs Briggs and Harriet whatsit – Kingsley. Old chums, obviously.'

'Yes, they are, school buddies.'

'Oh,' said Tom, disappointed at not being the first with that bit of news. 'Maurice Melton was lunching there, too. He joined me and talked shop throughout.'

'It all seems to happen wherever you are, Tom!'

'Yes,' he agreed. 'I'll be glad to get back to work for some peace and quiet.'

That was another good thing about corpses. They didn't insist on making conversation.

The library closed at five because the volunteers all had to get home. The club still hadn't decided on how best to display the selected work and everyone had got irritable. *As you'd expect!* thought Sally. She, personally, just wanted to leave without further delay. Gordon would fuss and argue all evening if he was allowed. It was already getting dark and she had to cycle to her rented cottage, about a mile outside Weston St Ambrose. It wasn't an isolated house, it was in a row of former farmworkers' cottages, and there were a couple of bigger houses nearby down lanes off the main road, but it was a lonely ride and there was little daylight left.

Everyone else, of course, wanted to socialise, to go for a cup of tea in Weston's one and only tearoom, or an early drink (what Gordon Ferris called 'a pre-prandial') at the Black Horse pub.

'Not the Royal Oak,' opined Gordon. 'The drinks are too expensive in the bar there. Tourist trap.'

Debbie and Sally were both for squeezing into the tearoom. But the men were all against that because of the lack of space and the fact that the two elderly women who ran the place didn't like people sitting around chatting if they weren't buying cake or sandwiches.

'They hover,' said Ron. 'And if you raise your voice above a whisper they glare and say, "Shush!"'

'They'll be closing now, anyway,' put in Debbie. 'They shut at five-thirty on the dot.'

So they all went to the Black Horse, which was the sort of pub Weston's rougher element drank in. Sally hated it, because it was dark and smelled of beer, and if you needed to go to the ladies', you had to go outside to an alley and into a separate little hut that had once been a stable, and there was no heating. Also, despite whitewashed walls and air freshener, there was a lingering odour of horse. She would really have liked to refuse altogether to join them, protesting rightly that she had a bike ride home. But that might be construed as some kind of criticism of the way things had gone back at the library. So she trailed along with Debbie, who said, 'I'm glad you're coming, too, Sally. I don't want to be stuck in the Black Horse with a bunch of men.' Sally managed not to reply *I just don't want to be stuck in any pub. I want to go home.*

The men all settled into the public bar quite happily. After about twenty minutes, Sally started looking surreptitiously at her watch. But they were all chattering away and Ron had bought her a packet of crisps.

At last, Debbie said, 'This is great fun, but I really need to get the supper started, Mike. We've got pork chops!'

Mike, who was one of those people who manage to put away regular large meals and remain as lean as a whippet, drained his glass and stood to bid the company goodnight.

'My wife's gone to her mother's,' said Desmond, 'so I might as well stay here for a while. She'll have left me something cold I'm supposed to put in the microwave.'

'I'll probably have a pizza here,' said Ron mournfully.

They understood his lack of enthusiasm, because the cooked-from-frozen pizzas served up at the pub weren't the stuff of gourmet dining.

So Debbie and Mike departed in an aura of domestic togetherness, and Sally took the opportunity to scurry out as well, before Ron invited her to join him for a pizza.

'They're well settled in,' said Mike, outside in the street.

'They've got no one to go home to,' replied Debbie, squeezing his arm and gazing up at him.

Oh, give it a miss! thought Sally. Aloud, she said robustly, 'Neither have I! But I don't sit about in pubs. Anyway, I've got to drive over to Stow on the Wold tomorrow to work.'

The Wilsons' home was within walking distance, and they set off linked, thought Sally unkindly, like Tweedledum and Tweedledee. Sally rescued her bicycle from the yard at the back of the pub to which she'd had to move it after the library closed. She was relieved to find it still there. It was an old bike and nobody should want it. But the Black Horse attracted a number of Weston St Ambrose's younger population, and they were generally out to make any mischief offered to them.

She pedalled off at a good pace and soon left the last buildings behind. This was the loneliest stretch, a four-minute (she'd timed it) ride to the cottages; not far, but far enough. There was no illumination other than the moon and her bicycle light. The moon's contribution was fitful, clouds scudding across it. The hedgerows to either side rustled, and the trees creaked. It reminded her of when she'd been in Crooked Man Woods that morning and heard all those creepy noises. That chap in the library, Tom, had told her to contact the police about it. It was the morning the dead man had been found. Tom had been in the woods and found the body. Tom himself seemed like a really nice person. It was too late to phone the police tonight, and tomorrow she'd have no time before leaving to drive to Stow on the Wold. But at lunchtime she would definitely follow Tom's advice and contact someone – Inspector Campbell, as he'd advised. Yes, she'd do that.

Out of the darkness a sudden beam of bright light played across her and she heard the sound of a motor vehicle approaching from behind, coming from Weston. The road wasn't very wide here, but wide enough for the driver to overtake her. But she made sure, riding in as close to the verge as she could. She wore a reflective jacket. He'd see her. He'd slow down soon. But he didn't. He seemed to have speeded up and now he was right behind her. A spurt of alarm sent a painful tremor through her chest. She couldn't pull off the road because there was a deep drainage ditch. He must have seen her.

Nearer and nearer. She took her right hand from the handlebar and turned in the saddle to gesticulate wildly at the windscreen creeping up on her. She couldn't distinguish the driver but it was then that the sick realisation flooded over her that not only could the driver see her, he was deliberately targeting her.

A split second before the impact Sally threw herself sideways. The bike slid away from her beneath the wheels of the oncoming vehicle. She hit the road head first. Her helmet took the first shock but she felt a stab of pain. Nevertheless, she managed to roll over in an ungainly, scrabbling way. The ground beneath her gave way and she was plunging down, down, into a wet, cold, watery trap. *I'm in the ditch*, she thought, before she lost consciousness.

Chapter 11

'It'll prove a wild-goose chase!' warned Ian Carter the following morning. 'You'll go all the way to Stow on the Wold just to find that this young woman was frightened by a combination of birdlife in the branches and her own imagination.'

'She seems to have impressed Tom as being sensible.'

'She seems to have impressed Tom, full stop!' muttered Carter.

'And we now know the identity of the missing cyclist.'

'Perhaps we ought to take Dr Palmer on to the force! He seems disinclined to attend to his duties at the morgue.'

'He's on sick leave!' Jess protested.

'So you keep telling me! It gives him plenty of time, apparently, for finding bodies, chatty lunches at the Royal Oak with Maurice Melton and amateur detective work. When's he going back to work?'

'Next week, I think,' said Jess.

'Thank goodness!' growled Carter.

He's certainly in a bad mood this morning, thought Jess. What's brought that on? I wonder. It can't all be to do with Tom. Aloud, she asked carelessly, 'Millie still OK at school?'

'What? Oh, yes, thanks, she's fine.' Carter paused. 'Her mother rang last night. She and Rodney didn't sell their house here when they moved to France. It's rented out. But now there's a problem with the tenant, so Sophie is coming over to sort it out. She wants me to meet her for lunch somewhere and, as she puts it, "touch base".'

Ah! thought Jess. So that's the problem! Sophie will be back in the UK and on the prowl, and if she's suggesting Ian and she meet up it could mean because of a problem with Millie. But Ian says Millie's fine. So it's some other problem. 'That'll be nice,' she said cheerfully.

Carter looked up at her, his face a picture. Forcing back what he obviously felt like saying, he merely advised: 'Oughtn't you to get going, if you're driving over to Stow on the Wold? No need to take all day about it, is there?'

When Jess had left, Carter immediately regretted having spoken so sharply. Being riled by Sophie didn't excuse discourtesy to a colleague, especially one whom he not only respected but also, well, liked very much. He shouldn't have been so rude about Tom Palmer, either. He was also aware that he'd only told Jess half the story with regard to Sophie's visit. His ex-wife was not just popping over from France to check out the rented-out property, which was well out of this area. She was going to be much nearer. She was proposing to stay for a few days with her aunt, Monica Farrell, who lived in Weston St Ambrose. 'Monica is getting on,' Sophie said. 'I'd like to see how she is.'

Ian liked Monica, who was a retired primary-school headmistress, and he'd always got on well with her. She'd also helped out in the past, looking after Millie when his daughter was staying with him and Carter had to work. He felt guilty that he'd not paid a courtesy call on Miss Farrell for some time. It made him look like someone who turned up only when he needed something. He would try and drop by Monica's cottage before Sophie arrived. For the next half an hour, he shuffled paperwork about, wishing something would happen to distract him from his own nagging guilt. Then it did.

A nerve-jangling squeak was growing louder, meaning someone was coming along the corridor towards his office. Could no one do anything about that floor? It struck him that the footsteps were rapid, and that could mean something had happened. A knock at the door announced a breathless Tracy Bennison.

'Sorry to disturb you, sir, but I thought you'd want to know. Someone called Derek Davies has just phoned in from the Old Nunnery. He says he's a carpenter working there. Two people, a man and a woman, have turned up. He says they are making trouble for Mrs Kingsley. He thinks it's to do with her stepbrother. Captain Kingsley isn't there. Mrs Kingsley has asked the visitors to leave and they refused. So Mrs Kingsley asked Davies to phone Inspector Campbell, but she's left.'

'I'll go!' said Carter immediately, starting up from his chair and reaching for his jacket. 'Is Phil Morton in the building? Tell him I need him, asap.'

Derek Davies, a squat, grizzled figure in work gear, was awaiting their arrival at the entrance gates of the Old Nunnery. He signalled wildly to their car to stop. 'You the police?' he was shouting.

'What's up?' demanded Morton, the driver, opening the door and leaning out.

'She can't make 'em leave, and I can't, either!' declared Davies, crouching down and putting one hand on the top of the car. 'And *he's* gone to Gloucester about something or other, so there's no use me phoning *him*. That's why I phoned you lot.'

'Who are they?' called Carter from the passenger seat.

'Blessed if I know! Man and a woman – townies. The woman is doing most of the talking – shouting, more like it. It's all about Mrs Kingsley's brother, the one what got shot over in Crooked Man Woods.'

'Leave it to us,' said Morton.

But Davies had already decided to do that and had set off back to his carpentry.

'What's the betting,' Carter asked, 'that the woman will turn out to be Natalie Adam?'

'Is she Finch's girlfriend? The one you saw in London, at the victim's flat?' Morton drew up before the front door with a swirl of gravel, alongside a Mercedes already parked there.

'That's the woman. I should have guessed we wouldn't have seen the last of her. We'll walk round to the back of the house, Phil. The kitchen door will almost certainly be open. I'd like to surprise the unwelcome visitors.'

They certainly made an entry. From the kitchen they could hear the raised voices coming from the sitting room. The voices stopped abruptly as Carter appeared in the doorway, Morton's burly frame looming behind him. Carter scanned the room swiftly, taking in the tableau presented.

An ashen-faced Harriet was standing by the Queen Anne chair, her refuge in times of distress. She rested one hand on the back of it and was clasping a handkerchief in the other, balled up and pressed to her mouth. A tubby fellow with ginger hair and a red face was over by the unlit hearth, looking as if he'd rather be a million miles away. Natalie Adam stood in the middle of the floor, hands on hips, dominating the scene.

All three occupants greeted the newcomers in individual manner. Harriet exclaimed, 'Oh, thank goodness you've come!' The ginger-haired man demanded, 'Who the hell are you?' and Natalie said simply, 'Damn!' She then turned to her companion by the fireplace and explained, 'It's the police.'

The ginger-haired man said, 'Oh, bloody hell! Why did I let you talk me into this, Natalie?'

'Pull yourself together, Henry!' she ordered him. She turned back to the new arrivals. 'Superintendent Carter, I see. Who called you?'

Harriet replied before Carter could. 'Derek did. I signalled to him to fetch some help.' Addressing Carter, she added: 'Luckily, I saw him in the yard, through the window. Otherwise, I don't know what I would have done. *She* was between me and the door over there, so I couldn't get to a phone. Derek came, took one look, and got the message.'

Natalie scowled. 'Who is Derek? I didn't see him.'

'You had your back to the door,' said Harriet. 'Dead keen on barring my way!'

Henry cleared his throat and said, 'If you mean a little whiskery chap with a pencil stuck behind his ear, I saw him.'

'Why didn't you draw my attention to him?' demanded Natalie.

'Bloody hell, Nat, he was only there for a split second, and then he ran.'

'Derek is the carpenter,' explained Carter to Ms Adam, taking over. 'Now then, what's all this about? Mrs Kingsley, were you expecting visitors? Did you know either of these people before this morning?'

'No,' said Harriet. 'I certainly didn't expect anyone. They just arrived and stormed in. I still don't know who they are. Well, *she'* – Harriet pointed at the fuming Natalie – 'she says she was Carl's girlfriend. But I never heard anything about a girlfriend.'

'That,' snapped Natalie, 'was because you wouldn't talk to him for the past six months, at least. I know he tried to get in touch with you. You wouldn't answer his calls or his text messages or emails or anything.'

Henry decided to put down his own marker. 'I'm Henry Knox. I'm a work colleague of Natalie's and I, er, just came along because she was nervous of talking to—'

'I was not nervous!' declared Natalie. 'Honestly, Henry, you know perfectly well I wanted you here as a witness!'

'You told me you were nervous of facing Kingsley and his wife together. You'd be outnumbered!' argued Henry.

'I understand, Mrs Kingsley,' interrupted Carter loudly, 'that your husband has gone to Gloucester on some business.'

'Yes, he wanted to—' began Harriet, but she was interrupted.

'We didn't come at this time because we knew that ghastly man, Kingsley, wouldn't be here!' snapped Natalie, tossing back her abundant mane of hair. 'We didn't plan to confront her alone, so don't get that idea in your heads. We fully expected to see him. Carl said Kingsley hung round the house all the time, inventing projects that never make any money. I know he's violent. It's because of this that I wanted Henry with me.'

Red flooded Harriet's pale cheeks. 'Guy, my husband, is not ghastly, and he is certainly not violent!'

'So what was he doing when he was in the army, then?' interrupted Henry unexpectedly. 'Natalie said he was in Afghanistan. He wasn't there to take photos of the scenery, was he? He's a trained marksman. Of course Natalie was wary.'

'Soldiering was his job!' stormed Harriet. 'It isn't now. He left the army ages ago. He doesn't go around attacking people now!'

'That,' said Natalie triumphantly 'is just where you're wrong! He attacked Carl. I was there. I saw it!' She whirled to face Carter. 'I've already told you this!'

'What rubbish! When?' demanded Harriet, turning to Carter. 'Do you know this woman?'

'In the course of our enquiries,' explained Carter as peaceably as he could, 'we searched Carl Finch's London home. Ms Adam arrived while we were there. She did tell us that your stepbrother and your husband had an altercation in the London house, in her presence, ending in a minor scuffle.'

'She's lying!' declared Harriet. 'Guy's never been to Carl's home. Just look at her! She's one of those loopy people who make things up and believe their own stories. She needs psychiatric help.'

'Steady on!' interjected Henry. 'If Natalie said it happened, I believe her.'

'More fool you!' Harriet told him crisply.

'The incident did happen,' Carter supported Natalie reluctantly. 'Captain Kingsley told my colleague Inspector Campbell about it.'

Harriet released her hold on the back of the chair and sat down in it abruptly. 'Guy didn't say anything to me. *When* did this – this supposed scuffle – happen?'

'I understand your husband went to London on some business—'

Harriet didn't let him finish. Her face had reddened and she put up both hands, palms outwards, as if she could physically push away his words.

191

'I won't discuss this any more until I've had a chance to speak to Guy. I want to hear about it from my husband, and not from anyone else! He should be home in about an hour. Superintendent Carter, I want these people out of my house before he gets back.'

'Oh, yes,' said Natalie nastily. 'It is *your* house, isn't it? Carl told me all about that, how you and your husband got your father to change his will—'

'That's enough, Miss Adam!' Carter ordered. 'I think you and Mr Knox had better leave.' He turned to Morton, who had been listening with interest. 'Sergeant, escort Mr Knox and Miss Adam out, would you?'

Harriet, her voice shaking with rage, shouted, 'My father did not change his will! My father was perfectly clear in his mind what he wanted to do! This is my family home! We've been here for generations! It's nothing to do with Carl. My father was very generous to him—'

'Not now, Mrs Kingsley!' ordered Carter. 'Your visitors are leaving.'

'Come along, folks,' requested Morton, advancing into the room.

Natalie wasn't leaving without a last verbal thrust. 'Henry's right. Guy Kingsley is a trained killer. What's more, he's got no money. It's all hers! Kingsley always hated Carl, and was eaten up with jealousy towards him. He didn't mean Carl to get a penny. If you want a suspect for Carl's murder, Superintendent, you don't have to look any further than Captain Guy Kingsley, in my opinion!'

Henry unexpectedly leaped into action. 'Come on, Nat!' He grasped her arm and marched her forcibly to the door.

'What the hell are you doing, Henry? Let go of me!' she stormed as she was pushed through the doorway into the hall.

'Shut up, will you?' Henry's voice drifted back to the listeners in the room. 'You can't accuse people without proof; certainly not before witnesses. It's actionable! If you go on like this, we'll both end up in the cells!'

They heard no more, as Morton had succeeded in escorting both visitors out of the house.

The room was suddenly quiet but for a lingering echo of the dispute. As it faded, Carter took a chair near Harriet and asked, 'When do you expect your husband?'

'Any time this afternoon, probably by three-thirty at the latest. He might grab some lunch, but it would only be a sandwich.' She swallowed and muttered, 'Horrid, horrid people!'

Carter glanced at his wristwatch. 'It's nearly one now. We'll make sure neither of those two comes back today. But perhaps it would be a good idea for you to have someone with you until Captain Kingsley returns. How about Mrs Briggs? Would she come up and sit with you?'

'Tessa? Yes, yes, of course, if she's free. I'll call her mobile.' Harriet faced him defiantly. 'It's all rubbish, everything that crazy woman said. If Guy did tell Inspector Campbell he and Carl had a – a sort of fight, then it must have happened. But I still want to hear about it from him.'

'You had no idea he'd visited Finch's home?'

'None at all. But I'm not going to talk about it until Guy's explained. Whatever happened, it couldn't have been much.'

'I understand it was just a scuffle.'

'I don't believe,' said Harriet fiercely, 'that she – Natalie, whatever – was ever really Carl's girlfriend.'

'Well, Miss Adam seems a rather volatile person. He might have wanted to keep her away from the Old Nunnery.'

'She's nuts!' said Harriet succinctly. 'Totally off her trolley.' She paused and added with less certainty: 'But Carl must have told her all that about the will. How could he be so stupid?'

'Perhaps he needed someone to confide in?'

'He didn't have to choose her!' muttered Harriet. 'Oh, this is awful!' She slapped the arms of the Queen Anne chair. 'I should have talked more with Carl before – before all this. Look, Superintendent Carter, Guy, my husband, is not a violent man! He didn't get along with Carl, but he wouldn't shoot him!'

Carter got to his feet. 'Call Mrs Briggs. Oh, it's rather chilly in here, if you don't mind me saying so. I think you should keep warm. Light that fire, perhaps.'

She glanced at the hearth. 'The house costs a fortune to heat. But I'll get the logs going. I was going to light the fire, anyway, before Guy got home.'

Carter nodded his approval. 'I'll go now and talk to your visitors. I'm reasonably certain they won't come back today, but I'll make sure.'

'Or come back ever?' she asked hopefully.

Carter pulled a rueful face. 'I don't think Mr Knox will return. Miss Adam's actions are less easy to predict. I'll do my best. Trespass, however, is a civil matter.'

'Can't I get a court order?' Harriet demanded.

'I don't think we're at that stage yet. She's only called here once. But you must let me know at once if she tries to contact you again in any way – phone, email, text, anything.'

Outside the house, Natalie sat sullenly in the Mercedes. Henry wandered up and down beside it, staring at his feet and dragging on a cigarette. Phil Morton looked on dispassionately. When she saw Carter coming, Natalie scrambled out of the car. Henry threw away his cigarette guiltily and straightened up.

'Right!' said Carter. 'I strongly advise you both to return to London at once. Did you drive down today?'

'Yesterday,' Knox told him. 'We stayed last night at a place called Weston St Ambrose. There's a hotel there called the Royal Oak. You can check with them.'

Carter nodded. 'I know the Royal Oak. If you still have luggage there, my advice to you is to go now and collect it. Then go home. I cannot prevent you remaining in the area, but I am telling you officially to stay away from this house, the Old Nunnery, and not to contact either Captain or Mrs Kingsley. This is a murder investigation, and your actions are not something we approve of. They could be interpreted as an attempt to interfere with witnesses.'

Natalie retorted defiantly, 'Do you at least have Guy Kingsley down as a suspect?'

'I cannot discuss the case with you or anyone else outside my team except a senior officer. I don't want you to attempt to go over my head, by the way. The chief constable is a busy man, and he doesn't like the general public interfering in police matters.'

'I'm a witness, too,' said Natalie sullenly. 'I was there when Carl and Guy had their scrap.'

'All the more reason for you to stay away from here and not discuss the matter with anyone, here or in London.'

'Get back in the car, Natalie, for crying out loud!' begged Knox.

Natalie, now evidently in a massive sulk, threw herself into the Mercedes.

They watched them drive away. Morton said, 'I don't envy

Knox having to drive all the way back to London with her fuming alongside him.'

'No,' returned Carter thoughtfully. 'Ms Adam has a somewhat aggressive disposition, Phil. She believes in action, not words. She doesn't like being thwarted or crossed.'

'She certainly doesn't. She's downright scary, in my book!' Morton cast him a questioning look. 'Do you believe her capable of falling out with Finch, grabbing a weapon, following him down here and blowing him away, in or near Crooked Man Woods?'

'If I'm honest, I have to say I can imagine it all too well. She's someone who wouldn't have taken it kindly if Finch had told her he wanted to end their relationship. Especially if she believed she'd stuck by him through his problems. But we don't know she fell out with Finch, so let's not get carried away, Phil. She's very keen to make certain we suspect Guy Kingsley.'

'She may really believe he did it,' said Morton.

'Possibly.' Carter added, 'On the other hand, she is a determined and headstrong woman. I wouldn't like to be on the wrong side of her. Nor is it impossible to get hold of an illegal weapon in London. She may even have access to a legal one, not held by her but by someone she knows. I'll get on to Sergeant Mullins and ask the Met to check her out. Henry Knox, too. I dare say he knows how to handle a shotgun.'

'Weekend shooting parties,' said Morton scornfully. 'Blasting birds out of the air.' He drew a deep breath, 'Just one thing, sir.'

'Yes?' Carter looked at him enquiringly.

'The morning Finch was killed, Mrs Kingsley, we now know, drove to Crooked Man Woods. She took the Range Rover, and that's the only car they have at the moment. I asked Mrs Briggs about that. Mrs Kingsley had her own vehicle but it's been traded in for a new one and she's still waiting for it to be delivered. So, on the morning in question, Captain Kingsley had no independent transport. His wife had gone off in their only vehicle. So, no matter what Natalie Adam reckons, he couldn't have driven anywhere to meet up with Carl Finch.'

'Unless he left very much earlier and got back before his wife left – and she didn't know he'd gone. Good point, though, Phil.'

'Or borrowed the carpenter's van,' offered Morton, unexpectedly cheerful.

'Yes,' Carter said. 'Check it out, Phil.'

Morton, looking disconcerted, exclaimed, 'I didn't mean—! Yes, sir, I will.'

'Well, go on, then!'

Morton set off for the rear of the premises and Carter stayed with his hands in his pockets, staring out at the view. He could understand that Carl Finch, having spent half his younger life here, felt it was his home. He must have resented Guy Kingsley. Kingsley had dispossessed him of what Carl saw as his rightful inheritance. Then Carter had a sudden nightmare thought. Suppose, just suppose, Sophie died at some future date while Millie was still a minor. He would naturally claim full-time custody of his daughter at once. But what if Rodney, Millie's stepfather, tried to contest his claim? He must check out French family law.

A crunch of heavy footsteps on gravel announced the return of Morton. His face wore a bemused expression.

'Well?' Carter asked.

'Yes,' said Morton dolefully.

'Yes, what?'

'Guy Kingsley borrowed the carpenter's van earlier that morning. He took it shortly after Davies arrived, around eight-thirty. He wanted to drive to a builder's yard and fetch some laminated board Davies needed. He didn't take the Range Rover because Mrs Kingsley wanted it later that morning. He was gone just under an hour and he got back shortly before Mrs Kingsley returned with the Range Rover.'

'Did he have the laminated board with him?'

'Oh, yes, he'd got that all right.'

'Then we'll need to check how long it would have taken him to carry out his errand. Find out where this builder's yard is located, Phil. Do a time check on how long it would have taken and whether it would have allowed him time to make a detour, shoot Finch, move the body and get back.'

'The trouble is,' Morton pointed out, 'we don't know exactly where Finch died. For my money, it was in or near the woods. But we don't know the actual spot, and that's what we need if we're to get anywhere.'

'We also need,' said Carter, 'to find Finch's car. Because if we find that, I have a hunch we'll know where he died. Where the hell is that Renault, Phil?'

When Guy Kingsley returned that afternoon, the first thing he saw was a familiar jeep parked before the front door. He found his wife and Tessa Briggs drinking tea in the kitchen, together with Derek Davies. Fred lay stretched out before the stove on his side like a hairy rug. The collie raised his head as Guy entered and flapped his tail against the floor tiles but didn't leave his warm spot. Guy didn't blame him. Davies scrambled to his feet.

'I gotta get going,' he said. 'If I can just have a word with you first, show you something . . .' He fixed Guy with a meaningful look and scuttled out of the back door towards the stable conversion.

'Be back in a jiff,' said Guy to the two women. They both nodded silently.

What the dickens has gone wrong now? Guy wondered as he made for the old stables.

Derek was waiting, anxious to tell him. 'Your missus had some visitors, come down from London, I reckon. Man and a woman. I had to call the police to get them to leave.' Derek squinted at him and then looked away, appearing embarrassed. 'The head copper came, the superintendent. He had that miserable-looking fellow with him, big chap. His name is Morton; he showed me his warrant card. He's a sergeant. He came and asked if you'd borrowed my van the day they found Mrs Kingsley's brother in the woods, shot. So I had to tell them you did, all right?'

Damn, Guy thought. 'Yes, you were quite right to tell him, Derek.'

Derek looked relieved. 'I told him you wasn't gone long.'

'Don't worry about it,' Guy reassured him. 'I should have mentioned it to them myself.' Yes, I should, he thought. Then it wouldn't have looked suspicious. Now it does.

'I'll be off!' said Derek, and promptly departed.

Guy went back to the kitchen and found Tessa making ready to leave.

'We've had visitors, I hear,' he said to his wife.

Before she could answer, Tessa said, 'Walk me out to my car, Guy, will you? Come on, Fred!'

When he was standing by the jeep, Guy said to Tess, 'Everyone's keen to talk to me before I talk to Hattie. What's been going on, Tess? Derek said a man and woman had been here and made trouble.'

'They did. Some girlfriend of Carl's turned up with a man friend in tow.'

'Natalie?' asked Guy sharply.

'That's the one. You *do* know her, then?' Tessa looked at him in surprise. 'Hattie didn't. They barged in and wouldn't leave. Hattie said they were throwing accusations around like confetti. The woman said you'd had a scrap with Carl at his place in London. You didn't, did you?'

'Unfortunately, yes. But it was a while ago, last September.'

'Oh,' said Tessa. 'Well, Hattie managed to signal to Derek she needed help, fortunately, and he had the nous to phone the police.'

Guy heaved a sigh. 'OK, Tess, I'll deal with it.'

'She's very – very – depressed about it all,' Tessa said in warning.

'I know. But I'll handle it, OK?'

'Just don't start barking orders at her. It wouldn't take much to make her fall apart completely.' Tessa gazed out at the same view Carter had stood before earlier. The light was already fading and the landscape was now under a dull veil. 'It seems,' said Tessa, 'as if there's no end to the amount of trouble Carl caused. But Hattie was very fond of him, you know. He could do that – be charming – if he wanted. He and Hattie were great pals when they were young; you've got to admit it. Hal had no time for him.'

'Hal?' Guy was puzzled.

'My ex-husband. You never met him.' Tessa paused. 'I told Sergeant Morton, when he turned up at my place, that I had no idea where Hal Briggs is these days. That's not quite true. He's living just outside Bath. I couldn't give you the address or contact number, but different people have told me that's where he is, running an animal-feed business. I wonder if he's heard about Carl?'

Tessa was still gazing out at the landscape. 'Hal was keen on Hattie once, when we were all young, probably keener on her than he ever was on me, if the truth's told! I sometimes used to wonder if he married me so that he'd see Hattie around the place when she came over to visit me.' She turned her head and grinned at Guy unexpectedly. 'I was never pretty.'

Guy said impulsively, 'You're a brick, Tess!' He leaned forward and kissed her cheek.

'I've got my uses,' said Tessa.

Guy waved her off and walked slowly back to the house. He went to the kitchen where they'd all been sitting but it was now empty. That meant he'd find Harriet in the sitting room, once her father's study. It was where she retreated to every time when there was any kind of trouble. But now that had been invaded by Natalie Adam, it might not offer Hattie the same kind of sanctuary.

But she was there, huddled in her father's chair, waiting. She said nothing when he entered and didn't look his way. Mindful of Tessa's words, Guy sat down near her and said, 'I'm sorry, Hattie, that I didn't tell you I had a – a bit of a scrap with Carl at his place in London.'

She turned her face towards him then and he was shocked by the desperation in her eyes. 'Oh, Guy, what's become of us? You don't tell me what you do, and I don't tell you what I do. We tell each other lies. Well, you didn't lie about going to see Carl in London but – but—'

'I was a lie of omission,' Guy said. 'I shouldn't have kept it from you.'

'Why did you go to see him, anyway?'

'I knew he was bothering you for money again and making you unhappy. I hadn't planned to go and see him. I went up to have lunch with a couple of old army pals. I told you that, and it was true. But lunch ended rather earlier than I'd expected and I had a bit of time on my hands. Going to see Carl was an impulse. Never act on impulse, they say.' Guy gave a wry smile.

'And you had a fight?'

'Hardly that, just a bit of a push and shove, playground stuff. Boys never grow up, you know.'

'It wasn't nice learning about it from her,' his wife said quietly.

'No, of course not. Wretched woman. She was there when I went to see him. I hadn't expected that. I rang the bell at street level and he let me walk up – and in on the pair of them swigging champagne and having a good time. It made me really mad. If that was the lifestyle he wanted, he should have funded it himself, not expected you to sub him. The Adam female had absolutely no business coming here!' Guy scowled. 'Bitch!' he said.

'Do you think she really was Carl's girlfriend?.'

'I doubt it was serious. She's pretty sharp, I'd say, and wouldn't waste serious time on a loser like Carl. Normally, he'd be well out of her league. But he was probably fun to be with if he chose. I'd say she's the sort of woman who'd enjoy a good time with him, if she fancied him, but she'd never let it go to her head.'

'Poor Carl,' said Harriet quietly.

After a moment, Guy said, 'Yes, I suppose you have to feel a bit sorry for him, silly sod.'

Jess had missed all this, because she had driven to Stow on the Wold. She took a cross-country route. Later in the year it would be a delight to the eye. But as yet there were few, if any, indications of spring on its way. The hedgerows remained dank and colourless in a winter sulk. The trees stretched out bare arms across the verges. But Stow is a busy market town all year round, so she took the precaution of leaving her car in the first official car park she came to. The dental surgery was not hard to find. The receptionist looked up as she entered and smiled.

'Have you an appointment?'

Jess took out her ID and showed it. 'I believe you have a dental hygienist called Sally Grove working here today?' The receptionist looked dismayed, so Jess added quickly, 'It's just a routine matter. I wondered if I could grab a few words with her between appointments.'

But she had mistaken the reason for the receptionist's dismay. 'But you can't!' she exclaimed. 'She's not here. She should be, of course, but I thought, being the police, you'd know!'

'Know what?' Jess asked quickly.

'About the accident. Poor Sally was knocked off her bicycle last night. She's in hospital. It was a hit and run. The driver just drove off and left her there.'

'I didn't know,' Jess told her. 'I'm not in traffic division. Where did this happen?'

'As far as we know, she was cycling home from the centre of Weston St Ambrose to the little cottage she rents just outside. It was quite dark, I believe, although it wasn't late in the evening – about six-thirty, we understand. I know Sally is a very careful cyclist,' the receptionist went on earnestly. 'She's got all the right gear – helmet, reflective body brace, all that sort of thing. But she was hit just outside the town. Sally was flung into a deep drainage ditch. She could have been there all night! But a farmer driving home on his tractor noticed, from where he sat high up, that there was something in the ditch, so he stopped to see what it was. Thank goodness he did. Sally's still unconscious. We're all terribly distressed.'

Outside the surgery, Jess got on her mobile to Phil Morton. 'Phil, Sally Grove's had an accident, possibly a hit and run. It happened early yesterday evening, just outside Weston St Ambrose. After she came off her bike, she was found in a ditch by a farmer. I've had an account from the receptionist in the surgery where Sally was expected today. But I suspect it's garbled and not reliable. See if you can get hold of the original report and then find that farmer and hear what he has to say. It may be a genuine accident, the driver might not even have seen her, but we have to check it out. She was in the woods on the day of the murder and it's possible she has information without realising it.'

Phil Morton looked at the leading cow and the cow looked at Phil. It lowered its head and uttered a long, drawn-out sound like a deflating set of bagpipes. Behind it, a herd of others bunched up and filled the narrow track leading to the farm. There was a stone wall between him and the field beyond. Phil wondered if he should scramble up and over it. The animals were clearly impatient; and they were very large and smelly.

'Hey!' shouted a voice from somewhere behind the bovine throng. 'You're stopping them. You want to get out of their way!'

'I'm trying to!' shouted back Phil. 'Are you Mr Biddle?'

'That's me! Who are you, then?'

'Police! DS Morton!'

'I already spoke to the p'lice! You an't got a dog with you, have you?'

'Dog? No!'

'Because they don't like dogs! You just stand back by the wall and they'll go on by.'

Morton supposed he could only trust Mr Biddle. He certainly didn't trust that leading cow. It had a very dodgy look in its eye. He pressed back as much as he could against the wall, the rough, uneven surface of its blocks jabbing his spine. Mr Biddle whistled and shouted. The herd lumbered forward. Phil was reduced to standing on tiptoe to avoid his feet being crushed as hairy bodies bumped into him. He'd stink of cows for the rest of the day. Last of all came Mr Biddle, now revealed to be an elderly sunburned man in dark blue overalls and a tweed cap.

'I'll just take 'em down to the gate,' he said, as he passed by. 'When I've let them through, I'll come back and talk to you. Won't take me long. You go on down to the house.'

Phil obediently walked down the lane to the farmyard, making a zig-zag progress because the departing cows had left plentiful evidence of their presence. The yard was also thick with mud, and more cow dung. There was a door open in the house. Morton peered in and saw a large kitchen, but no smiling farmer's wife presiding over a teapot, as he'd hoped. The only living creature in the kitchen was a brown chicken standing on the table. At the sight of Morton, it took up a combative stance, stretching its neck, flapping its wings and finally lowering its head in readiness to drive off the intruder.

'What's that dratted thing doing in there?' demanded Mr Biddle, who had returned and was looking past Morton. 'If the door's left open, they bloody hens always gets in. *Go on, get out of it!*' he roared at the chicken. The bird fluttered past Morton in a flurry of wings and uttering a discordant squawk. More sociably, the farmer added, 'I'll just take off my boots. You might like to wipe your feet – boot scraper over there.' He indicated an antique cast-iron device by the door.

Morton obeyed and Mr Biddle gestured him forward into the kitchen.

Morton took out his ID to show Mr Biddle, who peered at it and said, 'I an't got my reading glasses but I dare say you're what you say you are. The other copper what came here, he wore a uniform. He wasn't dressed ordinary, like you.'

'I'm CID,' explained Morton.

'Are you now? Like on the telly? Oh, well, you come about that lass I found in the ditch, I dare say. How's she doing, do you know?'

'She's in hospital. Would you mind if I recorded our conversation, Mr Biddle?'

'Funny old business, that,' said Mr Biddle. 'Hospital will put her right, I dare say. Record what I say, eh? You don't take no notes any more, then, pencil-and-paper job? The copper what came – the one in uniform – he wrote it all down.'

'In CID we find the recorded word is useful, should there be any difference of opinion later about what was said. I have read the original report of the officer who attended the scene and it does appear to have been a hit and run. I believe you told the officer you saw the driver speed off. So, lucky you spotted her in the ditch, sir.'

'Oh, well,' returned Mr Biddle. 'I spotted the other one first.'

Morton felt the hairs on the nape of his neck bristle. 'Other one, sir? I understand you saw the vehicle involved being driven away. But are you saying there was a third person at the scene, other than the injured cyclist and the motorist?'

'The driver was what I meant,' said Biddle, frowning. 'Perhaps I didn't describe it proper when I was talking to the other officer.'

Phil drew a deep breath. 'Take your time, Mr Biddle, and tell me everything you observed, even anything trivial.'

'Observed, eh?' repeated Mr Biddle, rolling the word round his mouth appreciatively. 'Let's see, then. I come along the road on my tractor – that one out there in the yard. It had got pretty dark. There was a moon, but quite a lot of cloud, so it didn't help much. Up ahead I saw there was someone by the side of the road, standing half in the ditch and half out of it, one leg down in it and the other bent and higher up, do you follow? He seemed to be bending over something, down in the ditch.

'There was a stationary vehicle further down the road, but I couldn't tell you what make it was because it was just a dark shape. Anyhow, any fool could see there'd been some kind of an accident. Then I spotted the bike, lying in the road mostly but the front wheel tipping into the ditch, twisted. The light was bad and it was all of a muddle.'

'I understand,' Morton encouraged him.

'There's a young girl I've passed before on that road, cycling along. I thought maybe it was her bike and the one bending over was her was the motorist – only I couldn't see for sure it was that girl in the ditch, not then, you understand?'

Biddle paused for reassurance and Morton again told him he followed and to please go on.

'Like I was saying,' Mr Biddle recommenced, 'I called out to ask if she was hurt bad. Then, it was a funny thing.' He leaned forward and an odour of cows struck Morton, who tried not to flinch. 'That one leaning over her made not a word of reply, just scrambled out of the ditch and ran like a streak of lightning down the road away from me, jumped in the other vehicle, whatever it was, and drove off! It didn't have no lights on,' the farmer added censoriously. 'No wonder there's accidents if folk drive round after nightfall without lights.'

'But you must have seen the running figure in the headlight of your tractor. Was it a man or a woman? You've been saying "he".'

'To tell you the truth, I couldn't rightly say. They all dresses the same in winter, don't they, trousers and them padded anorak things? Whoever it was, wore one of the woolly hats, pulled right down over the ears, down to the eyebrows. Couldn't see no hair. Someone fairly limber, though, to run off at that speed.'

Biddle paused for thought, frowning. 'Anyhow,' he continued, 'I climbed down from the tractor and picked up the bike to put it out of the road, before it was struck by some other vehicle coming along. Then I saw that there *was* someone in the ditch and she was hurt. That made sense, because if the other one, the one I spotted first, had a car, this must be the cyclist! So I scrambled down beside her and saw it was that girl – don't know her name, but she lives down in the old cottages. So I got out my phone and called the ambulance and the police to come quick. She was out cold, unconscious, but she was breathing. I didn't want to move her, not knowing how bad she was hurt, but I took off my jacket and put that over her to try and keep her a bit warm. I was worried because down in the ditch like she was, she was getting wet. Lot of stagnant water in the bottom, this time of year. I sort of forgot about the other one, I suppose, when the first police came. I was more worried about the ambulance coming, and getting that poor lass out of the ditch and off to the hospital.'

Biddle peered at the sergeant. 'It was a bit of a shock, you see, and I was bit confused when I spoke to the other officer.'

'I understand,' Morton assured him. 'Well, thank you, Mr Biddle, you've been—'

'There's something else,' the farmer interrupted. 'Not sure if I should mention it, because I could be wrong.' He scratched his chin thoughtfully.

Morton managed to stay patient. 'Anything at all, Mr Biddle, tell us about it. We'll decide if it's relevant.'

Biddle nodded. 'It was all so quick, you see. Me seeing there was a car stopped and someone in the ditch, then seeing the bike in the road. Then me calling out and the one I told you about running off like that. It all happened so fast it was nigh on a blur. So I could be wrong.'

'Even so,' encouraged Morton, finding patience more difficult to hold on to.

'Well, then, it was more of an impression, you understand. When I saw there was someone bending over the girl my first thought was, the motorist had jumped out and run back to help.

But afterwards I got thinking about it, and the way that motorist was moving his hands – supposing it was a man – it looked more like, well, like he was searching the body. Reckon he was after a wallet? Shocking thing, if he was.'

No, thought Morton, probably not a wallet, but something very important, important enough to take the risk of running down Sally Grove in a desperate effort to get hold of it.

'You don't never know, do you?' said Mr Biddle.

'No, sir, you certainly don't,' agreed Phil Morton.

Chapter 12

'It is, of course, terrible news,' declared Gordon Ferris.

The Countryside Artists had gathered that evening in an emergency conclave at the home of Mike and Debbie Wilson. The normal lively chatter was absent, no one talking about his or her latest work. They sat round in near-silence, broken at last by Gordon's words. His voice had boomed out unnaturally loudly. The others stared at him. Debbie, who had been sniffling into a hanky, wiped her eyes and then blew her nose. She pushed back her lank brown hair and sat up straighter.

Gordon, receiving no other reply, continued, 'But what we have to decide now is, do we continue with the exhibition?'

'It seems tasteless,' muttered Debbie, 'poor Sally lying there not able to speak or anything, and we just carry on as if nothing has happened.'

'It's been advertised and most of the pieces are already hung on display. We can't just take them all down again,' Ron Purcell pointed out.

'I'm sure Sally would want us to continue,' said Desmond Mitchell. 'We shouldn't be thrown off course—'

'Couldn't you find a different expression, Des?' snapped Mike.

Desmond reddened. 'I only meant we should carry on as a sort of tribute to a fellow member.'

'She's not dead!' burst out Debbie. 'You're talking as if she was!'

'Well, let's face it, she might – um – not recover for quite a while. She's yet to come round. She could be brain-damaged—'

'Des!' yelled Ron, his thin features suddenly suffused with a scarlet flush. 'Shut up! If you can't say something acceptable, don't say anything!'

'It's a possibility,' maintained Desmond, clearly taken aback by Ron's outburst.

'How about,' suggested Gordon, who had been stroking his beard as an aid to thought, 'we rearrange the display? We could group all of Sally's work together in the centre and put—'

'What?' interrupted Ron sarcastically, 'a black satin bow over the top?'

'No! Just a little note saying something like, well, "This member of our group is currently in hospital and very much in our thoughts."'

Mike spoke briskly. 'Look here! Sally would want us just to carry on. She wouldn't want us to do anything like put a notice up telling the world and his wife that she's been hospitalised.'

With a palpable air of relief all round, the others agreed; even, with reluctance, Gordon.

'So many things seem to be going wrong around Weston recently,' said Debbie. 'There was that poor man who shot himself in Crooked Man Woods.'

'He didn't shoot himself. Someone shot him,' corrected Gordon.

'That was Carl Finch,' said Ron unexpectedly. 'I remember him.' Seeing them all turn enquiring eyes on him, he added, 'Well, I'm a local man, aren't I? So was Finch, in a manner of speaking, years ago. He used to live at the Old Nunnery, that big old place. You know it.'

Mike gave a low whistle. 'So it isn't such a strange thing, him being found in Crooked Man Woods, after all.'

'The Kingsleys live in that house now, don't they?' Debbie asked. 'I see Mrs Kingsley from time to time in our little supermarket. I don't know her to talk to, of course, but I know who she is.'

Ron, the custodian of local knowledge, took it upon himself to continue his explanation. 'The house belonged to John Hemmings in the old days. They were a local family, been there generations. My grandad had a little butcher's shop in Weston back then, and he used to deliver meat up to the house. Some of the meat originated from Crooked Farm. Customers liked to buy local produce.'

'I wish we had that sort of thing now,' mused Debbie. 'I know we've got that supermarket, but it's not the same, is it? It would be nice to have local shops selling local produce. But I suppose they wouldn't do enough business.'

The men all stared at her. Ron took a breath and returned to his tale, 'Well, Mrs Kingsley was a Hemmings. She was John's daughter; her name's Harriet. *Now* she's Mrs Kingsley. Finch was part of the family, too. He certainly lived at the Old Nunnery when he was young. He used to turn out for the local cricket club sometimes, back in the days when I played, too. I was several years older than him, of course. He went to some public school or other and used to come home for the summer holidays. He was a big chap and, when he first appeared from school at the beginning of the summer vacation, his hair was fairly short. He'd let it grow and by the end of the summer it was down to his shoulders. Turned the heads of all the local maidens, I can tell you. He moved away to London later, after leaving school, and had to tell the cricket club he wouldn't be able to play for them any more. Not long after that I left the place to work further afield, too far to drive each day from Weston. That's what happens in villages. The younger people, and those whose jobs require willingness to relocate, leave. The cricket club found it couldn't muster a side, and that was that.'

'So what was he doing in Crooked Man Woods, if he'd left the place?' asked Desmond. 'Apart from getting himself shot, of course.'

'He used to come back from time to time,' Ron told them. 'He may have been visiting up at the Old Nunnery. I bumped into him, only a year ago, here in Weston. He was coming out of the Royal Oak. I recognised him at once; you couldn't mistake him. His hair was even longer, still blond, and he looked like a Viking. He seemed quite pleased that I had spotted him and we chatted a bit about the cricket club and what a pity it was it folded. He said he was living in London.'

'Public-school man? Got himself a top City job with a big salary, no doubt,' mused Desmond.

'I don't know about that. All I know is that, back in the cricket-club days, there was some sort of barney on one occasion, with Hal Briggs. Hal used to turn out for the cricket team as well. Do you remember him? His family farmed at Crooked Farm when it was a proper farm. Hal's wife still lives there. She got the house when she and Hal divorced, so she did all right.'

There was a note of bitterness in Ron's voice. They all understood that it had nothing to do with the Briggs's divorce settlement but with Ron's own.

But now he cheered up because, as a local, he knew a lot of old gossip the others didn't and had been given a chance to display it. 'But Hal wasn't married way back when he played cricket,' he explained to his audience. 'He must have been in his late teens, his father was still alive and Crooked Farm was still a proper farm. It's not now, of course. The land's been sold off and just the house remains.'

'What sort of a barney?' asked Mike curiously.

'A pretty spectacular one; they had a real old punch-up in the bar at the club and nearly wrecked it. They were young, but both big guys. There was blood and broken glass everywhere. It's a wonder they didn't do each other serious damage. I didn't remind Carl of that outside the Royal Oak!'

'Police called?' asked Mike.

'Lord, no! That would have been bad publicity for the club. We managed to separate them; told them to go home and come back when they were sober.'

'Over a girl, I suppose?' asked Gordon in a worldly-wise sort of way.

'I'm not sure.' Ron spoke unwillingly, as if there was something he'd have liked to say but had thought better of it. Instead, he leaned across the table and added in a low voice, 'I do know that John Hemmings came down to see the club captain and paid for all the bottles of booze that got smashed.'

'That was very good of him!' exclaimed Debbie.

'Was it, heck!' retorted Ron. 'He did it to hush up the whole business. Someone had to make good the losses, didn't they? You couldn't expect the other members to pay the bill. Word was' – Ron's voice sank conspiratorially again – 'old John Hemmings was always paying out hefty sums to cover up trouble Carl was in. He could afford it, mind you!'

Ron sat back, and they kept silence for a few minutes. Then Desmond spoke.

'Makes you wonder, doesn't it? John Hemmings isn't around any longer to pay hush money and someone blasted Carl Finch in the woods. So what else was going on?' Desmond drained his coffee mug. 'Leopard doesn't change its spots, does it?'

'It's my fault!' declared Tom vehemently.

'Don't be silly, Tom, how can it be your fault?' Jess protested. 'Unless you knocked Sally off her bike.'

'Of course I didn't knock her down!' Tom rubbed at his mop of black hair, as he often did when agitated about something. 'I mean, I talked to her in that library, where anyone could have overheard, and someone did! The place was packed out, Jess! There were people picking over the books and others who just seemed to have dropped in for a chat in a warm spot . . . and all those people arranging the paintings on the wall.'

'It sounds unlikely to me,' Jess argued, 'that in such a mob anyone could have eavesdropped on you and Sally.'

'Yes, they could!' retorted Tom. 'Because when she decided to tell me about what she'd heard in the woods, on the day of the murder, she drew me aside into a little den where they make the coffee. It wasn't private, because there was no door, just a bit quieter than the main room. We could be seen, and it would be obvious to anyone who did notice us talking in there that she had something to tell me. So, if that person was interested or curious, he or she could have sidled up and found a spot to eavesdrop, stood flat against wall beside the entrance, for instance.'

'Don't beat yourself up over it, Tom,' Jess tried to persuade him. 'You can't know that for sure.'

But Tom only gave a sort of growl and sat hunched and angry.

There was no distracting him but she could stop him brooding like that, thought Jess. She had to try to persuade him that the incident wasn't his fault. But it wasn't the moment to tell Tom that the police also suspected it might be a deliberate hit and run.

Instead she said: 'Those roads around Weston St Ambrose are narrow, the hedges are high or there are stone walls bordering the fields. There's no lighting after dark, only moonlight. I'm not surprised she was knocked off her bike. Frankly, she should use a car to get back and forth to Weston at this time of the year. She does have one. I've checked. She drives to and from her work in it.'

'Yes, she's got a car, but she rides her bike locally, she told me. She's probably trying to save on petrol. You can't blame her.' Tom sprang to Sally's defence.

'All the same, at this time of the year, she should have been using her car if she meant to travel after dark, even locally. It's only sensible,' concluded Jess. She knew as she spoke the last words that they would spark indignation in Tom, but they slipped out and couldn't be recalled.

'Now you sound like a moralising old biddy! Look here, that woman Kingsley was in the Royal Oak earlier, having lunch with that other female, the one who was in the woods with her dog. Mrs Kingsley nearly pushed me into a wall the day I found the body. If she drives like that all the time round those narrow roads, she could well have knocked Sally off her bike!'

His eyes glowed with the memory of his grievance. Now then, thought Jess, I think Madison has left it too late to return to the UK! But Tom's fraught love life was not the issue. The murder investigation was.

'Be fair. When Harriet nearly pushed you into a wall, she had just found her stepbrother dead in the woods. We don't know, or have any reason to believe, that she drives like that all the time. Listen, when you left the Royal Oak after lunch, was her Range Rover in the car park there?'

'There wasn't a black one like hers,' he admitted reluctantly.

'So she'd already left. Was there a jeep in the car park?'

Tom looked surprised. 'I can't remember. Who owns one of those?'

'Tessa Briggs. If that wasn't there either, both women had left before you decided to go wandering into that library.'

'I might not have noticed a jeep, especially if I was looking for the Range Rover. I did notice a spanking new Merc there, in the car park,' added Tom. 'I reckoned that belonged to the couple of loud-mouthed townies I saw in the restaurant.'

'It did – does. Ian Carter saw it out at the Old Nunnery. They were both there, and giving Harriet a bad time. The woman, her name is Natalie, is – was – a sort of girlfriend of Carl Finch. The car belongs to the chap with her.'

'Henry,' said Tom. 'I felt a bit sorry for him. So they were heading for a showdown with the Kingsleys, were they?'

'Apparently Natalie had brought Henry down with her for protection.'

'Protection!' yelped Tom. 'That woman, Natalie, from what I saw and heard of her, doesn't need protection. She would be well capable of knocking a cyclist into a ditch.'

'You're overwrought, Tom,' Jess advised him. 'Calm down, for goodness' sake.'

'Well, I feel so damn guilty!' Tom gave her an apologetic smile. 'I don't mean to yell at you or call you an old biddy. Sorry about that. What did they say at the hospital about Sally?'

'They are confident she'll come round. Things aren't as bad as first feared. But she had very nasty knock on the head and has a broken arm. They have promised to inform us as soon as she can be interviewed.'

Tom looked briefly more cheerful, then thoughtful. 'That woman Natalie, was she really Finch's girlfriend? Well, if she took the trouble to come down and tackle Harriet Kingsley, I suppose she must have been.'

'Don't ask me. All these people say whatever suits them. I'm getting pretty fed up with the lot of them, and so is Ian.'

Jess was also getting rather tired of encouraging Tom out of his state of gloom. She'd done her best. It had been a long day and she needed to get home. 'Things will look different in the morning,' she said, automatically repeating a favourite phrase of her mother's. She immediately regretted it. What am I doing? I'm not his mother!

'So cheer up, Tom!' she added aloud, before he could call her an old biddy again. Heck, she and he were much the same age! Old biddy, indeed.

He looked at her like a puppy that had been reproved for something it didn't understand it had done wrong.

Ian Carter was driving slowly towards Weston St Ambrose through the twisting lanes. He was mindful that Sally Grove had been knocked off her bike around here somewhere. Tonight, the rain-clouds had cleared and the moon shone as a bright disc in the night sky. Visibility was better than it had been the previous evening. Nevertheless, Carter could well imagine how easily an incident, like the one that had put Sally in hospital, could occur. If, of course, it had been an accident. The hedgerows cast deep shadows, pits of blackness. From time to time, his headlights picked up a pair of startled eyes in their glare.

Jess was unhappy with the careless motorist theory, and so was he. It was just that he disliked coincidences, and Biddle, the farmer, had told a very odd tale to Phil Morton. If someone had been searching the body of the injured cyclist, what had that person hoped to find? Or had the farmer been mistaken? Had the driver been checking the girl for the extent of her injuries? That might have looked as if he was searching the body. The light had been poor. Yes, Biddle could have been wrong.

Yet Sally Grove had been in the woods on the morning of the murder. Damn it, if she had any information, why hadn't she come forward at once? Because witnesses often don't, he told himself gloomily. They fear they will be disbelieved or, worse, cross-examined. And there was the natural disinclination to be drawn into anything unpleasant. It was so easy for such witnesses to persuade themselves that they really hadn't got anything important to say. Murder was well outside most people's experience. No wonder they kept their heads down.

But later, Sally Grove, given an unexpected meeting with Tom Palmer, had spoken of her unease. And Sally Grove now lay unconscious, unable to speak of what she might have seen or heard. Tom, said Jess, was distraught. It now began to appear almost certain that the accident was no such thing but rather a deliberate attempt to knock Sally down and recover – what?

Carter felt a fleeting sympathy for Palmer, who seemed to be very unlucky these days. However, he was one of those people who usually manages to land on their feet. Carter just hoped that Jess wasn't worrying too much about Tom in his present predicament. That was what really niggled. Every time Palmer had a broken relationship or was feeling lonely, or had a cold, he picked up the phone and rang Jess. When he had first met them both, Carter had imagined some sort of romantic link between them. But he now knew this wasn't the case. The knowledge ought to have made him feel better about it, but it didn't.

Carter had developed a theory about Jess's willingness to run round and comfort the pathologist. She missed her twin brother, who was out in some danger spot abroad, working with a medical charity. She worried about the risks her sibling ran. She couldn't do anything about it, but she could listen to Tom Palmer's woes. It made her feel better. This, anyway, was Carter's theory, and he knew he must never, ever, let her suspect it. She'd be furious. When Jess got angry, she was like a fizzing firework.

Then there was the other lead, suggested when he learned that Guy Kingsley had borrowed the carpenter's van early on the morning of the murder. He'd sent Phil Morton haring down that track, and it had got them nowhere.

'The people at the builders' suppliers remember him, sir. He was definitely there and collected laminated board previously ordered. But he couldn't have had enough time also to drive to a meeting with Finch, either in the woods or nearby, kill the bloke and drag the body to the place it was found. Plus, he would have needed to get back to the Old Nunnery before his wife returned. She'd told him she was only going to the supermarket in Weston. No one has mentioned seeing a tradesman's van in the vicinity of the woods,' Morton had added.

'Or the Renault belonging to Finch. We have to find that,' Carter had growled. 'We concentrate on that.'

Right now, he wanted to put the murder to one side and think about something else. To that end, he had phoned Monica Farrell, Sophie's aunt, earlier to ask if it was all right to call by that evening. She had been delighted, offering him a casserole supper. He was quite looking forward to it. They would talk about Millie, his daughter, of course, and that was all right. They would inevitably talk about Sophie as well, and that was not all right, but it was necessary. Sophie was always hatching up some plan, and he had a strong suspicion that her proposed visit to sort out some unspecified problem with the rented-out house veiled some other project. His headlights picked up another pair of eyes beneath a hedge, wild eyes reflecting green: a fox. He had a moment's superstitious feeling that it was trying to warn him, before the animal slipped away into the undergrowth.

He'd arrived at the outskirts of Weston St Ambrose. He couldn't help noticing how much it had grown in the short time he'd known the place. When he'd arrived in his present post, the village had become a shadow of what it had once been, little more than a name on the tourist trail. But over the past couple of years there had been significant changes. New businesses had opened. There was even a small supermarket. Weston St Ambrose was on the up. Perversely, most of the older inhabitants disliked all the new changes. Monica Farrell was one who had accepted them joyfully. 'Fresh blood!' she had declared enthusiastically.

The lights glowed in Monica's cottage. As Carter walked up the short path to the door a small, dark shape darted across in front of him, right under his feet. It nearly tripped him up before it vanished into the bushes. One of Monica's cats, he thought, setting out on its nightfall patrol. 'Watch out for Mr Fox!' he warned it, before raising his hand to the polished brass knocker. But his arrival had already been marked. The car's engine had probably been heard.

Monica, small, sturdy, grey-haired and sharp-eyed, opened the door. The enticing smell of the casserole drifted towards him. 'Come in, come in!' Carter bent his head beneath the low lintel of the door and allowed himself to be chivvied into the hall at speed. 'Don't let the cold air in! We're waiting for you.'

We? Foreboding gripped his heart. Monica was already pushing him towards the living room, where a comfortable chaos reigned and heat blasted from a wood-burning metal stove that had been installed in the hearth. Sitting by it, at her ease in a cretonne-covered chair, was his ex-wife.

'Hello, Ian,' she greeted him, and smiled up with a hint of triumph.

He'd been a policeman for too many years not to be able to deal with the unexpected. And he could have expected this, he thought. But Monica should have played fair and warned him. Had she thought he wouldn't come if he'd known Sophie was staying?

Still smiling and still enjoying having played a winning trick, Sophie raised her head to receive his greeting. He planted a chaste kiss on her cheek. She was looking extremely well, he thought, positively blooming.

'I hadn't realised,' he said aloud, 'that you'd already arrived. I didn't have a date for your coming over from France, only the info that you were on your way.'

Monica had disappeared into the kitchen to see to the casserole. There was a distant rattle and clang. A second cat, disapproving of an additional intruder, jumped down from an armchair and scurried away towards the sound of food being dished up. Carter slapped the cushions a couple of times in the vain hope of clearing away any cat hairs, and sat down.

'Good trip?' he asked politely. 'Did you fly?'

'No, I drove, using the Eurotunnel shuttle. I need a car here to get about.'

'Rodney well?'

'Fighting fit, thanks.'

Yes, he would be. When had Carter ever seen Rodney other than glowing with health and well-being?

'Seen Millie?' he asked.

'Not yet,' she admitted. Seeing the disapproving look on his face, she added hastily, 'I'll be driving up to the school at the weekend before going on to take a look at the house. I've got an appointment with the letting agency. I'll call back at the school again before I return to France.'

'What's the problem with the house?'

Sophie stretched out her long, elegant legs. 'A neighbour emailed us to say the tenants are giving wild parties. The house is full of people every weekend, and some of them bring dogs. The terms of the lease forbid the keeping of dogs in the house.'

'They will argue that the dogs are temporary, belonging to the visitors,' Carter suggested.

'They can try,' said Sophie, with the steely serenity he remembered so well. 'So, how are you, Ian? Still got that red-haired girlfriend?'

He felt himself flush and hoped it would be put down to the heat from the stove and not to anger. 'If you mean Jess Campbell, and I suppose you do, then she is not, and never has been, my girlfriend. She's a colleague and, I like to think, a friend. There's a difference.'

Sophie's smile was positively smug. 'Not according to Millie.'

'Millie's got it wrong.' He hadn't meant to sound so sharp.

But Sophie's smile had gone from smug to seraphic. 'You brought Jess here, I believe, when Millie was spending the day at Monica's, that time Millie was staying with you because of the asbestos in the school ceilings. You brought Jess along with you here so that Millie could meet her.'

'No! I brought Jess here that evening so that she could meet Millie. It's not quite the same thing.'

'Same difference, as they say.'

He didn't want to defend himself, because why the hell should he? But he couldn't do otherwise. 'Unfortunately, at that time, I couldn't take time off, so yes, while I was at work, Millie came here to Monica. And it wasn't just about asbestos being found in the school roof! If you recall, the reason I hadn't had any warning of her visit was because you and Rodney had suddenly decided to go to New York! Out of the blue, you asked me to take Millie.'

'I thought you'd be glad of extra time with your daughter,' said Sophie, making it sound as if he hadn't been.

'I was!' he growled.

'Well, Monica liked your Jess, too.' Sophie rose from her chair. 'That's all I meant. I must go and give Monica a hand.'

Alone, Carter suppressed the urge to rampage round the room throwing cushions at the walls. 'Don't let her do it to you,' he warned himself. 'She likes stirring it up. You ought to know that by now.'

Monica appeared to usher him into the extended kitchen, where the dining table was located, and they sat down to eat. Carter had a sense Monica was feeling a little guilty. She gave him surreptitious worried glances from time to time while Sophie chattered on about the house in France she and Rodney had bought, how well Rodney was doing in business, how well Millie was liking boarding school in England, and so forth. It wasn't until Monica's special chocolate cheesecake arrived that it struck Carter that more surreptitious glances were being exchanged, this time between Monica and Sophie.

Something's up. I knew it! Even as he told himself this, Carter was casting about feverishly for whatever it might be. He'd been set up. OK, that was obvious now, but what kind of bombshell was going to be dropped on him?

Sophie liked to tell people that she and he had had 'an amicable divorce', whatever that meant. It had been a bitter and miserable period in their lives, as Carter recalled. They'd tried to hide it from Millie, but Millie was bright enough to know what was going on, so she had suffered, too.

On the other hand, in his working life, Carter had seen enough cases where relationships had broken down and one or other of the parties had taken up a kitchen knife to express feelings, leaving the ex-partner in a sea of blood. Even if it hadn't come to murder, they went in for criminal damage on a truly ingenious scale. They cut up clothes, or poured bleach over them, vandalised cars and other property. In one case he recalled, the deceived spouse of a keen gardener had dug up and burned prized roses, before breaking every pane of glass in a greenhouse. Compared with all of that, their divorce had, yes, been a highly civilised affair. As if to confirm that, here they sat, eating cheesecake and behaving as if everything was hunky-dory. Only, it wasn't.

After the meal, Monica ordered them both out of the kitchen. 'I have my own system for stacking the dishwasher and I always wash the wine glasses myself by hand. They're very old and rather fragile. You two go and chat. Help yourself to a whisky, if you'd like one, Ian.'

They obediently trooped into the sitting room and retook the chairs they had been sitting in before supper. Sophie drew a deep breath, but Carter had decided to take charge of the conversation this time, if he was allowed to.

'So, what is it, your news? You haven't come over from France just because someone brought a dog into your house on a weekend visit!'

A flash of annoyance showed in her eyes. She had planned how she would inform him, and the plan had been ruined.

'I'm pregnant,' she said aggressively.

He'd thought how well she looked. How old was she? He did a lightning calculation.

'I'm forty-one,' she said, knowing full well what he was doing.

'Congratulations,' he said. 'Have you told Millie?'

'I'll be telling her when I go up to the school this weekend.'

'All right,' he said.

She looked surprised. 'Nothing else to say?'

'What should I say? My only concern is for Millie. I don't want her to feel she's been elbowed out of your half of her family.'

'She won't be!' Sophie snapped.

'Then I hope everything goes well for you and Rodney and the new addition. Will you have the baby in France or return to the UK?'

'We're thinking of having the baby in France. They have excellent maternity services.'

When he didn't say anything further, she added, 'What are you thinking about now?'

'About how your new family situation will pan out. I've got a case at the moment . . . well, the details won't interest you. But two of the people concerned in the matter are – were – stepbrother and sister. They weren't linked by a common parent, as Millie and your new baby will be. It was a question of a marriage between two people who already had a child each, quite different.'

Sophie sighed and said, quite sadly, 'Do you really know why our marriage didn't work out? It was because of the dratted police work. It got into everything! Even now, you see, when I'm telling you my news, you don't ask how I feel about becoming a mum again, or how Rodney feels about becoming a dad for the first time, a flesh-and-blood dad, not a step-parent. No, you link it to some case you're investigating and see my news filtered through that. Have you any idea how much I resent that, how I always resented it?'

There was a silence. Carter said, 'I'm sorry.' He didn't know whether she believed him, but it was true.

'Is it a murder case?' she asked after a pause.

'Yes, it is. It took place around here, as it happens. Not in Weston St Ambrose itself, but in some woods not far away. Crooked Man Woods, they're called.'

'I know Crooked Man Woods,' Sophie said unexpectedly. 'Who was murdered?'

'Someone called Carl Finch. He lived in London but had come down to visit his stepsister, who lives locally at a house called the Old Nunnery. Do you know that?'

'I know where it is. I never knew anyone who lived there. Monica might have done. Do you want to ask her?'

'No,' he said. 'Not tonight.'

Despite everything, the rest of the evening passed off quite pleasantly. Monica followed him out to his car when he left. She whispered an apology for the surprise he'd had on finding Sophie there.

'I know I should have warned you, Ian, but Sophie asked me not to. She's been worried about telling you her news, about the baby. So I went along with her wish. I hope you'll forgive me.'

'Don't worry about it, honestly, Monica,' he told her. 'It was a surprise to see her, I admit, and her news was a thunderbolt. Perhaps it was a good idea to combine the two shocks.' He stooped to kiss her cheek. 'But I should know by now to expect the unexpected from Sophie!'

'Come and see me again, after she's gone back to France,' she said.

He promised her he would, and set off back through the dark, twisting lanes. It was only when he arrived home at his cheerless flat, later that night, that the full impact of her news really came home to him. Sophie had not only made a new life with Rodney, she was starting a new family and had a full future ahead of her. He, on the other hand, was stuck here amid odds and ends of furniture, because he still hadn't got around to decorating and furnishing the place properly. It was like living in a theatre props room, all the bits and pieces to replicate a real home but nothing assembled, and no cast members to people it if it ever did get assembled. He must try and sort something out before Millie's next visit, make the place more welcoming. In the meantime, he had no wife, his child was away at school, and Jess was entirely taken up with the sorrows of young Palmer these days. Or so it seemed. He wanted suddenly, more than anything, to talk to her.

But it was too late to phone now. She might be at Palmer's place, still listening to him grouse, or be watching something interesting on the telly, or out with someone else. More likely, she was asleep. It was late, and he should turn in, too. But he didn't feel like sleeping, even though he was tired. He remembered the advice, often handed out, that a hot, milky drink at bedtime encourages slumber. But when he looked in his fridge, there was no milk. He'd intended to pick some up earlier, before going to Monica's. He'd have to have black coffee at breakfast. He did find in a cupboard a half-empty jar of instant chocolate drink, for which, the label promised him, he only needed boiling water. So he mixed that up but somehow got the amount wrong, or the jar was so old its contents had lost its chocolatey flavour. All he got for his trouble was a hot, sweet, lumpy brown sludge. He poured it down the sink and had a whisky instead.

Jess had arrived home earlier from Tom's and wondered if it was too late to phone Ian Carter. There was no real reason for doing so, other than that the conversation with Tom had both tired and irritated her that evening. She had never realised how self-centred he was. No wonder Madison had taken off for Australia. It had been tricky, too, not being able to tell him about the figure Biddle had seen, apparently searching Sally as she lay unconscious in the ditch. She just wanted to speak to someone else, someone she could talk to freely, even if it was just about work.

But a call to Ian went unanswered, and she remembered belatedly he had spoken of going out to Weston St Ambrose that evening to see Monica Farrell. She had no message to leave. She hung up.

Chapter 13

'There is nothing like shovelling muck for taking your mind off things!' Tessa Briggs muttered to herself, as she vigorously swept the floor of the loose box she had just mucked out. She'd risen at six that morning and been at work since seven-thirty. Outside, in the yard, a pile of gently steaming straw and manure bore witness to her diligence. The three horses were out in their paddock. The morning sun had now cleared the frost from the grass, and its watery beams brightened the scene. That was how the countryside looked first thing in the morning, fresh and pure, as if newly washed. Misty, the grey, was feeling skittish and cantering around by himself, kicking up his heels like a youngster. Yet, of the three animals, he was the oldest. The other two ignored him, nibbling the scarce grass. Stubbs had painted scenes like that and, out here in the English countryside, not a lot had changed from his day.

Fred was sniffing around in the far corner of the yard. Tessa suspected something had passed through during the night, a fox, probably. This was a lean time of year for Reynard and he called by to raid the bins, if he could knock the lids off. She'd given up keeping chickens because of the foxes. The deciding moment had been when one had burrowed his way into the henhouse and somehow squeezed up between loose floorboards to wreak bloody havoc. Hearing the commotion, she had rushed in her night attire with Hal's old shotgun, ready to blast the invader to kingdom come. But he had already got away, leaving nothing but blood and feathers and dead fowls. Foxes liked killing. They killed more than they needed, if they got the chance, just for the hell of it.

Yesterday, thought Tessa, had been lousy. What with that couple of troublemakers who'd turned up from London to throw accusations around, then the police poking their noses in at the Old Nunnery yet again. Poor Hattie was still in a dreadful state, and Guy Kingsley not there when he was wanted. When was he ever?

But this morning things didn't look so bad, at least not here. She'd ring Hattie later and hear how matters stood at the Old Nunnery today. The situation there wasn't getting any better, of course, and was even likely to get worse. The police wouldn't go away. Who knew what else might emerge from Carl's chaotic past? Natalie and Henry might prove the tip of the iceberg. Tessa paused and leaned thoughtfully on her broom handle. What to do next, that was the problem. Everything was in such a damn awful muddle. But just sitting and waiting for the next piece of bad news was like waiting for a thunderstorm to break.

The sound of a car engine was growing louder. She raised her head to listen. Someone was coming down the narrow road that led to the Old Farmhouse and nowhere else. It was early for a social caller. Hattie would have phoned ahead if she'd intended dropping by. Tessa wasn't one for praying, but she did utter up an involuntary muttered request: 'Please don't let it be that ruddy police sergeant again!'

The car stopped. The gate across the entry to the yard creaked and groaned as it was dragged open. Whoever it was, they weren't waiting to be invited in. She leaned her broom against the wall and walked out of the loose box into the yard, putting up her hand to shield her eyes against the sun's glare. She didn't recognise the car. But she did recognise the outline of the figure pushing the barrier shut and fastening it by dropping the metal loop over the gatepost. It wasn't Sergeant Morgan. It was someone even less welcome.

It's like those African wildlife films on the telly, she thought. The scent of a kill brings every carnivore to the spot, gathering to fight over the scraps.

The man had fixed the gate and turned to face her. He was a tall figure with thick, sandy hair, leavened with white, and was wearing an Aran sweater with corduroy trousers. The bulky sweater added to his already chunky build. And to think, when she'd first met him, he'd been as slim as a beanpole, thought Tessa, in a burst of nostalgia.

'Putting on a bit of weight, Hal!' she greeted him as he came towards her. 'What the hell are you doing here?'

'I was in the area. Thought I might cadge a cup of coffee,' Hal Briggs said. 'And check on how you are.'

He stooped. Tess graciously allowed him to kiss her on the cheek, which he did in a brotherly sort of way. Even so, it disturbed her more than she would have thought possible.

'Rubbish!' she said crisply. 'You haven't driven all the way from Bath for that. Go on into the house. I'll scrub up and join you. You can put the kettle on, if you want to.'

Fred had trotted up to inspect the newcomer and now accompanied him into the house. Tessa smiled to herself. Fred was keeping his eye on things! She followed man and dog to the kitchen door, where she paused to remove her wellingtons in the porch. Then she padded in her socks across the flagged floor past her visitor and made her way to the bathroom. Ten minutes later, changed into different trousers and sweater, and hopefully not still smelling of the stable yard, she went back to the kitchen. But it was empty now. She could hear Hal's voice from the living room. He was sitting comfortably in an armchair, making a fuss of Fred. Two mugs steamed on the low table.

Tessa took one and threw herself down on the sofa. 'How is the corn and feed business?'

'Doing well, thanks. You look fit.' He gestured generally in her direction and smiled.

'I am fit, thanks! You were always a straight speaker, Hal. I haven't seen you in Lord knows how long, and you don't say I look well, or, heaven forbid, that I look nice.'

He grinned. 'You look very well and, without the gumboots and smelly work gear, you look very presentable.'

'Right. Well, I know what's brought you. You've heard the news, I suppose?'

'It's been in the papers and on the local radio, not to mention the usual grapevine. Could hardly miss it.' He sipped his coffee. 'Odd business, especially since the police think it's murder.' He drained his coffee mug. 'How are things up at the Old Nunnery?'

'You could drive up there and see for yourself,' Tessa heard herself say waspishly.

'They wouldn't be expecting me. Hattie probably wouldn't recognise me now and I've never met the chap she married.' He managed a wry grin.

'Fair enough. You couldn't just turn up there, I suppose. Things are hellish, if you want the truth. Hattie is falling apart. Guy Kingsley – the man she married – is about as much use as a leaky bucket, and the police keep turning up and stirring things. Yesterday, it got worse.'

'Oh?' His voice sharpened. 'How?'

'Some woman claiming to be Carl's girlfriend turned up from London, with a man friend as back-up. She threw all kinds of wild accusations around. Guy wasn't there. But, luckily, a carpenter was and he called the police. They came up and sorted things out. But it was the last thing Hattie needed.'

'I see.' Hal leaned forward and replaced his empty mug on the table. 'I'm sorry.'

Tessa sighed, and said more mildly, 'Yes, I know you are. You were always keen on her.'

'Well, we were all young, and you know how it is.' He sounded apologetic.

'It doesn't matter *now*, Hal!' she told him.

He grimaced. 'Well, I'm sorry she didn't marry someone more supportive than the chap you describe. She could have had her pick. Nearly every male of suitable age in the neighbourhood fancied her. Yes, including myself, as you said. At least she didn't marry Carl.'

'What?' squawked Tessa. 'That would be preposterous! She'd never have done that!'

'I think it was in Carl's mind at one time,' Hal retorted. 'He'd never have admitted it, least of all to me, but he saw himself as lord of the manor, or at least calling the shots at the Old Nunnery. He was an envious sort of bloke, you know, and ambitious with it.'

He saw the expression on his ex-wife's face and added, 'Don't look so pop-eyed about it. And don't tell me you never had a moment's worry over it. He wasn't any kind of blood relative, or even a legally adopted brother. He was Nancy's kid, that's all. His natural father had vanished into the blue and his mother died five or six years after she married Hemmings. Carl had been hanging around the Old Nunnery, and it wasn't just because he had a sentimental attachment to the place. He was waiting his chance once Hemmings was dead. Only someone else got there first, this fellow Kingsley, and put his nose out of joint. He was always very good at manoeuvring others, Carl, but that time he missed the signs. Now then, if you'd told me Carl had taken a shotgun and blown away Kingsley, that would be believable.'

'You're talking rubbish, Hal!' Tessa said, but she looked shaken.

'OK, I won't mention it again. All theory now, anyway. But, talking of the locals, I passed Ron Purcell just down the road on my way here. I stopped to say hello. I was surprised to see him. I thought he'd moved away.'

'He did. He moved back when his marriage broke up. He didn't marry locally. I never met his wife.'

'He was another member of the cricket club, way back. He was a demon bowler.'

'Yes, well, now he paints.'

'Paints? Paints what?' Hal asked, surprised.

'There's some sort of an amateur artists' club in the village, and he belongs to it.' She pointed at the far wall. 'That's one of his.'

Hal got up and went to inspect the watercolour in question. 'It's this house!' he exclaimed. 'It's not half bad.'

'He came along one afternoon in the summer and asked if he could use it as a subject. He sat out there in the yard for a week.'

'And you bought it off him?'

'Actually, no,' Tessa told him. 'He gave it to me. I offered to pay him for it, but he wouldn't hear of it.'

'Well, well, old Ron, a man of hidden talents!' Hal returned to his seat. 'Harriet isn't the only one to be badly upset. It's knocked you for six, hasn't it?'

'Of course it has. Hattie is my friend. We were at school together.'

'You were always very fond of her, protective, mother hen!' He grinned.

Tessa glared at him. 'What's really brought you here, Hal?' she asked. 'Don't repeat that rubbish about being in the neighbour-hood. And it's not to catch up on old times with people like Ron. Please don't say that you're here on my account.'

Her former husband leaned back in the armchair and folded his hands. 'Well, now, Tessa, you might say that *is* why I'm here. Of course, I wanted to hear from someone close to the people concerned just what's been going on. This is my neck of the woods, too, you know! But also . . .'

He broke off, and was silent for so long that she began to redden under his steady gaze, and fidget. At last, when she could bear it no longer, Tessa burst out, 'Oh, for goodness' sake, Hal! Say what's on your mind!'

'All right!' He sat up straight and unfolded his hands. 'The whole thing has been worrying me. Tell me straight, Tessa, have you done something really stupid?' He held up his hand. 'Before you deny it and chew my ear off, listen, please! I am still quite fond of you, you know.'

'Thanks!' she managed, through gritted teeth.

'So if you've done something you now regret, I might be able to help.'

'Well, you can't!' she snapped, unwisely.

He heaved a sigh. 'So, then, you have done something bloody daft. What is it?'

Unwillingly, she admitted, 'I did try and arrange it so that Harriet wouldn't have to admit she found the body. She phoned me first, you see, after she'd found him. She'd driven back home, but she hadn't yet seen Guy. She was in a dreadful state over finding Carl and terrified of how Guy would react when he discovered she'd made a secret arrangement to meet him and discuss money.' Tessa paused. 'Carl was always nothing but trouble. I remember that scrap you had with him at the old cricket club, years ago.'

Hal nodded. 'It certainly was years ago. We wrecked the bar. Don't ask me what it was over.'

'Not over Hattie, then?'

Hal hesitated for the first time. 'I may have dropped him the word that I'd guessed what his long-term intentions were – warned him off, if you like. He didn't like that. Ron Purcell was captain that year, and he didn't like it either, when the furniture started flying around the bar. A couple of other members took it upon themselves to try and break up the fight and ended up in the thick of it. He was beside himself with rage, old Ron. He took the good name of the cricket club very seriously. John Hemmings paid for the damage.'

He gave her a shrewd look. 'So Carl needed bailing out again, did he?'

'When did he not? He was always running into debt and asking Harriet to help him. Anyway, after she called in a blind panic about finding the body, I told her to stay put but to keep out of Guy's way. I'd go down to the woods and find Carl. I'd phone the police and come back to the Old Nunnery as soon as I could so we could tell Guy together. That was the plan, anyway, and it might have worked.'

'But?' Hal raised a bushy eyebrow.

'But I was too late, wasn't I? Ruddy police had got there first. Someone else had stumbled over Carl and reported it.'

'And the police know this? About the little plan you and Harriet hatched up?'

'It wasn't Hattie's plan; it was mine. And yes, they know. There was another witness who saw Hattie's car driving away from the woods and he told the police. Now I've got a Sergeant Morton round my neck.' Tessa scowled. 'He's a gloomy-looking chap built like an oak wardrobe, and he seems to think it's his calling in life to pester me with questions. He even turned up here. I thought, when I heard your car, he might have come back again. Thank goodness, he hadn't!'

'And it was only me?' Hal's smile held no amusement. 'Why does he keep coming back, Tessa?'

'How do I know?' she retorted defiantly.

'All right, I'll hazard a guess. Because he thinks there is something else you're not telling him – and I think you're not telling me! Stop trying to give me the runaround, Tessa. I know you too well. So you tried to be the one to report the body, and you failed. But that's not all, is it? What's the other thing you've done?'

There was a silence. Then she said, 'I can't tell you, Hal. Not

241

because I'm being obstinate. I can't tell you because, if I do, you'll be an accessory after the fact, or whatever they call it. You'd have to go to the police. I don't want that. This isn't your business, Hal. I appreciate you wanting to help. But really, just go back to Bath and let things take their course here.'

After a moment, he said, 'All right. But you know you can pick up the phone if you need me.'

Tessa said gruffly, 'Thanks.' A little later, as she walked with him to his car, she asked, 'Just out of curiosity, you understand, are you still together with whatshername – Alison?'

'Yes.'

'Does she know you've driven here this morning to see me?'

'No, as it happens. She's in London for the week. She spends a lot of time at her flat there, because of her job, you know.'

'Still haranguing students about obscure bits of history?'

'Neolithic cultures of Western Europe.'

'How on earth—!' Tessa broke off, coloured, and said, 'Sorry, none of my business.'

'How on earth did we ever get together? We met at a mutual friend's place and got talking about farming and grain types. Men started clearing and cultivating the land in Neolithic times. They kept animals, mostly, of course.'

Tessa rolled her eyes. 'You've got something to talk about then. Thanks for coming over, anyway, Hal.'

'Not a problem.' He stooped and sedately kissed her cheek again.

His breath brushed her neck and she felt a pang of loss. They had not been drawn together by passion. They had married, she thought now, because all their friends were getting married; and they'd got on all right for a while. Then, one evening, sitting by the fire, Hal had announced he was moving out. Somehow, it hadn't surprised her. She wasn't daft. There had been someone else for a while. What did they say? 'A wife always knows.' She'd known because there was a spring in his step and a gleam in his eye that she hadn't put there. Nevertheless, you can't just dismiss from memory a time of shared togetherness.

'Remember what I said about the phone. Oh, and don't do anything else daft!' He was facing the entry to the yard as he spoke and suddenly straightened up and said sharply, 'Who is this?'

'Who is what?' Tessa turned and saw that, on the further side of the gate, a shiny black Mercedes had pulled up and a young woman was getting out. She was a startling apparition, in a tight red sweater, black trousers and shiny boots. She had a mass of artfully disordered tawny curls and was bedecked with various items of chunky jewellery. Even Fred, who had trotted forward to give the new arrival the once-over, had stopped, and was staring up at her in a bewildered way.

'Who's she?' hissed Hal, scowling at the vision. 'And what is she doing out here, done up like that?'

'Cat's whiskers, isn't she?' observed Tessa. 'Well, I don't know her, but if I had to hazard a guess, it's one of the pair of unwelcome visitors poor Hattie got yesterday. I told you about them. She – that girl – claims to have been Carl's girlfriend. I don't know where the man is – a beefy, red-haired fellow, Hattie said.'

'So, what's she doing here?' muttered Hal.

'How on earth should I know? I thought the police had warned the pair of them off and they'd gone back to London!'

'Are you Mrs Briggs?' called the newcomer loudly.

'She is!' retorted Hal, before Tessa could speak. She felt him give her arm a warning squeeze. *Let me handle this*, he was signalling.

'Any chance of a word? I'd appreciate it,' added the visitor, a touch belligerently.

Hal walked over to the gate and dragged it open.

'That dog OK?' asked the woman, as Fred gave an uneasy growl.

'He is. Come here, Fred!' Tessa ordered, and the collie trotted back to her. 'It's OK, boy.' She dropped her hand to touch his head, and Fred acknowledged the contact by briefly licking her fingers.

'I'm Hal Briggs,' Hal said in a flat voice, not offering any further information. 'What do you want a word about?'

The visitor flushed nearly as red as her sweater. Tessa thought, *she anticipated finding me alone, as she and her man friend found poor Hattie. Only they hadn't counted on Derek the carpenter yesterday, and she certainly hadn't counted on finding Hal here now!*

'I'm – I was – a friend of Carl Finch. My name is Natalie Adam. I want to know what's been going on, who killed him!'

'Then you'd better speak to the officer in charge of the team investigating the murder,' said Hal. 'He'll bring you up to date.'

Tessa spoke up, saying, 'His name is Carter, Superintendent Carter.'

'I've met him!' retorted the visitor. 'He didn't tell me anything.'

Tessa, unable to contain herself, burst out, 'You and your ginger-haired pal were at the house, giving Hattie a bad time. Superintendent Carter told you both to clear off. Where's the other one?'

'Henry – Henry Knox, who came down here with me – has had to return to London. He left me the car after I drove him to Gloucester, to the train station.'

'Carter meant for you *both* to go back to London!' stormed Tessa.

'Superintendent Carter,' came the icy reply, 'can't tell me where I can or can't go. I want to know what happened to poor Carl. I believe he was lured into a trap. I'm not going to give up until I know who's responsible.'

'That's enough!' ordered Hal. 'If you mean to interfere in a police investigation, Miss Adam, that would be a bad idea. You'll find yourself in a lot of trouble.'

'You let me worry about that!' Natalie snapped. 'I mean to see justice done.'

Hal drew a deep breath. 'In any event, you've no business here, so kindly leave. We can't help you.'

'I bet you bloody could!' challenged Natalie. 'If you wanted to. But you don't. No one down here does. You all had it in for poor Carl! Well, I'm not going to abandon him!'

'Ms Adam!' roared Hal. 'Your visit here is over.' His voice echoed around the yard, and even the horses in the meadow behind the house flung up their heads and stared curiously towards them.

Despite this, Natalie still looked for a second or two as if she would argue. But then she conceded defeat – for the moment. She tossed her long curls, causing her jewellery to chink, and stalked back to her car. As she opened the door, she turned her head for a last verbal volley at them. 'There's a conspiracy going on here, and you're all in it! Well, sod you all, I'm going to find out what's going on!'

They watched her back the Mercedes out into the lane and drive off.

'Bloody nerve!' exploded Tessa.

'Yes,' her ex-husband agreed. 'But listen up, Tessa. If she comes back, with or without her friend, call the police immediately. Don't muck about, and don't try and tackle her, or them, yourself!'

'I can deal with her!' retorted Tessa.

'Sure you can. But you shouldn't. She's half off her head, that's my impression. I don't know if it's grief or what it is. But I suspect she's liable to do almost anything. Here.' He took a piece of paper from his pocket. 'I've written down my landline and mobile numbers – and my office number, for good measure. If you need me, call. I'll come over straight away.'

'Thanks,' she mumbled.

'Still sure you don't want to tell me what you've done?' he asked, more gently.

'Absolutely sure.'

He heaved a sigh. 'Well, take care, old girl.'

'I'm not your old girl,' she huffed. 'But thanks, anyway, Hal.'

'You called my place last night,' Ian Carter said, when Jess appeared in his office that morning. 'I checked the list of missed calls and recognised your number. It was too late to call you back. Was it urgent?'

'No, not at all,' Jess replied evasively, 'and it was daft of me to call. I remembered too late that you'd gone to see Monica. You'd mentioned that was your plan when we left the office. I should have remembered. Anyway, it was nothing. I'd been talking to Tom, and he was a bit trying. He insists on taking the blame for

Sally Grove's accident, which is nonsense. I think he's on the right track and someone did overhear his conversation with her at the library and realised that she'd been taking snaps in those woods at the time of the murder, but neither he nor she could have known that at the time. Tom certainly couldn't have prevented what happened. But he's got it fixed in his mind that he could have. I think it's that head-cold thing he's been suffering from. It's interfering with his command of logic. I'm going to call the hospital in a minute and see if I can talk to Sally today. We need to, as soon as possible.'

'I thought Palmer was getting over his cold? If he wants to wallow in some sort of *mea culpa* fixation, let him. He'll get over it,' Carter said unsympathetically.

'I think he's fallen in love – well, just a bit.'

'Oh, has he? Well, good luck to him with that!' was the sharp retort.

'Everything OK with Monica?' Jess asked, eyeing him. He looked out of sorts and was fiddling irritably with papers on his desk.

He looked up. 'What? Oh, yes, well . . . to be honest, no. Monica is fine, nothing wrong with her. But when I got there I found Sophie sitting in a chair, looking smug.'

'Oh? You weren't expecting her, were you?'

'No, I wasn't. Well, I knew she had plans to come over from France. She spun me a yarn about the house they've let out and unsatisfactory tenants. I should have known there would be more to it than that.'

'Is she – and her husband – are they coming back to the UK?' Jess asked. Mentally, she was crossing her fingers and hoping that wasn't the case. Anything to do with his former wife unsettled Ian. Better to have her at some distance.

'No, they're staying in France but . . .' Carter drew a deep breath. 'Apparently, she and Rodney are to be proud parents. She's expecting a baby,' he added.

'Oh, I see. How do you think Millie will take that?' *And how are you feeling about it?* she wanted to ask, but couldn't.

'No idea. Sophie is going up to see her later today to break the news.'

'She might like the idea of a little brother or sister?' Jess suggested.

'She might, but I'm worried Millie will feel – well, side-lined. She's been dumped in that boarding school, where she seems perfectly happy, I admit. But her mother's gone off to France. I'm here. It's going to be hard for her. Anyway, as soon as Sophie's gone back to France I'll go to see Millie and have a chat with her.'

'I wish I could help,' Jess told him. She immediately wished she hadn't said that.

But she was relieved to see him smile. 'Thanks. Join me in having a drink somewhere tonight, after work? Unless you're seeing Palmer again, of course.'

'Tom can stew in his own juice for a bit. Of course I'll come for a drink. But I'd better go and ring the hospital now.'

The ward sister met Jess in the corridor and examined her ID with care. 'You're not going to stay too long, are you, Inspector Campbell? I'll be honest. The doctor is not too happy about you talking to the patient so soon after she's regained consciousness.

It isn't good for her, for one thing, and, in addition, anything she says may be – well, her memory will be hazy, let's say. So it won't be any use firing questions at her. And what she does tell you might be muddled, and even quite wrong. She may just fall asleep on you.'

'I won't stay long,' Jess promised. 'And I'll remember all you've said.'

'Very well,' agreed the sister briskly. 'You can have ten minutes, and then I'll be back to show you out.'

The curtains were drawn around the bed. Sister twitched one aside to reveal a very pale young woman with dark, curly hair propped up on the adjustable backrest. Her eyes were closed and Jess feared she was asleep now and that there would little chance the ward sister would let her wait.

But the patient's eyelids flickered and opened. Her eyes surveyed them with a faint expression of puzzlement.

'How are you feeling, Sally?' asked the nurse, stooping over her.

The patient's expression cleared, and she whispered, 'Still got a bit of a headache, but it could be worse.' She had a large dressing pad taped to her forehead and her left arm was in a sling. She managed a weak smile.

Jess was pleased to see the smile; Sister less so.

'Mm, well, this is Inspector Campbell, and she wants a quick word. I've told her it will have to be very quick. If you don't feel you're up to it, say so.'

'I can come back later,' Jess put in, hoping Sally would not ask this.

'It's OK,' said Sally. 'Only I'm afraid I might not make much sense. Frankly, I don't remember very much.'

The nurse departed, after a meaningful look at the visitor. Jess pulled the curtain back into place so that she was closeted with the patient in privacy. She drew up a chair to the bedside and invited, 'Please call me Jess. I don't want to bother you, Sally. I understand you won't recall much about the accident. But it's not that I want to ask you about just now.'

Sally looked perplexed.

Jess hurried on. 'I'm wondering how much you remember about something that happened earlier, several days ago, in Crooked Man Woods.'

The patient's brow began to crinkle in thought, but then she said, 'Ouch!'

'I really am very sorry, Sally,' Jess apologised. 'It's not nice of me to trouble you at this moment, but I do need all the help I can get in this case we're investigating.'

'That poor man who was shot in the woods?'

Jess couldn't disguise her relief. 'You do remember that?'

'I remember hearing about it. I didn't see anything. Or, if I did, I've forgotten. Sorry.' Sally paused, before going on, uncertainly, 'I think someone told me about it, or perhaps I knew before but the man I met at the library started talking about it. I belong to a group of artists. We're all amateurs, of course. We specialise in country subjects. We're showing our work at the library in Weston.'

'That man at the library was called Tom Palmer.'

'Tom, yes.' Sally's expression brightened. 'We were putting up our display pictures and I was arguing with someone, only I can't remember who it was right now.' She frowned again, and winced. 'It was probably Gordon Ferris. Gordon's our organiser. He founded the group, and he does tend to take charge. Anyway, Tom came up and started talking about my work, because I'd painted some trees in Crooked Man Woods and he recognised them.'

Sally leaned back on her pillows and closed her eyes. Jess's conscience pricked her, and she asked gently, 'Would you like me to come back later?'

'No, stay. I'm just trying to get my thoughts together. It takes me a while. I hope this gets better. I don't want to be going around in a fog for the rest of my life.'

'It will get better.' Jess paused. 'Do you remember seeing *anything* unusual in the woods that morning?'

'No – that is, not *seeing*, no.'

'How about *hearing* anything strange?'

Sally's eyes opened wide, suddenly alert. 'It was all strange!' she said energetically. 'I was scared, and I'm not usually scared out in the woods on my own.'

'What scared you?'

'I could hear things. Someone was there. But I didn't see whoever it was.'

Jess tried another tack. 'When you arrived there, you chained up your bicycle in the car park.'

'Ye–es, I suppose I did. I always do.'

'Did you see a black Range Rover parked there?'

'No – no, I didn't.'

'How sure are you, given you're not feeling a hundred per cent right now?'

'It wasn't there,' said Sally. 'There was nothing else there. The car park was empty. It was early. I do remember I was pleased, because people walk into shot, you know.'

As if on cue, on the far side of the curtain there came the rattle of a trolley being pushed into the ward and a voice asked if someone wanted tea or coffee.

Jess hurried on. 'Speaking of another kind of shot, one from a gun, did you hear one?'

'I think I might have done. There was a kind of small explosion just as I arrived, as I was getting off my bike. I don't know if it was a gun. There's some sort of shooting range nearby, and you do hear bangs from time to time.' Sally paused again.

Jess waited, taking a worried look at her watch. Any moment now, the ward sister would be back, or another nurse, and the trolley was on the move again. Whatever else they were keen on in that hospital, privacy wasn't high on the list, thought Jess irritably. She persevered.

'This bang or explosion, it might have come from the clay-pigeon-shooting place?'

Sally raised her undamaged right arm and pointed towards the wall to her right. 'No, that's over there.' She moved her arm across her chest to point to the left. 'Whatever I heard came from way over there, the other side of the woods.'

'You mean the shot, the explosion, came from the wrong direction for the clay-pigeon range?'

'Yes. Birds flew up, a whole flock of them, into the sky about the woods. I suppose it could have been a bird-scarer going off in one of the fields beyond the woods.'

'At this time of year?' Jess objected.

Sally looked momentarily confused. 'No, of course it wouldn't have been a bird-scarer. I'm muddled.'

'It's all right,' Jess reassured her hastily. 'What happened after that, when you were taking the photographs in the woods? Did you see or hear anything?'

Sally grew animated. 'I did, but I don't know what it was. I thought I was alone, but I wasn't. I kept feeling someone was there, watching me. It got worse because someone started moaning and breathing very heavily.'

'Where?' Jess asked eagerly.

'I don't know where. Somewhere in the trees, or beyond, on one of paths.' Sally paused again and added, 'And after that, there was a car.'

'You saw it? How would that get into the woods? Walkers have to leave their cars in the car park, don't they?'

'I didn't see it, I heard it. I remember now. The driver couldn't get into the woods from the car park, as you say, because there's a fence and a gate. But there is a way in from the far side. There's a short access road for the forestry workers.'

'How soon after hearing the moaning, as you call it, did you hear the car?'

'Oh, quite a bit later, after I'd taken some shots. I took a lot, snapping away, because I was so jittery. I kept swinging round to see if there was anyone there. Because of that, the shots I took weren't very good. I sort of thought that if there was someone, and that person saw I was making a record, he'd keep away. And I'm really sorry, but I can't concentrate any more now.'

The curtain was jerked aside and the captain of the tea trolley appeared. 'Tea or coffee, dear?' she asked Sally.

'I don't really—' began Sally.

'You got to keep your fluids up, dear!'

'Oh, well, tea then, please.'

'Biscuit?' A round tin was rattled under their noses. 'What about you?' the woman enquired of Jess.

'I'm fine, thanks,' Jess told her, willing the trolley to move on. The last precious minutes were slipping away – and here, looming up behind the trolley, was the familiar form of the ward sister.

'Time to go!' she said firmly to Jess.

'Yes, of course.' Jess got obediently to her feet. 'Thank you for talking to me, Sally, and I hope you feel much better soon. I would like to see all the photos you took that day in the woods some time.'

'Phone . . .' muttered Sally indicating the bedside cabinet.

'That's enough, dear,' said the ward sister.

'Jess can take my phone – I'll open it up for her.' Sally was still pointing at the bedside cabinet.

Jess moved quickly around the bed and opened the little cabinet, watched mistrustfully by the ward sister.

'All the photos I took that morning are on it. Mostly rubbish.' In Sally's hand, a picture of a group of trees suddenly appeared on the smartphone. She held it out to Jess. 'There you are. You can check it out . . . I need to go to sleep now, sorry.' She closed her eyes.

'I'm not sure I should let you take her phone,' said the ward sister anxiously to Jess. 'She isn't really compos mentis, as you can tell.'

'I'll give you a receipt and I'll see she gets it back as soon as possible,' Jess urged. 'This is a police investigation. Not just into Sally's accident, you know, but into a murder.'

The ward sister's expression would have turned a weaker mortal to stone. 'Is she a vital witness?'

'Well, no. That is to say, I can't say for sure. Her memory comes and goes. But the phone might have something of use on it.'

'Because,' said the nurse, 'it is very inconvenient when the police decide to put a guard on a patient. This is a busy hospital, and a police officer sitting outside a ward is most certainly in the way!'

Jess saw an opening. 'If there's nothing on the phone, that won't be necessary.'

Outmanoeuvred, the nurse conceded with poor grace.

Later, she and Ian Carter drove out into a darkening countryside to a small pub offering food and consoled themselves with calorie-laden fish and chips.

'I don't know about you,' Jess said, 'but I don't eat fried food too much – or I try not to. So I reckon I can indulge for once. It's comfort food, I know, but that's what I feel I need just now!'

'Likewise,' said Carter briefly.

'Sorry, didn't mean to be tactless. You're still worrying about Millie and her mother.'

'I'm not worrying about Sophie. I am, of course, worried about Millie. Sophie will do as she wants; she always did. No doubt Rodney will prove an excellent father. He seems to be good at everything he turns his hand to. But I'm not going to talk about that this evening. By the way, how is that brother of yours? Is he still in one of the world's danger spots, dispensing medical aid?'

'Simon? Yes, he is. But he's coming back for some leave next month.' Jess paused, and added, 'We're always relieved when we actually see him. It's never certain. Things are really bad where he is at the moment.'

'I understand,' he said sympathetically. 'How is your mother coping with it all?'

'Amazingly well, considering. She's always been very supportive of Simon.'

'And of you?' He raised his eyebrows.

'Yes, up to a point. She says she doesn't understand me.' Jess managed a wry grin.

'She doesn't understand why you chose a career in the police?'

'She's never understood it, but she does now accept it's my decision. What she'd really like are grandchildren. The way things are, Simon isn't going to be settling down any time soon.'

'And you?' Ian asked, lifting his glass of wine to his lips.

'I've no plans,' Jess said firmly.

After that, they both concentrated on eating and, when conversation started up again, it was, inevitably, about work.

'Perhaps,' said Jess optimistically, 'Dave Nugent, our very own computer whizz, will magic up something from those photos Sally took.' She paused. 'I was asked at the hospital if Sally was a vital witness. The nurse was concerned we might put an officer on watch at the door of the ward. The hospital finds that an inconvenience. I said it would not be necessary. But perhaps, in view of what the farmer, Biddle, told Phil, we should consider it? Someone knocked her off her bike deliberately and was searching her for something, presumably this phone, as she lay in the ditch. That person doesn't know I've removed Sally's phone from the ward.'

'A hit and run on a quiet country road in darkness is one thing,' Carter said. 'It's a cowardly act, even if driven by desperation. Marching boldly into a busy hospital, where anyone might see and remember you, is another matter. I don't think our killer has that kind of courage.'

But Carter, for once, was wrong. One of the many things about hospital routine to have changed over the years is the time allowed for visiting patients, now much more generous than in years gone by. One thing unchanged is serving the last meal of the day at an early hour. So, by six-thirty, dinner had come and gone, and now the dimly lit corridors and wards saw a continual to and fro of outsiders visiting relatives and friends.

No one took any notice of a slim figure in jeans and a leather jacket, with a black woollen beanie pulled down over their ears. It was cold outside, and any number of visitors wore such head-gear. The visitor glanced into one or two wards before reaching the one where Sally was.

Sally had fallen asleep again. It had taken the last of her energy to stay awake for supper. Her unconsciousness suited the visitor just fine. A hand reached out, the curtains glided along the rails surrounding the bed and made it into an individual private cubicle. Quickly, the visitor looked in the bedside cabinet, examining anything that might contain something small and flat, like a mobile phone. But there was nothing.

The visitor hesitated, looking down at the sleeping Sally. In the chair, on the other side of the bed, an extra pillow had been left. The visitor circled the bed, reached out and picked up the pillow. Sally stirred. The visitor froze, pillow gripped in both hands. Sally drifted back into slumber. The visitor, after a moment's hesitation, reached out with the pillow.

At that moment, a buzz signalled that the patient in the next bed had rung for attention. Sally's visitor froze again. Rapid footsteps heralded the approach of a nurse. Soon, voices were speaking, patient and nurse, right beside the visitor in the beanie hat, only the curtain between them. That was too close for comfort. The pillow was dropped back on the chair. The visitor slipped between the drawn curtains and out of the ward, walking rapidly away down the corridor.

The nurse attending to the patient who had summoned help saw, from the corner of her eye, a dark shape flit across her vision. She frowned, murmured, 'One moment!' to her patient, and pulled aside Sally's curtains and bent over the girl in the bed.

Sally slept on undisturbed. The nurse was satisfied.

But someone else wasn't. Tom Palmer, having sat at home and brooded about Sally's accident, had decided he had to do something. He'd drive to the hospital and visit her, satisfy himself she was on the mend. Jess had phoned him in the afternoon to tell him she'd seen and spoken to Sally. But that wasn't good enough. He had to see her for himself.

The hospital was full of those muffled sounds that echo through the corridors at the end of the day. Voices were pitched low. An elderly woman in a pink dressing gown was being wheeled along. There were a few visitors, either arriving or leaving, and no one took any notice of Tom. He didn't approach anyone for directions, because Jess had told him which ward Sally was in, and he set out confidently.

But as he approached the open doors with a view of occupied beds beyond, he saw, to his surprise, a figure slip out of the ward into the corridor in a manner that struck him as decidedly furtive. It was androgynous in appearance, wearing jeans and trainers, with a dark, leather-look jacket and a beanie pulled well down. The figure, exiting the ward, turned first in Tom's direction and then immediately spun round and made off at a brisk pace away from him.

'Hey!' called Tom instinctively.

The response from the receding figure was an increase in pace. Tom dashed into the ward and collided with an irate nurse.

'Did you shout out there in the corridor?' she demanded. 'Many of our patients are asleep—'

'Dr Palmer!' Tom said, dragging out his official pass. 'I don't work here. I work—' He stopped himself saying that his work was mostly in the morgue. Any patient overhearing might think he was up here hunting for bodies, like Dr Frankenstein's Igor.

The nurse, after a quick glance at his pass, understood. 'Yes, yes, Dr Palmer. What can we do for you?'

'I believe a patient named Sally Grove is on this ward. Has she had a visitor? Very recently, in the last few minutes.'

Uncertainty showed in the nurse's eyes. 'Well, I'm not sure. I was busy with another patient. I thought I saw someone leave. As a matter of fact, I did check on Sally, because a police officer was here earlier . . .'

But Tom had already darted past her and found Sally in the bed nearest the door. He bent over her anxiously. 'Sally? It's Tom Palmer. Can you hear me?'

To his relief, Sally mumbled, albeit incoherently, and then her eyelids flickered and opened. She looked up at him in confusion. 'Tom?'

'It's OK,' Tom said quickly. 'Take it easy. I'll be back in a minute or two.'

He spun round and hissed to the nurse, 'Call Security. Suspected intruder, slim build, leather jacket and woollen hat. Could be male or female.'

He hastened out into the corridor and down it in the direction he'd seen the visitor go. But there was no sign of that slim, dark figure and he realised that, whoever it had been, he or she had had time to reach an exit. There was one ahead of him. He hurried through it and looked around. It was night outside now and the artificial light provided gave sufficient illumination for traffic and pedestrians without allowing positive identification. Colours faded to a monochrome. There were dark figures all over the place. But then he saw one that was running away from the hospital building and had already covered some distance. Visitors didn't leave a hospital at a run, in his experience.

Tom dashed in pursuit, but the figure had vanished, apparently into one of the car parks. They were all fairly full. It was a popular visiting time. He ran up and down a few lines of vehicles, but the figure had disappeared. Frustrated, Tom returned to the hospital.

Security, in the form of one burly man and another, who was wiry and nervous-looking, had arrived now. He quickly explained the situation. While the two men set off to search the building, Tom took out his mobile and rang Jess Campbell.

Jess and Ian had finished their meal and moved on to coffee when Jess's phone rang.

'Sorry,' she said, and looked to see who was calling. 'It's Tom,' she added.

'Oh, for crying out loud!' exclaimed Carter. 'Can't he manage for one evening?' Then he saw that Jess was looking serious, and his expression sharpened. 'What?' he demanded.

'Tom went to visit Sally Grove, and it seems there may have been an intruder, trying to get to her. From Tom's description, it sounds very like the same person Biddle saw running down the road after Sally's accident.'

Within forty-five minutes the ward sister's worst fears were confirmed and a uniformed officer stood guard outside the ward where Sally lay.

Chapter 14

The examination of Sally's photos had taken on a new urgency, and they got to work early to begin. But it quickly proved frustratingly uninformative.

'Trees,' said Ian Carter. 'And more trees.'

'She specialises in painting trees,' Jess explained.

'I thought artists set up their easels or took their sketchpads out with them into the countryside?' said Phil Morton.

'Sally doesn't. She takes photos on her mobile phone and goes home and, if she likes one, she makes a painting out of it.'

'Run through them again!' ordered Carter.

They stood in a little group before DS Nugent's beloved computer as, once again, the sequence of photos taken by Sally Grove in Crooked Man Woods on the day of the murder appeared on the screen.

'Most of them are pretty good shots,' said Nugent. 'Until you get to the last ones. She seems to have gone a bit wild then and taken anything. Some of it is out of focus, and some of it is skew-whiff.'

'That was when she panicked,' Jess told him. 'She thought if the mystery person saw she was taking photos, they'd clear off.'

'If he was up to no good, isn't it more likely he'd try and grab the phone there and then?' argued Carter. 'Why wait and go to all the risk and trouble of knocking her off her bike later?'

'Because Sally was mistaken. The mystery visitor to the woods hadn't seen her snapping away among the trees. He didn't know anything about it until Tom got talking to her in the library and drew attention to the subject of the paintings. She explained to him about being in the woods and hearing something spooky.'

'So the murderer was in the library and—'

Nugent exclaimed, 'There's someone!'

They all leaned forward and peered at the screen. 'Where?' demanded Jess. 'Can you zoom in on it, Dave?'

'There's someone standing by that tree trunk,' muttered Carter. 'You can only see half of the outline, but I think it's a woman.'

'It might be a thin man,' warned Jess. 'It's not Tom Palmer, although he was in the woods that morning.'

'And it's not Carl Finch. He was broader than that, altogether beefier. That's a woman, for my money, but we can't see any detail of her. She has her back to the camera, but where is she looking?'

'Towards one of the paths, or he or she's standing on the side of one of the paths with his or her back to the trees. But the image is too fuzzy. The phone wasn't being held steady. I still think that could be a thin man,' Jess argued.

Further efforts by Nugent to improve the image proved fruitless.

They all stepped back from the computer and stared at one another.

'Well?' said Carter in exasperation. 'This is supposed to be a team effort! Perhaps someone can come up with *some* suggestion?'

'Team effort,' Jess repeated softly. 'Yes, you're right, sir, that's exactly what this has been!'

'Go on,' he said tersely.

'Didn't you say, right at the outset of this, that someone was playing games?'

'I did.' Carter nodded.

'They've all been giving us the runaround. I've said so from the beginning!' Morton put in aggressively. 'They're playing us for a set of idiots!'

Jess said slowly, 'Possibly some of them.' She turned to Carter. 'It's that Renault belonging to Finch. It's ridiculous that we can't find it. It has to be in the area. Someone's got it hidden. That has to be the answer.'

Morton said diffidently, 'I've got an idea. I don't know if it's haring down the wrong track but, well, it might be worth a try.'

'Go on, Sergeant,' Carter ordered.

'That woman, Tessa Briggs, she lives on a big property. It's not the size it was when it was a farm, but it's still a fair amount of land. When the place was a farm it was called Crooked Man Farm, the same name as the woods. So I reckon, if we consulted an old map showing the various agricultural holdings in the locality, we might find that the farmland once extended right down to the edge of the woods. There could be an old track from the woods to the farmyard. It could be disused now and overgrown but if someone knew where it was—'

'An old ordnance survey map of the area, that's what we need!' Jess burst out.

'There must be a set of those for Gloucestershire somewhere in the building,' Carter said. 'And unless they've been updated very recently, they will show Crooked Man Farm as it was before Briggs sold off most of it.'

The maps were indeed there, but it still took a while to find them. When they had been run to earth and the appropriate one spread out for inspection, they all bent over it eagerly.

'There you go!' said Jess triumphantly. 'There's the farm, and there's the woods. As the crow flies, it's scarcely more than half a mile across the fields from the boundary of the woods to the house where Tessa Briggs still lives.'

Morton pointed at the map. 'The farmyard buildings are used to garage her car and, apparently, there's a workshop that was once used by her former husband. But this big piece of land behind the house still belongs to her. She lets people graze their horses on it and provides stabling for them in the yard. There's an old barn – more of a large shed – about here' – he tapped the map – 'in the field where the horses graze. It's less than a quarter of a mile from the house and, according to this map, not much more from that to the woods. The land dips down to where the house is, and the woods are probably just over this ridge. But, for all that, you should be able to see the tips of the trees on a clear day from the house.'

They straightened up and looked at one another.

'We'll need a search warrant,' Carter said. 'In theory, Mrs Briggs should have no objection to us looking in a disused outbuilding on her property. But she's a lady who knows her rights – especially if she's got something to hide. We can't risk giving her time to move the car, if it is there.'

'So you're back!' Tessa greeted them. She stared at Jess. 'You've come along, too, I see. Usually, you just send the sergeant there to talk to me.'

266

She stood in the yard in working clothes, including her grubby gilet and boots, arms folded, and Fred in attendance at her side. The grey horse was tethered by the stables and, judging by the brush in Tessa's hand, she had been busy grooming him.

'We haven't come today just to talk, Mrs Briggs. We've come to take a look around the outbuildings on your property. We have a search warrant.' Jess held it out.

Tessa took it and scanned it briefly before handing it back. 'Go ahead!' she said briefly.

There was a note of resignation in her voice. Jess thought in triumph, *we're going to find the car! She knows that, and she can't prevent it.*

'We'll begin with the barn and the stables here,' she said.

'Then give me a minute to put Misty back in the paddock.'

As she was being so co-operative, they waited while Tessa untethered the grey and led him past them to the meadow beyond. When she returned, she said briefly, 'All yours.'

They started with the barn Tessa used as a garage but, predictably, they found nothing unexpected, only her jeep and some sacks of pony nuts and chaff. There was a work bench in one corner with some cobwebbed, stained paint pots. Tessa stood watching them, her arms folded defensively. The collie, Fred, had come to press himself against her legs and looked up at her anxiously.

'We'd like to look in that other building over there, in the meadow,' Jess said.

A curious expression crossed Tessa's face, half a smile and half a grimace of resignation. 'Go on, then.'

'You know what we're looking for, I think, Mrs Briggs.'

'Do I? What if I say I don't?'

'I believe you do,' Jess told her gently. 'That's why we brought the search warrant.'

'Don't tell us,' Morton put in, 'that you don't know what's in your own shed there.'

'I might not. It's not in use these days. But that isn't going to wash with you, is it?' Tessa took a deep breath. 'Am I allowed to make a phone call?'

'You're not under arrest, Mrs Briggs. Do you feel you need a lawyer?'

'I'm not intending to phone my solicitor; at least, not yet. It's someone else.'

Jess considered her. 'Perhaps better not. I'd rather you came with us to the shed.'

The three horses threw up their heads and watched curiously as the little group of people made a slow but inexorable progress across the meadow, Fred running back and forth around the humans, as if he wanted to herd them.

The building was dilapidated but it still had its double doors, and they were padlocked. Jess peered through a gap in the planks. A large shape, covered with a tarpaulin, could be distinguished in the dim interior.

'If you don't have a key to this padlock on you, Mrs Briggs, perhaps you'd fetch it from the house? Sergeant Morton will accompany you. Please don't say it's lost. We'll break in if you do.'

Tessa said nothing, only turned away with a sullen expression and set off back across the meadow, Phil Morton following close behind and Fred the collie circling them both anxiously.

When they returned with the key and the doors were pulled open, dusty air and a strong odour of ancient hay and other animal foodstuffs once stored here filled their nostrils. Jess stifled a sneeze and Morton took out a handkerchief and blew his nose noisily. 'I've got an allergy,' he muttered. 'This won't do it any good!'

The empty space beneath the steepled roof, and the silence, suggested a deserted church, but without pews or pulpit. The building contained only the draped shape of a car. Morton dragged away the tarpaulin and the Renault was revealed, neatly parked.

'We believe this to be the car driven by Carl Finch,' Jess said.

'Do you now? Well, I'm not going to argue about it.' Tessa sounded quite resigned, but there was still a trace of the old combativeness, mostly in her attitude. She stared Jess in the face. 'How did you work it out? I mean, that it was here?'

'The car had to be somewhere, Mrs Briggs, and not too far from the woods. We consulted a map.'

'Simple as that, eh? Oh, well, if I'd left it where it was, you'd have found it. So it comes to the same thing, in the end, doesn't it? I've only delayed things.'

'You've tried to delay our investigations from the start, Mrs Briggs.'

'Not much good at it, though, am I? You got to the woods ahead of me and now you're here. Fred! Leave that!' The collie was scratching at the floor in the corner of the building. 'Probably smells of rats,' said Tessa. 'We used to get them in here in the old days, when the feed was stored here.'

'We'd like you to come with us now, Mrs Briggs, for a formal interview on record.'

'Can't I just make a statement?'

'You made one of those before, Mrs Briggs, in the woods, when the body was found.'

'And it was a load of codswallop. Yes, I know.' Tessa swallowed.

'And this new statement will be recorded, for use as evidence.'

'All very official, eh? Then I'll have to come with you. Now do I get the one phone call, to my solicitor?'

'If you wish.'

'Better have him there, or Hal will kick up a rumpus.'

'Who is Hal?' asked Jess.

'My ex-husband. He turned up, first time in years. He'd heard about Carl, you see. Bad news always travels fast. What about the car?'

'It will be taken away for forensic examination. You may have cleaned it up, but if there's the smallest fingerprint or hair, or anything, Forensics will find it.'

'Bully for them!' snapped Tessa. 'And Fred? I can't leave him here for an indefinite length of time. Can we drop him off at the Old Nunnery?'

'I'd rather we didn't call by there,' Jess said.

'All right. Well, Ron Purcell lives about a quarter of a mile down the road, towards Weston St Ambrose. 'Perhaps he'd look after Fred for a few hours. He's a local man,' she added. 'He used to play in the cricket team with my former husband – and with Carl. Everyone knew everyone else in Weston St Ambrose, in the old days.'

Morton remembered that thin, ascetic-looking man gazing out at the landscape. *You could have told me a lot more than you did, if you'd wanted to*, he thought. *But, like she says, they all know one another – and they all stick together.*

Aloud, he asked, 'Do you really want your neighbour to know that you've been taken in for questioning, Mrs Briggs?'

Tessa shrugged. 'It'll get about pretty quickly, anyway.'

You're darned right it will! seethed Morton. *Jungle telegraph has nothing on it!*

'Anyway,' Tessa added, 'I want to know Fred's all right, and he will be, with Ron.'

'Right, Mrs Briggs, perhaps you'd like to tell us about it from the beginning.'

Tessa sat upright on a chair beside her solicitor. 'This is being recorded, like you said?'

'Yes, it is.'

'Well, then, there isn't much to tell you. I came across the car and realised it must be Carl's.'

'Where and when did you find it?'

A gleam appeared in Tessa's eye. 'Oh, straight away! I found it while you coppers were still blundering about around the body. I'd hoped to get to him before you, after Hattie told me about it. But you know all about that, don't you? All right, it was a daft idea and it messed about with your investigations. But we were trying to keep Guy Kingsley out of things.

'Anyway, as you know, it didn't work. I got there only to find you – the police – all over the scene. It shook me pretty badly. I did manage to get a good look at Carl, and I recognised him, even though his face was such a mess. I needed to think it out, calm down, pull myself together. I also knew I had to get to the Old Nunnery before you did. You'd taken my address and then clearly wanted me out from under your feet, so I left. I walked on through the woods with the dog and came out at the service road. The Renault was there, parked up under the trees. That must be Carl's, I thought.'

'But you didn't come back and inform the officers at the scene.'

'No,' said Tessa briefly.

'Why not?'

'Because I didn't know what the hell was going on! As far as I could see, the wretched man had blown himself away. He was always a nuisance. That doesn't mean I didn't feel any pity for him. It was sad, of course. Not least because it made problems for everyone else! Don't forget, I didn't have time to think it through. I wanted to get to Guy and Hattie before you did, and I didn't have much time. I didn't want to waste more, trailing back to where you were and leading you to the car, so I just acted on instinct. People don't always act sensibly when they're in shock, do they? Well, I was very shocked, and I thought I'd take a look inside the car, to see if there was anything in there confirming it was Carl's.'

'It wasn't locked?' Jess asked.

'No, if it had been, I couldn't have taken it. I'm not one of the local tearaways. I don't know about breaking into locked cars and fiddling about with the wiring.' She leaned forward slightly. 'What's more, it wasn't just that it was unlocked. The driver's door was *open* – ajar. The key was in the ignition. It was as if he'd just got out, walked into the woods, abandoning the car, and killed himself.'

Tessa heaved a sigh. 'It helped confirm to me that that's what must have happened. "Farewell, cruel world! Don't need the car any more. Just leave it." Well, that's what I suspected, then.

'Before I'd thought about it, I'd pushed Fred into the back, got in and driven it on down the track. It peters out when it reaches the farmland, but there's a gate. I opened it, drove through, and carried on driving across open country until I got to my place. It was all one farm at one time, you see, and there's an old dirt road the tractors used.

'By then I'd panicked, realising what I'd done. I needed time to work out some plan of action. The disused feed store was the obvious place to hide it, until later. So I drove it in there. Then I went back to the car park at the woods for my own car. I didn't walk all the way round by the road. I cut across the fields and through the trees. I could hear you all, and more of your vehicles arriving. But I kept clear of that spot and managed to slip into the car park and retrieve my jeep. I drove over to the Old Nunnery to tell Guy and Harriet what had happened to Carl. I didn't tell them about the Renault, because I hadn't decided what to do about it. I needed time to think about that, and I wouldn't have had time, if I'd told Guy Kingsley. He'd have taken over, insisted on phoning you immediately. He did that when I told him I'd recognised the dead man as Carl.

'The reality, of course, was that I was stuck with the wretched Renault. I just left it there in the feed store, where you've just found it.'

'Did you attempt to clean it up? Inside, or on the door handles?'

'Yes, of course I did. I started rubbing away to clean off my fingerprints, and I swept out the back where Fred had been. My long-term intention was to come back when you'd all gone and move the car again, wearing gloves, and abandon it somewhere else, put a match to it, possibly. But I didn't get a chance. You were all over the place. He—' she pointed.

Jess said, for the benefit of the recording, 'The witness has indicated Sergeant Morton.'

'He turned up at the house. I was afraid then he might go poking about the place, in the outbuildings. But he didn't. He pushed off, and I breathed a sigh of relief – but the relief didn't last long. I should have owned up there and then, shouldn't I? I could have taken your Sergeant Morton to the car. But I didn't, and that made the situation worse.' Tessa paused, and added quietly, 'It felt like being stuck in a quagmire. I couldn't get out, and I was sinking. I was desperate to get rid of the car, but it just seemed too risky to try moving it. Once you'd gone, Sergeant, I relaxed a bit. It gave me some breathing space. I decided to wait a while, until things had calmed down. But they didn't quieten down. People kept turning up. Even that harpy from London, Natalie Adam, she turned up.'

'She's still in the neighbourhood?' asked Morton, startled.

'You bet she is,' returned Tessa gloomily. 'She came here, making a fuss. Hal – my ex-husband – was here, as it happens, and sent her packing. She was yelling at us until the last.'

'Was her man companion with her? Fellow with ginger hair?'

'No, she was on her own. She said the chap who was with her before, at the Old Nunnery, had gone back to London. Well, anyway, that's it.'

'There is nothing else you'd like to add?'

There was a brief silence. Then Tessa said, 'In case you're wondering, I didn't blow Carl Finch away.'

'Mrs Briggs!' exclaimed the solicitor in alarm.

Tessa glanced at him and shrugged. 'Well, it's going to be the next question, isn't it? Did I kill him? I'd felt like doing it often enough over the years.' She ignored the solicitor's frantic protests. 'But it's like lots of things you fantasise about doing and know you won't. I didn't blast Carl away. I can't give you a logical explanation of why I moved the damn car. I just did it. It just, well, seeing it sitting there with the door open and the keys in the ignition . . . It was a sort of invitation.'

'Yes,' said Carter grimly later. 'That's exactly what it was! An invitation to any youngsters, travellers, any wanderer about the countryside, to take it for a joyride and, with any luck, torch it afterwards. If it had been left in a more frequented spot, that would have happened within an hour or less. But the killer didn't have time to move it to the side of the main road. The killer needed to get out of there fast, so the car was abandoned to its fate. Unfortunately, Tessa Briggs came along and decided to drive it away. She meant to hide it. What she actually did was preserve it intact. You might say she did us a favour.'

Jess said thoughtfully, 'Why do you think she moved it?'

'You don't accept her explanation that she was in a fog of shock? It led her to act on the spur of the moment?'

'Not really, no.' Jess took time to marshal her argument, and Carter waited. 'She had already hatched that plot with Harriet Kingsley to go to the woods and "find" the body. She was thinking clearly enough at that point. That doesn't mean it wasn't a daft idea, but she's got it all worked out, even so. Off she goes to the woods. She knew Carl Finch's body would be there. Harriet had told her exactly where to find him and had described his injuries. It must still have been a distressing sight for Tessa, but she was prepared for it. And she's a pretty tough lady! So *that* wasn't a shock, either. The only thing she wasn't prepared for was to find us already on the spot. That *was* a shock. So, what does she do? Answer: she thinks fast. She immediately tramples the area around the body, under pretence of trying to catch the dog, until she's ordered away. That took care of any footprints. She then left us to walk on down to the service road – she knew where it was, she walks her dog in those woods all the time – and there's the car. She doesn't hesitate, doesn't doubt for a minute it's Finch's car. She gets in and drives it away. She hides it and, despite having the opportunity when Phil called by her house, she doesn't admit it. She does admit to trying to clean away her own fingerprints, and the dog's hair. But I'm beginning to wonder if it's more than just her fingerprints she's worried about.'

'Go on,' Carter said quietly when she paused.

'She wanted to hide that car and clean it out because Finch's blood is in it.' Jess leaned forward. 'It's been a puzzle from the first to know exactly where Finch died. It wasn't where he was found. The other puzzle was the missing Renault. Doesn't it make sense that the two puzzles are linked? That's where he died. In the car.'

Chapter 15

Guy Kingsley intercepted them at the front of the house. 'Now what do you want? And why so many of you?' He looked past Carter, Jess and Phil Morton towards the figures of Tracy Bennison and Dave Nugent emerging from a second car. 'Every time you come it's more bad news! Hattie's had enough!'

'It's your wife we've come to talk to,' Carter told him.

'Look, is this absolutely necessary?' Guy's face reddened, the muscles around his mouth twitched and his voice rose to a shout.

'Calm down, Captain Kingsley,' Carter advised him. 'Losing your temper won't help, and it won't prevent us talking to your wife.'

'Not unless I'm there!' Guy told him hoarsely. 'The state she's in, she could crack apart and shatter like a piece of glass. What is it you want to talk to her about?'

'We must see your wife now,' Jess said. 'You are impeding us.'

There was a wild look in Guy's eyes, and he stood with his back to the front door like an animal at bay. Jess knew that Phil Morton, standing to the rear of the little group, had tensed. Then Guy muttered, 'All right, but I repeat: not without me!'

'Sorry, can't be done. We need to speak to her alone. Later, perhaps, you can join us.' Carter's tone brooked no opposition. 'So, if you'd just wait here with Sergeant Morton?'

'I'm phoning our solicitor!' Guy snarled.

'That might be advisable later, sir, if Mrs Kingsley wishes it. But now, if you please, allow us to see your wife.'

Harriet was sitting in her father's former study, now the sitting room, huddled in the Queen Anne chair, her favoured refuge. She looked pale and tired and, when she saw her visitors, very frightened.

'It's all right, Harriet,' Jess soothed her. 'We've come to tell you we've found Carl's Renault.'

Harriet whispered, 'Where?'

Jess ignored the question. 'It will be subject to forensic examination. That will be thorough. People often think they can clean away evidence. But that's seldom – almost never – possible.'

Harriet made an almost imperceptible movement of her head, signifying disbelief or refusal.

'We believe we'll find traces of Carl's blood, and that he died in the car, where it was originally parked on the service road on the far side of the woods. The car was later moved.'

Harriet was shaking her head as Jess spoke. 'No, no! He was in the woods. He was sitting on the ground. His back was against a tree trunk.' Harriet spoke the words with a dogged resolve. 'I saw him. Tessa saw him. You all saw him.'

'Because someone dragged his body into that position. Someone who didn't want us to know he'd died in the car.'

Harriet was shaking her head. 'No, no.' She swallowed and struggled for some composure. 'I don't understand. Why wasn't it – why couldn't you find it earlier? Someone moved it, you say. Who? How did you find it?'

'Mrs Briggs has owned up to driving it across the fields to a disused building on her land. She also tried to clean the interior.'

Harriet let out a long, low, almost animal moan. 'Oh, no! Tessa! Why didn't she leave it? Why did she do it?'

'She says she had hoped to move the car again at a later date, torch it, possibly. But there was too much going on to do that safely.' Jess paused. 'However, Mrs Briggs denies killing Carl.'

Harriet gripped the arms of the chair and leaned forward, infused with a sudden burst of energy. 'Of course she didn't! She wouldn't kill him!' The energy drained out of her, and she became as listless as before. She sighed and leaned her head against the chair back. Her gaze drifted past Jess, towards her mother's portrait on the far wall.

She's been sitting here, in that very spot, over many years, looking at that portrait, Jess thought. For all she claimed to be happy for her father when he remarried, had she resented the coming of Nancy – and Nancy's child? She and her father must have been close after her mother's death. Or had he been often absent, leaving her to that succession of nannies she spoke of before? Had she hoped that, when he remarried, and Nancy and Carl moved into the house, her father would spend more time at home? Everyone agrees she and Carl were close as children.

Then something about Harriet's line of vision struck her. A tingle ran up Jess's spine. Without turning her head, she mapped the further wall in her head. The bookcases, two with modern volumes in them and one with tightly packed old leather spines. Spines! It was as if a bright light suddenly lit the room. The spines of old volumes did not necessarily mean the books to which they had once been attached were present. Harriet wasn't looking towards the portrait. She was staring at the bookcase.

Jess got to her feet and, under Carter's surprised eyes, walked across the floor to the bookcase. She touched the old leather spines and tapped them. They were hard and ungiving, and there was a faint noise, as if knocking on wood. She turned to Harriet, who was watching her, as if mesmerised.

'It's false – it's a door,' Jess said to Harriet. 'How does it open?'

'It just swings out,' Harriet replied in the same low voice. 'There used to be a catch, but it was broken years ago.'

Jess put out her hand and pressed the leather spines on the right. Nothing moved. She put her hand on the spines to the left and tried again. Now the wooden door, with its rows of false books, pivoted on a hidden metal pole and swung open, as Harriet had said it would. Carter, behind her, gave an exclamation of surprise.

Revealed was a recess the thickness of the old wall. It was empty, but marks in the dust on the floor indicated that something had been there until recently.

Jess returned to Harriet and sat down again before her. 'You told us your father didn't have a shotgun,'

Harriet made no reply.

'Someone in this house did.'

'Guy,' whispered Harriet. 'But you've seen it.'

'We think there was another gun. Is that where it was kept, in that hidden cupboard?' Jess prompted. 'Let me ask you again. Did it belong to your father?'

Harriet replied in a voice little more than a murmur, 'No – yes, in a way. It was my grandfather's.'

'Did your father ever use it? Show you how to use it?'

'When I was little, he sometimes used to go out early and shoot rabbits. They – the rabbits – used to get into our vegetable garden. But he didn't do that after Nancy came to live here. She didn't like guns, or any weapons, and she wouldn't have let him kill anything! She was a vegetarian, and all about nature being sacred, and so on, as I told you. She'd been a peace campaigner, too, at one time, marching with a banner, that sort of thing. So my father hid the gun away.'

'Did your husband know it was there?'

Animation flooded Harriet's face. She leaned forward, gripping the arms of the chair. 'No! No, Guy didn't know anything about it! I'd almost forgotten it myself! I only remembered it when—' She broke off.

'Mrs Kingsley,' Jess asked gently, 'would you like to come with us and make a statement? You can have a solicitor present, if that is your wish.'

Before Harriet could reply, they were rudely interrupted. There was a shout from Phil Morton outside. 'Stop right there!'

But the door to the room flew open with a crash and, like an avenging angel, Natalie Adam appeared. Her face was white, her eyes huge and staring. She raised a trembling hand and pointed at Harriet, who shrank back into the chair.

'You – you killed him, you cold-blooded, grasping bitch!'

Morton, almost purple with rage, appeared, panting, with Guy Kingsley on his heels. He grabbed Natalie's arm and she spun to face him, shrieking, 'Let me go, you ape!'

'How did she get past you?' Carter demanded angrily of Morton.

Morton, wrestling with the furious Natalie, gasped, 'She came

281

in through the kitchen, sir, at the back of the house. She ran up the corridor from that direction and got this door open before I could get past Kingsley! He was blocking the way.'

'Miss Adam, you are under arrest!' Carter snapped. 'Read her her rights, Sergeant!'

'Rights?' Natalie yelled. 'Yes, everyone has rights, don't they? Except poor Carl! She killed him! She killed my brother!'

There was a stunned silence. Carter found his voice first. 'What do you mean? *Your* brother?'

'That's right! *My* brother!' Having succeeded in temporarily silencing them all, the words came tumbling out of her. 'Nancy, my natural mother, made the decision to put me up for adoption at birth. I don't blame her. It must have been a tough decision, and she thought she was doing the best thing for me.'

Harriet, in the chair, was swaying back and forth, muttering, 'No, no.'

Natalie carried on. 'I grew up in a comfortable, middle-class household, and everything was fine, except in one way. There was a gap in my personal history. I'd been told the truth of my origins very early on. My adoptive mother believed it would be less of a shock if I knew pretty well from the start. It didn't worry me. I was happy. But when I was twenty, my adoptive parents retired to live in Italy, and I decided that I'd like to find my birth mother. By the time I'd traced Nancy – it took quite a while – it was to find out I was too late. She'd died. But a former neighbour told me she remembered Nancy and her little boy, Carl, very well. Carl? I hadn't known anything about him! I had a brother!'

Behind them all, in the hall, Guy had overheard, and they

heard him exclaim, 'Nancy! I might have guessed she was at the root of all this!'

Harriet had wrapped her arms around herself and was swaying to and fro.

Natalie demanded of her, 'Can you imagine what that meant to me?'

Harriet whispered, 'Yes.'

'I wasn't going to lose him again! It took me ages to track Carl down, and there were gaps when I couldn't devote as much time to the hunt as I wanted because of other commitments. But three years ago, I found him!' Nancy's voice rose in triumph. 'When I told him who I was, do you know what he did? He cried. He told me all about himself, and how happy he'd been after Nancy married John Hemmings, because he had a great childhood here in this house, and John had treated him in every way as a son. Then, when Hemmings died, the ground just collapsed under his feet. He'd been cut off with a measly sum and just abandoned by that other sister – her.' Natalie pointed at the cowering Harriet. In a voice that echoed with hate she said, 'I believe she killed him. Or her husband did. I'd found my brother, and she – *she took him away from me again!*'

So fascinated had they been by this story that all of them were watching Natalie. Harriet was temporarily ignored. Now, the Queen Anne chair rocked on its feet as Harriet was suddenly galvanised into action, leaping up and pushing it away from her. She crossed the room, darting past them before they could stop her. A second later and she was through the open door and in the hall beyond.

'Stop her!' Carter shouted.

Morton was still gripping Natalie by the arm. The few seconds it took to release her and turn to pursue Harriet were enough for Harriet to reach the open front door. But there, she came face to face with Guy Kingsley.

Guy shouted, 'Hattie, darling, no!' He stepped forward, his arms held wide open to stop her running out of the house.

Harriet whirled and fled away from him, across the hall and up the wide staircase.

'What the hell—' muttered Carter, as he and Jess started in pursuit. 'Where's she going?'

He, Jess, Morton, Natalie and Guy were now all in the hall, and tangled together. Carter was bellowing at Morton to take Natalie outside. Jess tore herself from the group and raced up the staircase. She could hear the thud of Harriet's feet above her head, climbing higher and higher. When Jess turned the newel post at the top of the stair on to the upper floor, she had a fleeting sight of Harriet at the far end of a long corridor, beginning to climb another, narrower staircase.

Jess ran down the corridor, realising that Guy was at her heels. He was shouting to his wife to stop. But by the time they reached the small staircase, Harriet had got to the top, where there was a door. She pushed it open, dived through it and slammed it in their faces, seconds before Jess could grasp her. They heard the click of a key turned in the lock.

'Harriet!' Jess shouted. She rattled the handle of the door, fruitlessly. 'Harriet, open the door!'

She turned to the panting Guy and demanded, 'What's up there?'

'Former maids' rooms, and the rest of the attic.'

When the Kingsleys had spoken of old furniture and unwanted

items stored in the attic, Jess had automatically imagined one long, large open space. But, of course, a house this size had had, years ago, a permanent staff. Bedrooms for them had been created above their heads, beneath the roof.

Carter had caught up with them.

'She's locked herself in the attics,' Jess told him briefly. 'Where's Natalie?'

'Morton's taken her outside to give into the charge of Bennison and Nugent.' He glared at Guy. 'Have you got a key?'

'For the attics? No, there's only the one, and it's kept in the lock. Well, there might be another – probably is – but I have no idea where.' Guy's expression was one of desperation, but also resolve. 'I'll break the door down.'

'That will spook her even more,' Jess argued. 'We'll try and persuade her to open it.'

'You don't understand!' Guy burst out. 'She'd have time to get out.'

Carter asked quickly, 'There's a second point of access? Where?'

Guy shook his head, his face desperate. 'There's no other way *in*. There is a way *out*! It's through a trapdoor in the ceiling. It lets you get out on to the roof.'

Pounding footsteps announced the arrival of Morton. 'She's in the car, and Tracy is doing her best to calm her down,' he said. 'Where's Mrs Kingsley?'

Jess pointed to the locked door. 'In the attics. We'll have to break the door down if she won't open up and come out.' In a lower voice, she added, 'She's able to get out on to the roof, and she's very distressed.'

She turned back to the door and knocked on it. 'Harriet? It's

Jess Campbell. We understand you're scared, but just open the door and we can talk.'

There was no reply. Carter asked Kingsley, 'What is the roof like? Very steep?'

'It slopes from the eaves up to the chimney pots. But the incline isn't too bad and, if you slip, there is a parapet. It's not very high, but it would stop anyone working up there – doing repairs, or maybe a chimney sweep in the old days – from falling right off. But it's only a low parapet. Anyone could climb over it,' Guy told him miserably.

'You think your wife might climb over it and jump off?'

'She's bloody scared!' Guy snapped. 'You've frightened her out of her wits, and that damn woman claiming to be Carl's natural sister was the last straw!'

'Go down and outside, Sergeant,' Carter ordered. 'See if you can spot her up there on the roof and phone up to us her exact position.'

'Yes, sir!' Morton clattered away.

'We need a trained negotiator,' Carter said to Jess.

'With respect, there's no time to wait for that,' Jess replied.

'Of course we can't hang about here doing nothing while you wait for some other person to get here from miles away!' Guy exploded. 'Hattie!' he roared at the door. 'Hattie, please, open up and let me in!'

From the other side of the door came a clatter, and they held their breaths. But Hattie didn't come to the door. Then Jess's phone jangled.

'She's climbing out on to the roof!' Morton's voice said in her ear. 'I can see her head and shoulders.'

But Guy had overheard. He lunged forward, hurling himself at the door, and it splintered around the lock and flew open. Carried forward by his weight and impetus, Guy tumbled through it, blocking the space for the others. By the time they had scrambled into the attics, Harriet had disappeared.

The trapdoor was open, and a ladder leading up to it had been pulled down. Light was pouring through the open hatch, together with a cold fresh breeze sweeping through the attics.

'She's on the roof,' Jess muttered to Carter. 'We can't wait for a negotiator.'

'If one of you goes up there, you'll spook her even more and she – she could do something . . .' Guy's voice stammered into silence. 'Let me,' he begged. 'Let me talk to her.'

'I can't do that,' said Jess quietly. 'It's my job.'

Unexpectedly, Guy replied in a quite a different tone, calm, authoritative. 'Sorry, Inspector Campbell, but it really is mine, you know.'

Before she could prevent it, he had dodged past her and Carter, crossed the floor and was climbing the short hatch ladder.

Jess started after him, but Carter caught her arm. 'If Harriet hears a scuffle, it will unsettle her even more. We have to let him try.'

'Phil?' Jess put her phone to her ear. 'Can you see her now?'

'Yes,' came Morton's voice in her ear. 'She's standing just above the eaves, behind a sort of ornamental stone parapet, not very high. She's just staring out. Hang on a minute, someone else is coming through the hatch, a man – it looks like Kingsley!'

'It is Kingsley,' Jess told him.

'Damn!' muttered Carter beside her. 'We should have prevented him.'

'He's talking to her,' said Morton's voice.

'How near is he to her?'

'Too far away to grab her. He's just talking to her.'

In the attic, at the foot of the ladder leading up to the roof, Carter and Jess held their breath and strained to catch the sound of Guy's voice. It came faintly, drifting down from above their heads.

'Take my hand, darling. Just move a little to your left and you'll be able to do that. I won't move. I'll stay here. Hattie?'

Then Harriet's voice, even fainter, replying, 'It shouldn't have happened. I didn't want it to happen. It was an accident.'

'Of course you didn't mean it, darling. Nobody believes that you did. I don't care what happened at the woods. You were under great stress, and Carl was a fool. He should have kept away. Hattie? I don't care what you did, we can sort it out, but please, just move a little to your left so I can take your hand.'

'He's holding out his hand,' said Morton's voice in Jess's ear. 'But she's not moving. She's still standing there like a blooming statue, staring out.'

Then Harriet's voice again, asking, unexpectedly, 'Where is that woman?'

'Natalie?' Guy sounded surprised but then went on calmly, 'The police have taken her into custody. You don't have to worry about her any more.'

'Is she really Carl's sister?'

'She says so.'

'How much she must hate me.'

'I wouldn't let that trouble you, Hattie. She's a pretty fierce sort of person and probably has a list of people she hates. They probably can't stand her! Come on, Hattie. Does it matter? About Natalie? I'm here, and I love you. Does anything else matter?'

Morton's voice spoke in Jess's ear again: 'She's turned her head towards Kingsley. Otherwise, she hasn't moved, but she does seem to be paying attention to what he's saying.'

Kingsley pleaded, 'For my sake, Hattie, please? Forget the others, they don't matter. They never did.'

Morton, his voice full of suppressed emotion, hissed, 'She's moving! I think, yes, she is! She's edging towards Kingsley – oh, hell!'

'What's happening?' Jess demanded.

'She's wobbling . . . she looks as if she's going to faint . . . she's tipping forward . . .'

There was a scrabbling from above their heads, the sounds breaking into the quiet, like a salvo of gunfire. Carter called up the ladder, 'Kingsley! I'm coming up there.'

Then Guy's voice in reply, panting but triumphant, 'No, no, it's OK. I've got her. There isn't room for another person. Come on, Hattie, bear up! I'll guide you. Hold me and put your foot on the top rung . . .'

So they descended, Harriet clinging to each rung of the ladder with a limpet grip and having to be cajoled into descending to the next lower one. At last, both she and Kingsley had reached the bottom rung and then the solid floor.

'OK, Phil,' said Jess into her phone. 'She's down safely. If anyone asked for a trained negotiator, cancel it.'

Chapter 16

'I've been trying to think,' Harriet said, crinkling her forehead, 'when it started. I suppose Carl began to ask for money as soon as the terms of my father's will were known. But I knew that Carl's envy and resentment had begun much earlier. For a while, I thought it started when I married Guy. Now I wonder if it was always there, even when we were children and I thought we were such good friends. It's a terrible thought.'

'It's hard to know what's going on in another person's mind,' Jess told her.

To herself, Jess was thinking, *it started when John Hemmings met Nancy and her little boy on that train.*

They sat in the small interview room, Carter and Jess on one side of the small table, Harriet and her solicitor on the other. The solicitor was an elderly man with silver hair and a moustache. His attitude towards his client seemed fatherly. *Family friend as well as family legal advisor*, thought Jess. *He must have known Harriet most of her life. Natalie guessed right about that. Or Carl told her the truth about that small point, at least.*

As for Harriet, she looked pale but seemed calm, almost resigned. *It's easier for her now we all know about it*, Jess's thoughts ran on. *Concealing what she'd done was worse, much worse, an intolerable strain. That's what sent her up on to the roof. I wonder, if Guy hadn't talked her down, I could have done it, or even a trained negotiator, if one could have been brought there in time.*

Aloud, she said, 'Let's start with Carl's last request for money.'

Harriet had seemed sunk in thought. Now she stirred and looked up. 'I'd told him so often,' she told them earnestly. 'I couldn't give him any more money. Guy and I – Guy's projects have cost us a lot. We've been hoping the guest accommodation plan would earn some of it back. But all the building work, furnishing the apartments – everything cost more than we'd originally expected. More than the money, Carl's continual grumbling and pestering threatened my relationship with my husband. Guy couldn't stand Carl. It was a mutual thing. I always knew Carl hated Guy. I suppose it was jealousy. At first I thought he was jealous because I cared more for Guy than I did for him. But then I began to realise it went deeper. He envied what we had – chiefly, the house. The house represented something special to him. I suppose it was security. Something he wanted and couldn't have. But in the end, I have to accept it was basically about money.'

'It very often is,' said Ian Carter. 'But this last time, you said, you were determined not to give Carl any more.'

'That's right. I couldn't, and I didn't want to. What Guy had said from the first was true. Every time I helped Carl out, it encouraged him to think I always would. He'd begun to consider it his right. He'd always said we influenced my father at the end of his life, but that's not true. My father had underestimated Carl, that's all.'

She fell silent again. The solicitor leaned towards her and asked quietly, 'All right, my dear?'

Harriet nodded. 'This time, I meant to make him really understand that the days when he could come to me with his money
troubles were over. I knew it would be difficult. He was begging
me to help him. I believe he was scared. But I had made up my
mind so I hardened my heart and told him "no".'

She paused. 'I didn't mean to kill him,' she said, looking them
full in the face. 'I never meant to do that. You have to believe
me. I didn't even know the gun was loaded.'

How many times have I heard that? thought Carter sadly. She
might not have meant to shoot him dead; perhaps only fire a
warning shot or to signal her resolve not to give way. But she'd
fired and Carl was dead. He realised that Harriet was looking at
him entreatingly, wanting him to say he believed her. But the
truth of her claim would be tested in court, and the decision
would not be his.

When he said nothing, Harriet plunged on. 'He was a dreadful
nuisance, and I knew he was behaving badly, but I loved him,
despite it all. But I still had to say I couldn't give any money.
"Tough love", they call it, don't they? He insisted on coming to
Gloucestershire to see me; and I knew I had to face him. Every
time that happened, it ended with my giving in. So I had to do
something to make him understand how determined I was.

'That's when I remembered my grandfather's old gun and where
Dad had hidden it, in the secret cupboard. He didn't want Nancy
to see it, you understand. If he'd put it in a normal gun cupboard,
she'd have known about it and insisted he got rid of it. But he
didn't want to do that because it had been his father's.'

'So you arranged to meet Carl in Crooked Man Woods?' Carter
prompted.

'Yes, so that Guy wouldn't know. I didn't want Tessa to know, either. She was as difficult as Guy about Carl. I arranged to meet him on the access road the maintenance workers use. This time of year, there isn't much going on in that line and I was fairly certain no one else would be parked there.'

She spread out her hands in a gesture of resignation. 'It went exactly as I'd dreaded it would. Carl refused to accept anything I said. He started on about Dad's will again. He was horrible about Guy. I had to do something. I turned and ran back to my car, grabbed the shotgun from the back seat, where I'd put it – and I pointed it at him.'

'That must have given him a shock!' observed Carter.

'I meant it to give him a shock. I wanted to make him understand I really wouldn't put up with his nonsense any longer. He was startled for a moment. Then, he asked, "Where the hell did you get that antique, Hattie?" and he laughed. Just laughed! I felt stupid and angry and – hopeless. Wasn't there anything I could do to make him understand?

'Then he shrugged and said: "Oh, all right, I can see there's no use talking to you now." He walked back to his car and opened the driver's side door. If he'd just got in and driven off, it would have been all right. But he paused and turned to face me, and called out, in such a casual way, "We'll discuss it again when you've calmed down."

'I yelled, "No, we won't!" The gun jumped in my hand – and it went off.'

There was a longer silence. Harriet drank some water. The solicitor asked her again if she wanted to go on, or to recommence later.

'No, I can go on,' she said. 'I just want to tell it all now. He fell back into the car. I ran up to him . . . his face – his face was dreadful. The lower half of it was a red mash. Above that his eyes were open, and he looked so surprised. But I knew he was dead. If he'd still been alive and badly injured, I'd have called an ambulance, I really would! But he was dead and I was standing there with a corpse.

'I tried to think what I should do. I know I should have called the police immediately, or Guy, but I had an insane idea I could cover up what had happened. People shoot themselves, don't they? I mean, if they're desperate or something? Surely I could make it look as if Carl had shot himself?

'I had driving gloves in my car so I went back and got them, put them on. Then I went back to his Renault. I pushed his legs into the car and shut the driver's door. Then I went round to the passenger side and opened that door. I leaned in and somehow managed to drag him across – not completely, but enough to allow me to go back to the driver's side and squeeze into that seat. I drove, with him slumped against me, down one of the tracks into the woods. I pulled him out. It was unbelievably difficult. I can't tell you how hard it was. He was so heavy and unwieldy. I thought I'd pull my arms out of the sockets trying to haul him out. But sheer panic and desperation gave me the strength, I suppose. I propped him against the trunk of a tree that had been felled. I wiped my fingerprints off the gun and tried to put his on them. That didn't work, did it?' she asked suddenly of Carter.

'No, Carter said. 'It didn't. It's a difficult thing to do.'

Harriet sighed. 'I behaved stupidly in every way. I knew he was going to be found, but if I could delay any link with me or the

Old Nunnery, that would give me time to – well, think out what I was going to do. I looked in the inside pocket of his jacket. I took out his smartphone because it might have information, or photos, on it, and I looked in his wallet. There were snapshots in there, of Carl and me, when we were children, larking about and looking so happy. I didn't want anyone to see those, because they were so private – to Carl and to me – so I took them.'

'What about the keys to his flat in London? Were they in his pocket?'

Harriet nodded. 'Yes, and I took those, too. I wasn't sure what I was going to do with them. Perhaps I had a crazy notion of going up to London, to his flat, and looking around in there for anything private to him and to me. But I didn't get the chance. People have been hovering around me ever since that day.'

'And where are they, all the items you took?'

'In the stream at the bottom of the meadow, to the rear of the house. I threw everything in there. The photos floated away. The heavier things – the phone and the keys – I pushed under a large rock in the water. I hoped the current would work them deep into the gravel at the bottom.'

'Was that before or after you and Mrs Briggs concocted that yarn about her finding the body?' Carter asked.

'Oh, not until the next morning. I had no chance before, what with Tessa and Guy fussing round me, and then the police coming.'

Harriet rubbed her hands over her face. 'Can we stop for a bit, please? I'm very tired, and my brain's almost aching.'

'Certainly,' said Carter. 'Interview is suspended at . . .' He added the time.

'Send someone down there to retrieve those items she pushed

under the stone in the stream,' Carter ordered when he, Jess and Morton were alone.

'I remember that stream,' said Morton. 'It's at the bottom of a grassy slope. I'll go now.'

When they resumed later, Carter began, 'Perhaps, Harriet, we could talk about Sally Grove.'

Harriet looked puzzled for a moment, then said, 'Oh, yes, the girl on the bike. Is she going to be all right?'

'Yes. Did you cause her accident?'

Harriet was infused with another of those spurts of animation Jess had noted in her before. She wondered whether these odd bursts of energy, as sudden to fade as they were to erupt, had always been part of Harriet's make-up. Had such a moment led her to press the trigger?

'I didn't know anything about that girl, Sally, at all!' Harriet told them. 'I didn't know she existed. I didn't know anyone was in the woods, so near to where I'd dragged Carl. I certainly didn't know she was taking photos! I never would have known, if Tessa hadn't insisted I come out with her to lunch in Weston St Ambrose, at the Royal Oak. I didn't fancy going, because I had no appetite. But Tessa said I shouldn't mope. As if anything could take my mind off what had happened!

'As I would be going to the village, anyway, I decided to stop at the churchyard and check on my parents' grave. My father bought a double plot when my mother was killed, because he wanted to join her there. So, that's where he was buried.'

Jess asked, not really intending to interrupt, 'What about Nancy, your stepmother? Where's she buried?'

'She was cremated,' said Harriet briefly. There was a moment's silence, during which she seemed to be lost in thought. Then she said, reminiscently, 'We all had to go down to Stonehenge with her ashes in a box and scatter them without anyone seeing us. She'd asked Dad to do that, so he did.'

She gave herself a little shake and carried on more briskly. 'I parked up by the church and went to the grave. I still had a few minutes in hand before the time I'd agreed to meet Tessa, so I strolled along the main street to the Royal Oak. Lunch was as grim as I'd expected. I didn't want to eat anything. Tessa kept fussing and urging me, like a demented nanny. So I forced something down. I can't even remember what it was. When we left, I felt quite sick and couldn't get out of the restaurant fast enough. I parted from Tessa in the hotel car park, and she drove off. I set off to walk back to the church, where I'd left my car.

'I still felt nauseous. I didn't feel like driving home. I walked past the old library. It is still the library, but it's staffed by volunteers now. Anyhow, there was a poster outside advertising an exhibition of paintings by local artists. I could see in through the door and there were people arranging the display and arguing among themselves about it. There was a bald-headed man with a big, bushy beard bossing them all about, or trying to. A small girl was kicking up a fuss, and another, younger man with dark hair was standing by them, looking at the paintings and generally listening in. I wanted something to distract me so I went in.

'Nobody took any notice of me. Then I heard the man with the dark hair ask the girl about her painting. It was of trees, and he said he recognised Crooked Man Woods. She said that was where she'd taken the photos on which she had based the painting.

They began talking about the dead man in the woods. They'd both been in the woods that morning. He – the dark-haired man – had found Carl and called the police! I'd thought there wouldn't be anyone there that morning but Carl and me. But there were at least those two others. It's a miracle we didn't all fall over one another!

'Anyway, as soon as they began to talk about the woods I slipped behind a bookcase so they couldn't see me but I could hear them. Then their voices faded, so they must have moved. I peeped out from behind the bookcase and saw they had gone into a kind of large recess, a sort of big cupboard with no door. I took a book off the shelf and moved to stand by the wall near the gap, pretending to read. I could hear them. I was horrified. He was telling her to contact the police. She'd been taking photos all morning in those woods! I had no idea what she might have snapped. I knew I had to get hold of that phone.'

'So you waited for her . . .' Jess prompted, when Harriet fell silent.

'I had to wait ages . . .' Harriet told her crossly. 'She went with some other people to that dingy pub, the Black Horse. It was getting dark when she left, but that suited me. Also, she left on her own and on a bicycle, so I thought it would be easy. She set off, and I followed.'

'And you knocked her off her bike, in the lane,' Carter said.

'I didn't mean to hurt her, just – just knock her into the ditch and get the phone. I nearly did it. She did fall in the ditch and I started to search her for the phone.'

'Was she conscious? You can't just knock someone off a bike and trust to luck they won't be badly hurt!' Jess exclaimed.

'Well, she wasn't badly hurt, was she?' Harriet retaliated, with another flash of that energy that seemed to send an electric impulse through her. 'And then that wretched farmer came along on his tractor. I had to leave her and run for it. I got into my car and drove off. My car is black. It was pretty dark. There's no street lighting along there and it was cloudy. I thought there was a good chance the tractor driver wouldn't be able to identify me or the car.'

'And did you try again later to get your hands on the phone?'

'Oh, at the hospital,' admitted Harriet, sinking back into her more usual lethargy. 'But I had no luck there either, and someone chased me down the corridors. I got out and hid in the car park until he'd gone.' She looked up at them. 'Things kept going wrong,' she said. 'It all just spun out of control.'

Chapter 17

'Tell me, Tessa,' Jess asked, 'when did you realise that Harriet had killed Carl? Was it when you found his car? Is that why you drove it away? Or had you known or suspected it from the first?'

Predictably, Tessa's reaction to this blunt question was to snap back, 'If you think I'll ever believe that Hattie deliberately set out to kill Carl, I can tell you now: not in a million years! Whatever happened, it was an accident, a horrible bit of bad luck!'

'So then, when did you start to think this "bit of bad luck", as you put it, had happened?'

Tessa subsided and ran her fingers thoughtfully through her mop of greying hair. 'To start with the car, I told you exactly what happened. I drove it away on instinct, because I wasn't thinking straight, just like I told you, and because it sat there, door open, keys dangling, just like I said.'

She paused and heaved a sigh. 'But I'd had a funny feeling in the pit of my stomach about how Carl had died ever since I drove over to the house to tell Guy that Carl was dead as part of that little plan I'd hatched with Hattie. Guy expected her to be distressed, so it was easy to pull the wool over his eyes.'

Tessa hunched her shoulders. 'Well, for a very short time only, you know. Guy's not a fool. But at that point *I* didn't doubt she'd

301

told me the truth and that she had found him sitting there dead, just like she said.

'Anyway, I put her to bed. It seemed the best thing. She was on the point of collapse. I helped her undress. She just sat on the edge of the bed like a child and let me. There was blood on her clothes, but I thought, well, she'd found him, she must have bent over him. Bloodstains were to be expected. Then, when I went downstairs, I picked up her jacket from the floor of the hall. There was an awful lot more blood on that. That was when I began to wonder if she'd left something out of her account. It would be quite understandable if she had done, the state she was in. Anyone would be incoherent and anyone would omit details!'

'So what did you think she might have omitted from her account?' asked Jess.

'Frankly, I did just start to suspect that there had been some awful accident.' Tessa glared at Jess. 'For heaven's sake, I didn't think she'd shot the wretched man! I thought perhaps she'd wrestled with him to get the gun off him and it went off. Because I believed the gun must have belonged to *Carl*, you understand, and he'd brought it with him to the meeting. How should I think anything else? I didn't know Hattie had access to any gun. The gun found with Carl wasn't Guy's. So it followed it must be Carl's own weapon, and that confirmed that he must have shot himself.

'That her *grandfather's* old weapon was still in the house – well, we none of us knew that! I don't suppose Carl knew. If he had, he'd have pinched it and sold it, along with the books he filched and anything else he took and turned into ready cash.'

Tessa added grimly, 'It's a racing certainty that he'd been through those attics with a fine-toothed comb over the years, unbeknown to Hattie and Guy. Lord knows what he'd sold. The out-of-favour odds and ends of generations were up there. Or must have been up there once. We'll never know, given Carl's depredations. No wonder, when Guy and Hattie wanted to start up an antiques centre, there was nothing of any value left!'

She looked down at her folded hands, resting on the table between them. 'When I went back to the old feed store to clean the car of my prints and Fred's hair, I found smears of blood inside it. I knew then that Carl had died in the car, there where I found it, on the service road. It was like being hit by a thunderbolt. He was in the car when he was shot. There hadn't been any wrestling match for possession of the gun, as I'd imagined. Someone had blown him away and subsequently moved him. After that, I honestly didn't know what to think. It was the gun, you see,' Tessa finished miserably, 'I didn't know she had her grandfather's gun.'

'You'll be charged, Tessa, probably with perverting the cause of justice,' Jess told her. 'But the actual charge will be decided by the Crown Prosecution Service.'

Tessa said quietly, 'I *couldn't* take your Sergeant Morton to the car. I couldn't do that to Hattie.'

'It's been decided,' said Carter, 'that now Ms Adam has been given a severe warning about getting in the way of police investigations, there will be no further action taken against her. She's been told to stay away from newspaper reporters. I have a horrible feeling she won't, not once Harriet's trial is over and the matter no longer *sub judice*. Her story has everything a press hound could want in a human-interest story.'

'And Natalie really is Carl's sister?' Jess asked. 'She's not the sort of person to claim she was, if she wasn't, but even so . . .'

'Oh, yes, she's his sister, all right. It's all been checked out. She originally set out to find her natural mother, as many adopted children do. Discovering a former neighbour of Nancy's was the vital link that set her on the right track. The neighbour remembered Nancy giving birth to a baby, father unknown, and surrendering the infant for adoption. But then she revealed the astonishing news – to Natalie – that Nancy's reason for giving up the new baby had been that she already had a little boy to look after and very little money to support herself and her son. Carl had been five at the time of Natalie's birth. The neighbour had looked after him while Nancy was in the maternity ward. So Natalie set out to track down her brother. It took her years, and it was a remarkable piece of detection. But she's a thorough sort of woman. When she first found Carl, she insisted they have private DNA tests done to confirm the relationship.'

They both sat in silence for a while, sitting over the remains of a pub Sunday lunch. Around them, people, many of them in family groups, chattered noisily as they cleared plates of roast meat and potatoes, Yorkshire pudding and assorted winter vegetables. A chalked notice on the wall invited them to finish their meal with sticky toffee pudding or apple tart and custard.

'I wonder,' said Jess, her gaze taking in this scene of normality, 'how Carl really felt about Natalie turning up in his life. Pleased, in a way, I suppose, because he must have felt he'd lost one sister – the stepsister – to Guy Kingsley. Now he discovered he had a real flesh-and-blood sister to replace her. But Natalie's a successful career woman and – well – it must have underlined for Carl what a precarious existence he led. By the way, when my brother, Simon, gets home, I'd like to put in for some leave so that I can spend some proper time with him.'

'Of course.'

'Can I get you a dessert?' asked a fresh-faced young waiter brightly.

Probably a student earning a bit of money, thought Jess. They declined his offer, settling for coffee.

When the lad had gone, Carter mused, 'Guy Kingsley always believed Nancy had secrets she hadn't told John Hemmings. John had believed her completely open and frank. Let's face it, not many people are that. I don't mean we all have a guilty or embarrassing secret. But, well, there are always little things – trivial, perhaps, but we'd rather other people didn't know them . . .'

He looked at Jess and announced firmly, 'But I'm not in confessional mood, so don't expect to hear tales of my younger disasters!'

'Fair enough,' agreed Jess. 'Don't look forward to hearing about any of my embarrassing moments, either!'

They sat in silence for some minutes. Then Carter said, 'First thing in the morning, I'm going to get on to the cleaners. I don't know what they've put on the surface of the corridor outside my office, but there must be some way of removing it. I'm not putting up with that squeaking for weeks until it wears off!'

'It's very kind of you to give me a lift home from the hospital, Tom,' said Sally. 'They tell me my bike is a mess. I won't be able to get it fixed. I'll have to look out for a second-hand one to replace it.'

They were driving towards Weston St Ambrose. It was one of those pleasant, mild days that pepper the dull early-year climate and lead people to hope, usually in vain, that spring might not be far away.

'It's up to you,' said Tom, 'but, possibly, you'd do better to stay clear of bikes for a while, until you're totally recovered.'

'I *am* recovered, thanks!'

'Yes, yes,' agreed Tom hastily. Sally had that militant sparkle in her eyes. 'But you don't need to take another tumble and bash your head again, do you?'

'I don't normally fall off my bike, you know! I only came off that time because that screwy woman knocked me off deliberately.'

Seeking to make the peace, Tom said, 'The Kingsley female nearly forced me into a stone wall on the day of the murder. She was driving like a bat out of hell then.' After a tactful pause, he went on, 'I thought, you know, since you've been existing on hospital food, you might like to stop for lunch somewhere.'

'Oh,' said Sally. 'Well, thank you, Tom, that would be very nice.'

'Only not the Royal Oak, please!' Tom requested. 'As soon as I get in there I seem destined to meet up with people who know me.'

'Preferably nowhere in Weston St Ambrose,' agreed Sally. 'Too many people know me there, too. Only, later on, if there's time, I'd like to look in the library and see what's become of the display of our paintings.'

'I went to see it. It looks pretty good. Your tree paintings have pride of place.'

'Great! Gordon must have a guilt complex.' She looked out at the passing countryside. 'It's a lovely day,' she said.

'Yes!' agreed Tom happily.

'I don't come into the centre of Oxford often,' remarked Edgar Alcott. 'Too many people, from all over the world, and my health suffers in crowds. Shall I be mother, hmm?' He put a proprietary hand on the teapot.

Natalie bit back a sharp retort. 'Go ahead, Edgar!'

They were seated in the comfort of the lounge of the Randolph Hotel. Outside, the sky was overcast and even the graceful classical frontage of the Ashmolean Museum across the road, clearly visible through the long windows, seemed grey and forbidding. A school visit was underway. A harassed teacher was herding a small group of schoolchildren up the flight of steps. Natalie leaned back in her chair and let her eyes travel round the walls and the series of paintings showing scenes of Edwardian mayhem. Anything rather than watch old Edgar fuss about as if presiding over a Japanese tea ceremony.

'I'm obliged to you for coming,' Edgar said, tea dispensed, 'and for telling me all about it in person. There is nothing like an eyewitness account.'

'I told you I'd let you know what happened when I got down there, if you were interested.'

'As indeed I was! You have been my eyes and ears, my dear, my eyes and ears. Most valuable, and I am deeply appreciative.'

Natalie brought her gaze down from the pictures to his face. 'I'd have gone, anyway, for my own reasons!'

'Of course you would, dear girl. But I am so glad you got in touch with me.'

'After I found those coppers in his flat I knew they'd find their way to you, once they started checking out his business deals. So I took a short cut, if you like, and gave Superintendent Carter your name. I knew you'd bought some books from Carl and he must have filched them from that house. Not but he wasn't entitled to take something, after the way they'd treated him, cheated him . . .'

Natalie put her hand briefly to her mouth and paused to sip tea while Edgar nodded understandingly.

She went on, 'When they told me the awful news about what had happened to Carl, I can't tell you . . . I knew I had to do something myself. I couldn't leave it to the local police. They were very much against Carl down there in Gloucestershire, you know. He told me all about it. They'd stand together; they clammed up in front of the police. I wanted to stir things up. The police would tell the sister and her grasping husband about the books, and that would give them a nasty moment, thinking how, under their noses, Carl had slipped in and out of the Old Nunnery . . . what a name for a house! He had a key, you know. He said to me once, "Only a key, Nat, and I should have half-ownership of the whole place!"' Her voice trembled.

'Well done, Natalie, well done,' Edgar soothed. 'You flushed out the quarry, eh?'

In command of herself again, she went on, 'I wanted the police to get a flavour of what went on in that family.'

Edgar turned his gaze across the room towards the view of the portico of the museum. 'Carl, poor boy, such a loss. Foolish in business, of course, and needing to be taught a lesson. But murdered? No, no, never! He could have inspired any of the world's great sculptors.'

Natalie suppressed a wry smile. Putting down the teacup, she said briskly, 'Nevertheless, you must have hated the police coming to your house.'

'It was inevitable,' murmured Alcott. 'It doesn't matter now, anyway. The important thing is that justice has been done by your brother. Don't worry about those detectives coming to my house. One gets used to the police, you know.' He sighed. 'They are so very predictable.'

If you enjoyed ROOTED IN EVIL, look out for the other
Campbell and Carter mysteries in the series…

For more information visit Ann's website www.anngranger.net or
www.headline.co.uk

Discover Ann Granger's latest thrilling Victorian mystery featuring Inspector Ben Ross and his wife Lizzie...

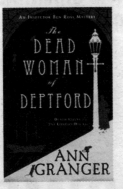

On a cold November night in a Deptford yard, dock worker Harry Parker stumbles upon the body of a dead woman. Inspector Ben Ross is summoned from Scotland Yard to this insalubrious part of town, but no witness to the murder of this well-dressed, middle-aged woman can be found. Even Jeb Fisher, the local rag-and-bone man, swears he's seen nothing.

Meanwhile, Ben's wife Lizzie is trying to suppress a scandal: family friend Edgar Wellings has a gambling addiction and no means of repaying his debts. Reluctantly, Lizzie agrees to visit his debt collector's house in Deptford, but when she arrives she finds her husband is investigating the murder of the woman in question. Edgar was the last man to see Mrs Clifford alive and he has good reason to want her dead, but Ben and Lizzie both know that a case like this is rarely as simple as it appears . . .

And don't miss the previous novels in the series:

A Rare Interest in Corpses
A Mortal Curiosity
A Better Quality of Murder
A Particular Eye for Villainy
The Testimony of the Hanged Man

www.headline.co.uk
www.anngranger.net

THRILLINGLY GOOD BOOKS
FROM CRIMINALLY
GOOD WRITERS

CRIME FILES BRINGS YOU THE LATEST RELEASES FROM
TOP CRIME AND THRILLER AUTHORS.

SIGN UP ONLINE FOR OUR MONTHLY NEWSLETTER AND BE THE FIRST
TO KNOW ABOUT OUR COMPETITIONS, NEW BOOKS AND MORE.